Praise for the Novels of Lisa Verge Higgins

One Good Friend Deserves Another

"Reminiscent of the *Sex and the City* TV series...easy and fun, chock-full of humor and entertainment...relays the necessity of taking risks and the power of friendship to pick you up when you fall."

—*Norfolk Daily News* (NE)

The Proper Care and Maintenance of Friendship

"A life-affirming novel...A happy reminder that life is all about taking risks."

—*Publishers Weekly*

"This well-written contemporary buddy book contains plenty of depth...the premise of friends knowing you at times better than you want to admit makes for a strong tale."

—*Midwest Book Review*

"Quirky, original, and startlingly refreshing, this is a novel about friends. It's a novel about risks. And it's a novel about dreams, what we thought they were and what we discover them to be... [Higgins is] gifted and talented... Great novel. Great reading. Great characters and plot."

—TheReviewBroads.com

"A lovely novel with moments of deeply moving insight into what it means to be a mother, a wife, and a friend. Read it and share it with your own friends—you'll be glad you did!"

—Nancy Thayer, *New York Times* bestselling author of *The Hot Flash Club* and *Beachcombers*

Friendship makes the

heart grow fonder

ALSO BY LISA VERGE HIGGINS

The Proper Care and Maintenance of Friendship
One Good Friend Deserves Another

Friendship makes the heart grow fonder

LISA VERGE HIGGINS

five
spot

NEW YORK BOSTON

5 Spot
Hachette Book Group
237 Park Avenue
New York, NY 10017

www.5-spot.com

Printed in the United States of America

RRD-C

First Edition: March 2013

10 9 8 7 6 5 4 3 2 1

5 Spot is an imprint of Grand Central Publishing.
The 5 Spot name and logo are trademarks of Hachette Book Group, Inc.

The Hachette Speakers Bureau provides a wide range of authors for speaking events. To find out more, go to
www.HachetteSpeakersBureau.com or call (866) 376-6591.

The publisher is not responsible for websites (or their content) that are not owned by the publisher.

Library of Congress Cataloging-in-Publication Data

Higgins, Lisa Verge.
 Friendship makes the heart grow fonder / Lisa Verge Higgins. — 1st ed.
    p. cm.
 ISBN 978-1-4555-0031-4 (trade pbk.) — ISBN 978-1-4555-1775-6
(ebook) 1. Widows—Fiction. 2. Bereavement—Fiction. 3. Self-realization
in women—Fiction. I. Title.
 PS3558.I3576F75 2013
 813'.54—dc23
                                        2012029383

*To Tom . . . for showing
me the world.*

Friendship makes the

heart grow fonder

∽ chapter one

Four years, two weeks, and three days. To Monique, grief was still a familiar guest, arriving without warning.

She sat on the edge of her bed. She knew she shouldn't be here, alone in her house, engulfed by shadows. She should be outside enjoying the waning light of the evening with Judy and Becky and the whole neighborhood. Through the screen window, she smelled the mesquite-smoke scent of barbecue. She heard the rippling of her friends' laughter as they gathered on the deck next door. It was the last Sunday of the summer. Everyone was home from the beach, the lake, and the mountains. Swarms of kids squealed as they jumped on the trampoline. In the driveway, an empty garbage can rumbled to the ground as if someone had stumbled against it.

Earlier Monique had made an appearance at the gathering, like she always did. She'd brought over a nice batch of *doubles*, her grandmother's Caribbean-island version of spicy hummus sandwiches. It was a crowd favorite. She'd shown up because Lenny would have wanted her to. Lenny had always loved these casual get-togethers, sitting back with a beer and laughing with Judy's husband, Bob, over some golf game. He'd tease Becky's husband, Marco, for doting so much on his own young kids, even as Lenny leaned forward to allow those same giggling children to peel open the winged seeds of maple trees and stick them on his nose.

Four years, two weeks, and three days. Everyone expected her to move on, whatever the hell that meant. Yet here she was, sitting in the gloom with Lenny's bucket list on her lap. Fingering the crackling edges of the paper in the hope that, if she stared long and hard enough at it, then Lenny would come.

He did not disappoint.

She drew in a long, deep breath, smelling the faintest whiff of Brut. She let her eyes flutter closed. She detected a rustle in the room, like the sound of curtains blown by a breeze. She imagined she felt a pool of warmth, just behind and to the right of her, where the mattress canted a bit, sagging under an unseen weight. She heard Lenny's rumbling baritone in her mind.

Taking that thing out again, huh? Second time this week.

She made a stuttering sound like a half laugh. Her heart began doing that strange pitter-patter thing, the one that reminded her of the swift skitter of a premature baby's heart, the fierceness of it in the preemies she worked with in the neonatal intensive care unit. Her doctor had told her that palpitations sometimes happen when a woman approaches menopause. But she didn't think it had anything to do with menopause. She was only forty-six years old, and everything else was working right on schedule. But she'd been feeling this sensation on and off since the day Lenny died.

I left you money to do that list years ago, Monie.

She smiled into the darkness. This list lived in the drawer of her bedside table, along with Lenny's Mass card, his watch, and the case with the diaphragm she hadn't touched since. "You left me with a thirteen-year-old daughter too, remember?"

Oh I remember she's a handful.

"It just didn't seem the right time, to flit off to Europe, me, a widowed working mom."

Monie, when did you ever "flit"?

"Is it wrong to want to spend as much time with Kiera as I can? In less than a year, she's leaving for college."

Kiera will be all right. She's like you, Monie. She's strong in the middle.

A prickling started at the back of her eyes. The paper rattled in her hands. She didn't feel strong, sitting here in the dark with her heart romping in her chest. She couldn't help thinking about a biology lab she'd done while she was studying to become a nurse. She and her lab partner had put dissected heart cells into a petri dish and fed them an electric current to set them beating in dissonant rhythms. Within only moments, the cells began to adjust their throbbing to sync with the ones closest.

The heart closest to hers was dead.

She battled the urge to turn around and burrow into his burliness, to smell the scent of cut grass on his flannel. She'd succumbed to that urge once—the very first time she'd sat in this empty room, bent over, crying out for him. She'd sensed him then. She'd jerked up at the sensation. In her elation, she'd whirled around and found, instead of the man she'd buried, nothing but cold and silence and an empty bed. So she'd learned to hold her breath when she felt him, lest she scare away the ghost of his memory.

Her Trinidadian grandmother would have called him a *jumbie*—a lost spirit—and in her island patois she would have urged Monique to go to an Obeah woman to collect the herbs and the talismans needed to send the spirit of Lenny away.

She didn't want Lenny to go away.

You should do the whole list, Monie. All of it, just like we talked about.

Monique read the odd things they'd written. Slogging through the catacombs of Paris. Rappelling down an alpine ledge. Hitting 100 mph on a German autobahn. She could barely remember what they were thinking when they dreamed up this list. The project had just been something to do to pass the time between chemo sessions or while the doctors were waiting for test results before they prescribed more pills. These trips were something to busy their minds with, something to joke about, so that Lenny wouldn't completely lose hope, even while his burly body melted away in the hospice.

Lenny never lost his sense of humor, not even in the end.

She ran her fingers across his spidery scrawl, noticed how shaky his handwriting became at the bottom of the list. "This was just a lark, Lenny. You don't even like motorcycles."

Maybe I just wanted to see you wearing leather.

She choked down a laugh. Her chest squeezed, muscling out all the oxygen. The truth was that the things on this list bore no resemblance to any part of the wonderful life she'd led with her husband. Their life was here, in their center-hall colonial on a street swarming with children. What vacations they'd taken had been modest—cabin-camping in western New Jersey, a week in a beach house in Wildwood, one splurge to Disney World—always tempered by the need to pay the mortgage and his medical school loans, and fatten up Kiera's college fund.

She'd give up a thousand trips to Paris to have Lenny back, laughing as he hiked Kiera on his shoulders so their daughter could reach the red apples on high.

"I can't do this, Lenny."

She clumsily folded the paper, running her fingers along the weakened seam. His disappointment was a chill as his presence faded from the room.

"I just can't do this without you."

Judy poked her head in through the open front door and called Monique's name into the darkness. Monique's muffled response rippled down from second floor gloom. Judy gripped the banister and headed up the stairs, noticing, as she reached the landing, that a light suddenly went on in the master suite. She rounded the bedroom door just in time to catch Monique slipping something into the drawer of her bedside table.

Monique shot off the bed and started pulling clothes out of the laundry basket, folding them with brisk efficiency. "Hunting me down already, Judy?"

Judy noticed three things at once: Monique wasn't meeting her eye, her friend's graceful neck was tight and corded, and the photo of Lenny on her side table was angled perfectly for bedside viewing.

"Well, Monie, you did pull your vanishing act again."

"You usually let me get away with it."

"Yeah, but this time you left me sitting next to Maggie talking about her most recent skin melanoma."

Monique flashed her hazel eyes, begging her not to probe. Judy considered. She never should have let Monique drink that second glass of wine tonight. The neighborhood gatherings often set the widow off. Four years was too long to be grieving this strongly, but then again, Judy missed Lenny too. Bob missed Lenny. Everyone in the whole darned neighborhood missed Lenny.

Judy gestured to the basket of clean laundry. "I suppose you're determined to finish that?"

"It's not going to fold itself."

Judy wandered to the bed to pull a pair of pajama bottoms out of the basket. "You know, you're not the only Franke-Reed who was noticed missing in action tonight. Becky's kids were asking for your daughter."

"Kiera's still in the city, working with that filmmaker. She's going to stick with that internship until the director kicks her off the set."

"Ah, yes. Unpaid internships: The twenty-first-century way to work around child labor laws. At least it'll look great on her college applications."

Judy glanced over her shoulder to where the door to Kiera's room yawned open across the hall. Kiera's computer monitor was on, the screen-saver a kaleidoscope of warping neon cubes. A pile of textbooks teetered on the desk. A blow dryer lay on the top of the bureau amid a cascade of cosmetics. A hoodie was tossed carelessly across the unmade bed.

Proof of occupation.

Judy's ribs tensed. She remembered what it was like to have a teenager at home. She remembered what it was like to have *five* kids at home, to have an oversized calendar on the kitchen wall aflame with ink—blue, green, yellow, red, purple, orange, brown—one color for each body in the house. She'd been the captain of the Good Ship Merrill, full of purpose, blissfully ignorant that her entire adult life was sailing by in a blur of parent-teacher conferences and Tater Tot casseroles and crew-team meets.

Now her empty calendar, a ghost in the kitchen. Audrey's empty bedroom, like a sucking black hole. Judy's sense of purpose a wisp she kept searching for, while whisking the dust bunnies from under unused beds.

Judy forced her gaze away from Kiera's room. Laying the folded pajamas down, she reached for a pair of jeans and shook them with excess vigor. "So," Judy said, "has Kiera whittled down her list of schools?"

"She's working on the NYU application already."

"Clearly I'm going to be useless to both of you. Kiera has already started early, which is the first piece of advice that I would have given you."

"You can still help. She's stuck on a list of odd questions. You know, 'what's your favorite word?' And 'describe your most life-altering experience.'"

"Oh, yeah. Audrey and I spent a whole afternoon vying

to come up with the most outrageous opening lines for that one."

Monique winced. "Please tell me Audrey didn't use the story of her teammates trying to sneak a bottle of cheap vodka into the crew-team hotel suite."

"No, no, we made everything up." Judy fixed her attention on smoothing the seams of the jeans, to hide a pang of remembrance. "I think Audrey won with 'It took me awhile to convince the natives to make me their god.'"

Monique's smile was subdued, but at least it nearly met her eyes. Post-Lenny Monique was a hard nut to crack.

"Monie, don't worry. Kiera's a super candidate. She'll fly right through this, just like she does with everything."

"I hope so. Because, I tell you, it's really not fun."

Judy felt her smile tighten. It hadn't seemed fun at the time, she remembered. It had been stressful and difficult. She probably complained about it at every opportunity. Amid the raucous chaos of her home life, she had taken for granted the affectionate intimacy, the warm, busy togetherness that had been jettisoned abruptly three weeks ago when Audrey walked to the gate of the plane that would take her to California and tossed her mother a casual, breezy wave.

Bob kept telling her she should be grateful for the new freedom. Bob kept saying she was acting like a bird who didn't yet realize that the cage door was yawning wide open. Well, she remembered that they'd owned a parakeet once. Her older daughter Maddy, appalled at its incarceration, had flung open its cage door.

The bird flew out . . . and then flew right back in again.

"You all right, Judy?"

Judy snapped her attention to her friend and found herself in the crosshairs of Monique's hazel gaze. She dropped her attention back to the yoga pants she was folding. Oh, yeah, she would love to talk to Monique about this—if the idea didn't fill her with shame. Monique worked as a nurse in a NICU. She cradled premature babies fighting for life every day. After Kiera left home, Monique would have a meaningful vocation to return to, not just a house that felt so hollow and quiet that Judy felt compelled to vacuum obsessively just to fill the place with noise. Monique wouldn't have to fight a constant, low-grade pall by starting an attic-cleanout project, or replastering the battered, crayon-streaked walls of the hallway, or planting perennials on the edges of the lawn. "Damn hot flashes," Judy muttered, picking up the pile of Monique's active wear so she could turn away from those all-seeing eyes. "I swear, if you could plug me in, I could light up half the neighborhood."

"You're not looking pink to me."

"It's just starting."

"Um-huh."

Monique's mutter was low and drawn-out and supremely doubtful.

"You just wait." Judy crouched to pull the lower drawer of the black lacquered chest-on-chest to slip the yoga pants and workout shirts into their proper place. "In five minutes, I'll have mottled cheeks and beads of perspiration on my upper lip, and I'll be generating enough heat to put steam on these windows."

Monique gave her a narrow-eyed look. "Did you leave the

barbecue because you didn't feel like listening to Joe Davis's latest fishing story?"

"You mean the one about the two-hundred-pound marlin?"

"It was one-eighty when he boasted to me." Monique rounded the bed to carry Kiera's things across the hall. "The point is, you clearly used me as an excuse to slip away."

"Your powers of observation are extraordinary, Sherlock."

"It comes with the nurses' training."

Judy paused outside Kiera's room, assaulted by the scent of nail polish and coconut shampoo, of dirty socks and ink. "Actually," she said, "I wanted to talk to you about Becky. She came by tonight."

"Yeah, I heard the tumbling of the garbage can that heralded her arrival."

"Actually, that was Brian's Big Wheel, which she knocked into the garbage can. The thing is, Becky came by, but then left right away."

"Did she forget to bring that red velvet cake? If she brought that cake, I'll reconsider my antisocial tendencies and put up with Joe's fish tales."

"She didn't bring the cake." Judy frowned, concern filling her anew, the concern that had urged her to seek out Monique in the first place. "Something's up with her."

Monique wandered toward the doorway and tilted her head in unease, her fall of tight braids brushing against her throat. "It's Marco, isn't it?"

"That's where I'd put my money."

Marco, Becky's husband, had been put on unpaid furlough three weeks ago as a cost-cutting measure imposed by the architectural firm he worked for. The company was struggling to hold on to its talent through a grim economic time, but couldn't afford to keep everyone on full payroll. Marco was one of the architects with the least seniority, one of the later hires. Gina, his eighteen-year-old daughter from a previous marriage, was now in college, while Becky stayed home raising the younger kids.

"The timing is right," Judy said, "for the financial strain to show."

"It can't help that Becky dented the car again."

"Body work is expensive."

"It couldn't have happened at a worse time."

"Yes, and Marco's not home tonight. He took the train to his brother's house in Hicksville so he could borrow their second car while theirs is in the shop."

Monique paused. "So she's alone."

"Yup."

"And her kids are next door, having fun on the trampoline."

"Monie, I saw her through the window tonight. She's sitting at her kitchen table with her head in her hands."

She could do this.

Becky pushed herself up from the kitchen table and slipped into the den, rounding the couch to confront the usual scattering of toys. She picked up the Matchbox fire truck and little yellow car, and then she scooped up the Spiderman and Green Goblin action figures and tossed them unerringly into the big wicker bin in the corner. She gathered the fashion dolls. She squinted at the rug, searching for the little shoes, belts, and sparkling fabric purses. She lifted pillows off the carpet and tossed them on the L-shaped couch, pausing to fold the throw blankets and tuck them in the lower shelf of the coffee table.

See? She was perfectly fine. She could take care of her house. There was nothing wrong with her at all. She'd finish cleaning out this den and then she'd move back to the kitchen and make sure the last of the flour had been scrubbed from the counter. She would hand-dry the bowls she'd used to make the cake. By then the pans should be well-soaked enough that she wouldn't have to scrub to loosen the baked-on crumbs.

After that, it'd be time to call Brianna and Brian home from the trampoline. On summer nights, they always tumbled in streaked with grass stains, sticky with mosquito repellent, and sweaty around the hairline. She'd have to bathe them tonight because early tomorrow morning they were going to her mother-in-law's house for the annual Labor Day weekend cookout. She should probably start packing snacks for the car.

A knock on the back door startled her. Shadows shifted through the window, and then someone turned the door handle and stepped right in.

"Hey, Becky."

She recognized Monique's voice before her friend stepped into the light of the kitchen. Monique wore a tank top that showed off her arms, honed by kickboxing. Judy, a shorter, sturdier shape, followed behind.

"I told you she was an alien." Judy hiked her fists onto

her hips as she scanned the room. "Mothers of three children aren't supposed to have clean houses."

"It's only two of the monsters now. I can't blame Gina for this." Becky pulled open the lower cabinet to toss a paper towel into the garbage. "I haven't seen hide nor hair of Gina since she left for Rutgers. But I'm not complaining."

Becky smiled tightly. No use bringing up that other concern about Gina—that, if Marco's unpaid furlough stretched much longer, the college girl might actually have to move out of the dorm at Rutgers and back into this house. She and her step-daughter didn't have the best of relationships. If Gina came home again, the girl would take inordinate pleasure in flaunting the tongue-stud she had done on her eighteenth birthday.

But Becky had bigger things to worry about now. She let Gina slip away, like water through her fingers.

Monique pulled up a chair. "We missed you at the barbecue, Beck."

"That's quite a trick," Becky said, "since you weren't there either, Monique."

"I bailed when I thought your red velvet cake wasn't coming."

Becky turned toward the sink to avoid those clear, all-knowing eyes. "I think you bailed when Mrs. Davis started talking about her colonoscopy. I hear the Miralax powder is thorough."

Judy asked, "Marco not home yet?"

"The charmer won't be back until ten or eleven."

Monique said, "You want to talk about it?"

Becky concentrated on pulling one of the cake pans out

of the sink and attacking it with the scrubbing side of a blue sponge. No, she really didn't want to talk about it. She hadn't even told Marco what was bothering her. For so long she and Marco had been living in strained little silences. The act of keeping explosive information from him had been easier than she'd expected. The financial squeeze they were feeling was only the latest hit in a long string of odd distrusts and not-so-subtle misunderstandings. And he'd been so angry lately, for the fact that his salary had been cut to nothing, for the bills piling up, for the car accident. It didn't help that she'd just found out from the dentist that Brianna was going to need braces. She hadn't yet dared to mention that, if Brian was going to play hockey this season, he would need all new equipment because he'd grown so much. And no matter how many elaborate fantasy-castle cakes she made for friends and their referrals, she couldn't bake and sell them fast enough to fill the gap between what Marco had been paid and what the mortgage demanded. It was a long list of worries.

They all seemed so silly now.

"Hey, Becky," Judy said, peering at the calendar hanging over the desk in the corner of the kitchen. "Don't you have a birthday coming up?"

"Yeah. In April." Becky held the pan up while water dripped into the sink. "I didn't think you'd so quickly forget the margaritas at Tito's last spring."

"April, September, whatever. It's close enough for a celebration." Judy wandered over to the table and ran her hand over the back of a chair. "Don't you agree, Monique?"

"I think I could talk Kiera into donating a little community service time toward watching your two little monsters."

Judy added, "I hear that new tapas place on Main Street is great."

Monique murmured, "A little Spanish guitar..."

"A little Spanish wine..." Judy nodded in decision. "I think you and Marco could use a fun night out."

A night out. Becky shifted her gaze to the window over the sink, to the smudgy, shadowed reflection of her own face.

Nights were the worst.

She gave the dripping pan one last shake and then slipped it onto the drainer. At least she tried to slip it onto the drainer. Somehow instead, she cracked the corner of it against a glass mixing bowl so precariously piled that the force made the bowl tumble over the edge and knock a whisk and two wooden spoons out of the utensils bin. While the bowl clattered on the wet counter, one wooden spoon flipped into the air and then rattled onto the tile floor.

In the uncomfortable silence that followed, Becky felt a hot prickle of embarrassment. Clumsy Becky, again. Always tripping on uneven sidewalk pavements, stumbling over garbage cans, knocking over wineglasses, and dropping whole trays of cupcakes off the edge of tables.

So adorable.

"Hey, nice flip." Judy turned the bowl upright and pushed it deeper onto the counter. "Did you see the spin on that thing?"

Monique retrieved the spoon and handed it to her. Becky took it and saw the flicker of a look that passed between her friends. It was a subtle thing, a quiet zipping of information. The kind of nonverbal communication that would, soon enough, pass right by her, unnoticed.

Monique flicked a drop of water on her arm, to get her attention. "Are you going to tell us what's wrong, girl, or do we have to do this kabuki dance until we tease it out of you?"

Becky picked the other cake pan out of the water, setting the sponge upon it with new ferocity. She wished they would just go away. They knew her too well. Just like Becky could tell by the strain in Monique's voice that something was bothering her, or by the way Judy acted crazy when she was upset, Becky knew they saw the signs in her, too. When you form an alliance to mutually raise a passel of curious, risk-taking, hormone-crazy teenagers, you become comrades in a very narrow foxhole. She, Monique, and Judy had survived raising-a-teenage-daughter boot camp. They were bonded for life.

But Becky wasn't in the mood to share. She hadn't yet wrapped her own mind around the news. Every time she looked at Brianna and Brian, her throat closed up. She found herself cataloging the tangle of their lashes, the way Brian's nose tilted up at the tip, Brianna's shoulders dusted with freckles.

If she spoke the words out loud, then it would be real.

"Marco didn't believe me," she said, casting about for any reasonable excuse for her behavior. "About the accident."

Judy wandered to the far cabinet where, by stretching her solid frame up on her toes, she could just reach the bottle of whiskey on the third shelf. "Beck," she said, "you aren't the best of drivers."

"So I'm repeatedly told."

"I mean," Judy continued, "it's not like this was your first fender bender."

"It was a deer." At least, she thought it was a deer. It might have been a big beige dog. Or an odd-colored garbage can. It had all just happened so fast, and the sun was right in her eyes. "I clipped it on that road just by the nature preserve." Twenty-five-mile-an-hour speed limit and she was riding just under it. "The place is lousy with deer."

Monique shifted her stance, a line appearing between her eyes. "How bad is the damage?"

The damage to the car, at least, was repairable. She shrugged. "It's more than we can afford right now. Marco is understandably angry."

Judy nudged her and held out a whiskey on ice. "Listen, when Bob had his so-called retirement and was home for four months, he took every frustration out on me. Thank God he was hired by this start-up online news corporation or we'd have killed each other by now." Shrugging, she pushed a lock of brown hair behind her ear. "Marco is tense, Becky. He's feeling like he can't provide."

Becky let the pan drop right back into the water as she took the drink. "Marco made me go to the eye doctor to get my vision checked."

"That's like when I sent Jake to get his hearing checked." Judy rolled her whiskey glass in little circles on the kitchen table. "Perfect hearing, the doctor told me. Apparently my kid just doesn't listen to me."

"Becky, you're coming up on forty, yes?" Monique said. "Well, it's a sad, dreary little fact that you'll be wearing rhinestone-studded reading glasses before long."

Judy took a sip of her whiskey. "Hey, it'll raise the chance that *one* of us will remember our glasses when we go out to eat. We'll be like those three witches in that Disney movie, sharing one eye."

Becky clattered her glass onto the table. Her hand was shaking, and she'd already spilled some of the liquid onto her fingers. She tried to rub it off, but only succeeded in spreading it over her other hand. Maybe Monique would understand all this, she thought, digging her nails into her palms. At the very least Monique could explain it to her in a way she might be able to comprehend.

Becky strode to the small desk in the corner of the kitchen and riffled through the permission slips and flyers she'd pulled from her kids' backpacks until she found the information sheet she couldn't bring herself to read. She glanced at it briefly and then, closing her eyes, thrust it behind her, toward Judy, who was closest.

Judy took it and held it at arm's length. "Wouldn't you know I didn't bring my reading glasses?" She squinted as she moved her head back a little. "And it's in Latin, no less."

Monique started. She came around the table to peer over Judy's shoulder. Becky watched Monique's face as she swiftly read the text, her eyes moving back and forth. As Becky watched Monique read to the bottom, she noticed that her friend's lips went tight, revealing a pale line around the edges.

"I don't get it," Judy murmured, squinting ferociously. "All I can see is the title. What the hell is retinitis pigmentosa?"

"It's a disease." Monique lifted her troubled gaze to Becky's. "A degenerative one."

Becky saw the shock in Monique's eyes and the dawning dismay in Judy's. Then she spoke before her throat closed up.

"Apparently, ladies . . . I'm going blind."

∽ chapter two

Monique pushed the curried chicken around the iron skillet. The scent of onions, garlic, diced tomatoes, and green seasoning rose up with the steam. Through the kitchen window, she glimpsed Becky's kids playing in her backyard on the old wooden swing set, the one she couldn't bring herself to take down though Kiera hadn't gone near it in years. At least Becky's kids were enjoying it, their laughter bright and sharp.

Monique stopped stirring, her fingers tightening on the wooden spoon. She knew that Becky still hadn't told the kids. Kids that age would struggle to grasp the meaning of such bad news. They wouldn't really understand the incremental progression of the disease, or what it all meant to them on a day-to-day basis. With the diagnosis so fresh, Monique suspected that even Becky and Marco hadn't fully absorbed the consequences—certainly not enough to explain to Brianna and Brian in plain terms the grim, long-term repercussions.

Dread shifted within her, a solid weight that pressed against her spine. Earlier in the week at the hospital, she'd spent a coffee break with a specialist in degenerative eye diseases, pumping him for information. Monique knew the prognosis. She knew how it would play out. She knew more than she wanted to know—enough to break her heart three times over.

"Hey, Mom."

Kiera busted through the back door. With a solid thunk, she dropped her backpack onto the floor of the mudroom. She sailed into the kitchen and gave Monique a quick peck on the cheek.

"Hey, baby girl," Monique said. "How did the physics test go?"

Kiera rolled her eyes. She scooted to the sink, rolling up the sleeves of her hoodie. "Let's just say I wouldn't mind pushing Mr. Orso off a cliff to calculate how long it would take for him to reach terminal velocity."

Monique suppressed a smile, momentarily grateful for the spoon in one hand and the oven mitt in the other, because they prevented her from running her palm over Kiera's hair to smooth down the short pieces that stuck up from around the braided headband. Such fierce, affectionate motherly urges were usually repaid with affront. "I'll make sure not to mention that at the next back-to-school night. You hungry?"

"Starved. That smells awesome." Kiera peered into the skillet as she ran her hands under the open faucet. "Curry chicken?"

"And callaloo." She lifted the top off another pot to show the greens simmering in coconut milk. "Swiss chard and spinach, though. Don't go expecting dasheen leaves like *Grand-mère* would have made you, hunting them down in some side-alley Caribbean grocer."

"So what's the occasion?"

The kid had a sixth sense. "Since when do I have to have an occasion to whip up some comfort food for my hard-working high school senior?"

"You're still in scrubs."

Monique shrugged as she glanced down at the duck appliqués on her blue scrubs. She'd had one of her colleagues cover for the last hour of her shift because she was no fool. She hoped Kiera would adore what she was going to ask her, but since it involved her father, there was no way to tell. "Takes a long time to chop all these vegetables, you know that. Didn't have time to change."

Kiera narrowed her dark-chocolate eyes as she shut the faucet off, grasped a dishtowel, and worked her hands dry. She made a little mumbling sound, the kind of sound Lenny might have made if he had an opinion and was tamping it down for the time being.

The similarity was like a needle in her heart.

"I know what this is about." Kiera tugged the dishtowel through a cabinet handle below the sink. "You shouldn't poke around my room, you know."

Monique gave her daughter a raised brow. Kiera was a good student, a strong-minded individual who rarely got in trouble. Her daughter's room was an oasis of privacy Monique had allowed her, one that Monique had never felt compelled to invade.

Course, that didn't mean she wouldn't let her daughter think she *would* invade it—if she had due cause. "Is there something in there that your mother shouldn't see?"

Kiera flung herself in a kitchen chair. "I *was* going to tell you. I was just waiting for the right time."

A cold tingle washed up her spine. She ran through the usual dangerous possibilities—body piercings, tattoos, sexting with strangers, drug paraphernalia. She pulled the oven mitt off her hand and turned toward the cabinet, more to hide her expression than to pull down plates.

"And just for the record," Kiera said, "it's not going to work."

"What?"

"The great meal, the whole nice attitude, your aura of unshakable calm. I've made up my mind."

"Kiera," she said, placing the first plate on the counter, "when have I ever tried to talk you out of anything?"

"Well, I *know* you're going to try to talk me out of UCLA."

Monique fumbled the second plate. It slipped out of her grasp and onto the counter. She pressed it to stop it from clattering.

Los Angeles. Three thousand five hundred miles away.

Monique feigned calm as she dished a chicken thigh on each plate, smothering them in the onion, garlic, and diced tomato sauce. This wasn't what she'd planned to talk about tonight. But she'd been a mother of a teenage daughter long enough to understand the importance of seizing the moment.

"I'm glad you're telling me now, Kiera." She added a healthy helping of the dark green callaloo. "You have to admit your mother deserves to have a voice in this discussion, since I'll be writing the checks."

"It's trust money, Mom. Daddy put it aside for me."

Her throat tightened at the sound of the word *daddy*. "Yes, it is. And we're both lucky that your father had prepared so well to take care of us, long after he couldn't physically do it anymore. But you know he'd want to discuss this with you, too, if he were still here."

"Low blow, Mom. Guilt is not a fair weapon."

"But it's ageless and ruthlessly effective."

Turning around, Monique gave Kiera a little smile as she slipped both dishes on the table in the breakfast nook— where they took all their meals now that there were only two of them at home, and the dining room table had morphed into a staging surface for the college search. Kiera chose that moment to drop her gaze and fuss with her napkin.

Monique settled down across from her, watching her daughter with the word "Los Angeles" echoing in her head. She looked lovingly at Kiera's hair, shining with raven-blue highlights. On weekends, Kiera took great care to fluff and condition it into a flattering cascade of relaxed curls, but during the active sports season, she just pulled it back flat. Monique liked it better this way. With the stub of a ponytail, the open plaid shirt, the tank top and ripped-knee jeans, Kiera retained some remnant of the active little girl who once tore swaths through the backyard, catching ladybugs and sorting them by spots.

Sometimes she missed that little girl, hidden within the perceptive, years-ahead-of-herself teenager that Kiera had become.

Monique waited for Kiera to say something. Kiera straightened in the chair and switched her knife and fork from one hand to another, before idly digging into the chicken thigh. Her daughter was a deep, deep well. Monique knew this. Monique loved this.

Finally Kiera glanced up through sullen lashes. "You know it's the best film school in the country, right?"

Monique didn't argue the point. UCLA had always come up on their early searches for the best film schools, and it was just as quickly waved off as geographically undesirable. She also knew that two of the other best film schools in the country were in California, a fact she would pointedly not mention. "A month ago you were saying the same thing about New York University."

"NYU has one of the top film departments too," Kiera admitted, "but I'm applying from New Jersey."

"Yeah?"

"It's a disadvantage. Lots of people from New Jersey will be applying to NYU—I mean, it's right *there*. We can commute." She chewed another bite of chicken. "But there won't be nearly as many people from New Jersey applying to UCLA, so I'll have the advantage of geographical diversity."

"You should be choosing a school because it's where you want to go, Kiera."

"Duh."

Monique absorbed the hit. Her ego wasn't so large it couldn't survive a few bruises. "You've never even visited it."

"Audrey's there. She loves it."

"That doesn't mean you will. And you shouldn't be choosing a place just because you think you'll have better odds of getting in."

Kiera started to roll her eyes and then, abruptly, stopped herself. "I *have* to work the odds, Mom. It's hard to get into any film school. " She stabbed a piece of meat. "And it's going to help that daddy is an alum."

"He went to the University of California in San Diego, not UCLA—"

"—doesn't matter. I checked."

"Did you check the cost? It's more expensive for out-of-state students. Just as you said, for NYU, you could commute."

"Not sure I want to commute."

Monique stilled a little, soaking in that revelation, staring at the sliver of onion stuck in the tines of her fork.

"I mean," Kiera added quickly, "Daddy left us enough money, right? You always told me that college was one thing I'd never have to worry about."

"I did say that." *Damn fool.*

"If it hadn't been that way, I'd just be making you fill out financial aid forms. We'd have found a way to work it out. *You* always told me that."

The girl was warming up to the debate. Monique could tell by the swirls Kiera was drawing in the air with the tip of her knife.

"And living away from home the first year is sort of part of the whole college experience. You know, dorm life, learning to get along with different kinds of people from all over the world and all that."

Monique raised a forkful of callaloo. "At UCLA it's not like you'll be able to pop home for some curried chicken."

"Yeah, but when I do, it'll be all the more special."

Kiera leaned over the plate, her smile slowly stretching wide. Monique gazed at the full round cheeks that her daughter had inherited from Lenny, at the steady intelligent eyes pleading for understanding. And it came to her that her daughter was behaving more and more like Monique's own father, who'd worked thirty-two crazy years as a district attorney in Newark. Dad had claimed his ability to argue his way around the cleverest of defense lawyers was a product of hard work, plenty of preparation, and good old German-American logical thinking.

Monique suddenly realized she shouldn't have started this conversation. She was utterly unprepared. And outmatched.

"Let me think about this for a while," she said, completely changing tactics. "There was actually something else I wanted to discuss with you tonight."

"Oh?"

That was a light-hearted, hopeful, high-pitched kind of "oh?" followed by a little wiggle in the chair and a fresh attack on her dinner, and Monique sensed that Kiera believed she'd just won the argument.

Monique didn't want to think about that right now. "Remember the other night," she said, "when I told you about Mrs. Lorenzini's diagnosis?"

"Yeah. Major bummer. Gina texted me after her dad gave her the news. She was all freaked out about it."

Monique checked her surprise. She couldn't imagine that Becky had asked Marco to give Gina the news. Gina was Marco's daughter from a relationship he'd had when he was just out of high school. The relationship quickly went bad, and after twelve years of drama, Gina had finally ended up in Marco's custody. Gina had been, hands down, the most difficult of the three neighborhood teenage girls to handle, and it had been years before she began behaving in a way that wouldn't give Saint Theresa gray hair.

"I mean," Kiera added, grimacing, "Gina used to say some really nasty things about Mrs. Lorenzini. She used to go on about how stupid she was, how clumsy, how *blind*."

"Maybe this will make her reassess her relationship with the stepmother who welcomed her in her home and raised her."

Kiera gave her a look that said otherwise.

"In any case I've been thinking about doing something for Becky. Something special."

"Oh, Mom, I can't do a fund-raiser." Kiera shook her head. "If it were any other time, I *totally* would. I love Mrs. Lorenzini. But you know how important these first-quarter grades are, and now that I'm coaching freshman crew—"

"I'm not asking you to hawk brownies at the next PTA meeting."

"No?"

"It's not like someone is actually *sick*." Although Becky was behaving like a mad housewife, endlessly picking up toys and cleaning floors. "There's no use in rallying the casserole brigade. Becky's just fine making dinner." *For now.* "And with Marco home on work furlough, she has all the driving help she needs. No, what I'm thinking, well… frankly, it's a little crazy."

"Crazy? Like, what, buying her a seeing-eye dog?"

"The bucket list."

There. She'd spoken it aloud. Just the act of speaking the words to another human being caused her pulse to race and her breath to hitch in the back of her throat and the curried chicken in her stomach to roll. She'd spent every spare minute of the last two days searching airline fares and calculating approximate hotel costs and mapping possible routes and then checking exactly how many vacation days she had and whether she could take the time off without causing chaos on the neonatal floor.

Kiera looked at her with a face that had gone utterly blank.

"You remember," Monique prodded, "that list your father and I made, in those last weeks?"

Kiera dropped her gaze to her plate. "Oh. That."

"Your father put some money aside so I could do all those things—"

"I know."

"So," Monique continued, "I started to think about Becky. About all those cakes Becky bakes to earn a little money on the side. She models them on castles from all over the world. You remember on your sixteenth birthday she—"

"—made me a cake like Cinderella's castle in Disney World." Kiera tapped her knife against the edge of the plate.

"Right. But Becky has never actually *seen* any of these castles. Not a single one. And I thought, wouldn't it be a wonderful thing to bring Becky to Europe? Show her the Tower of London or Chambord or Neuschwanstein?"

Monique left out the obvious addendum: *before Becky goes completely blind.*

Kiera hunkered a fraction farther over the table. "So is this it? You want to take Mrs. Lorenzini to Europe?"

"I want to take her," Monique said, as she stretched her hand across the table, "and I want to take *you*."

Kiera stilled. Her hand curled up underneath Monique's palm. Monique tried to read the shifting currents of Kiera's expression, sensing storm clouds of danger ahead but not quite sure of their source.

Kiera slipped her hand out from hers. "Mom, it's my senior year."

"I know it won't be easy to schedule."

"I've got applications due at the end of November, and more in January, and semester grades are going out to those schools."

"I've already looked at our calendar. We can arrange it over the Jewish holidays, the parent/teacher conferences, and stretch it into Columbus Day. You'd miss a total of six full days and one half-day—"

"To go tripping across Europe with you and Mrs. Lorenzini, fulfilling your and Dad's silly bucket list?" Kiera pushed away from the table so hard the chair screeched against the floor. "Wow, Mom, what a teenage dream."

Monique narrowed her eyes. Her senses were tingling. "It's Europe, Kiera. This is a wonderful opportunity. You might find another idea for a college essay."

"My college essay already rocks. And I told you, I'm coaching the freshman crew team. We're just starting the season."

"Then let's just work it out for when the timing is better." Monique suppressed a spurt of worry. Becky's disease was degenerative, and there was no knowing the rate at which her tunnel of vision might tighten. "Maybe during the April vacation—"

"My college acceptances will just be in. I'll have to visit schools to make a final decision."

Monique squashed the urge to ask about next summer.

Next summer Kiera would be working in the city again, interning with the producer she'd met through one of the neighborhood block parties. Monique mused that there once was a time when she and Kiera planned everything together, a time just after Lenny died when they spent a whole month in Trinidad, seeking solace in the sun and the easy living, braiding each other's hair.

Now her daughter had plans of her own, appointments and schedules.

"Let's do it right after you graduate then," Monique conceded. "Before that producer sucks up your summer."

"Mom, you just don't get it. I'm *not going*." Kiera pushed up from the chair. She seized her plate and strode to the counter, where she pulled open the cabinet for the garbage and started violently scraping the remains. "Why do you always have to *finish* things, Mom? Why can't you just leave something undone?"

Monique went very still. The question made no sense. She and Kiera were most alike in this particular way: Neither one of them ever left anything undone.

"This has nothing to do with Mrs. Lorenzini going blind." Kiera tossed the plate on the counter next to the sink. "That's an *excuse*. You just want to do that bucket list."

Her daughter's feelings billowed over her, and Monique struggled to parse them out—anger and frustration and, most upsetting, a deep sense of confusion and hurt. None of this made sense. She and Kiera had discussed Lenny's list no more than two or three times since his death, and then only in passing. Monique thought she'd been clear: she'd always intended to do the list, someday. It was Becky's diagnosis that drew her, for the third time in one week, to seriously consider the idea. Becky *deserved* to go away.

So she looked at her tight-jawed daughter and answered the only way she could. "Kiera, you know I promised your father I would do it someday."

Kiera's eyes narrowed with incredulity. "And what's going to happen when you're all done with that list? Are you going to set up an account on Match.com? Start bar-hopping with that crazy divorced nurse in your ward? Bring home skeevy younger men to meet your grown daughter?"

Monique blinked. She didn't just hear those words come out of her daughter's mouth. It was...absurd. She would laugh at the idea of dating, if she could muster air into her lungs. The sad, sorry truth was that no matter how many people told Monique she should move on, get herself out there, start dating again—Monique knew she could never, ever bring any other man into this home.

"Kiera." Monique took a deep breath, striving for equilibrium. "Clearly, you're upset—"

"Yeah, I'm upset." Kiera pushed away from the counter. "It must be nice, Mom. I mean, it really must be nice. You know, to just check things off a list, and then completely forget about Daddy."

∞ chapter three

"So Kiera threw that comment like a punch and then—like a true diva—made a dramatic, sweeping exit."

Judy shook her head in sympathy as Monique finished relating what had happened last night. Judy's two oversized and hyper-energized dogs propelled her along the park path, past women jogging with strollers, kids biking with their backpacks lurching, and seniors perched comfortably on benches. "Boy," she said, "that daughter of yours sure chose her career well."

"She wouldn't talk to me all night." Monique kept pace along the path, swinging two-pound weights in her hands. "She wouldn't even open her bedroom door. She just stayed inside, blasting her emo rock."

Judy fixed her gaze on the dappled path. In her experience, teenagers during this difficult year before college shifted their behavior like quicksilver, from cruel mockery to icy distance. It was an evolutionary impulse—at least that's what she'd told herself while she'd been suffering through the same fluxing emotional banishment, five times over. It was the only way teenagers could handle the fact that they'd soon be leaving home.

But Judy sensed Monique was too distressed to absorb the truth. "C'mon, Monie, you must have figured that your proposal was going to take her by surprise."

"I thought she'd be thrilled. It's a trip to *Europe*, not a root canal."

"It has something to do with her father, which means it's a minefield."

"And it blew up in my face. Can you believe what she said to me?" Monique's ferocious striding threatened to outpace Judy's chocolate lab and her lunging golden retriever. "Kiera really seems to think once I'm done with Lenny's list, I'll be dressed in leopard skin leggings and strutting on the singles circuit."

"You *do* own a pair of leopard skin leggings."

"Halloween costume." Monique shook her head in dismay. "You have a memory like an elephant."

"You and Lenny sporting the Tarzan-Jane thing seven years ago at the neighborhood Halloween party? I'll be taking that image to my grave."

"I haven't even looked sideways at a guy since Lenny died. Honestly, if I weren't still having my period, I'd wonder if I had any hormones at all. As far as I'm concerned Lenny's still *here*."

Monique tapped her chest with the ball end of one of her weights. Judy imagined she could hear a hollow, unhealthy thump.

"Maybe Kiera will come around." And maybe Kiera would, Judy told herself, when *Monique* finally came around. "Maybe she just needs a little time to think about it."

"Time." Monique let out a frustrated sigh. "The one thing

Becky doesn't have. She'll be losing more of her vision every year."

Judy's insides did a sliding drop like they did whenever she imagined Becky rendered, by slow and unpredictable degrees, into utter darkness. The dogs, sensing weakness, plunged onto the grass in pursuit of a squirrel. She put the whole force of her shoulders into restraining them, and the whole force of her mind not to think how this villain of a disease would steal from Becky the sight of her own children's faces.

She'd Googled the disease after Becky's bad news, but her mind just couldn't grasp the kind of scientific and medical jargon that, in her early academic life, sent her fleeing to the humanities. So she'd focused most of her Internet searches on what she really wanted to know: the possibility of a cure. The only one she could find lay in retinal implants, a speculative and untested therapy that might not be viable for decades.

Judy often found herself these past weeks trembling in the living room in front of the bookshelf, staring at the photographic history of her own scattered brood.

"Here's the kicker, Judy." Monique's feet scuffed across a patch of gravely path. "I was getting a little excited about it, you know? Before I spoke to Kiera I'd been mapping out a couple of possible routes, thinking about the castles Becky might want to see. Trying to squeeze in all those things on Lenny's list." Monique tipped her head back, closing her eyes for a moment under the light of the sun. "And I'd so really, *really* wanted to do this for Becky."

Judy understood. The whole neighborhood was trying to

find a way to help the Lorenzinis. Everyone was offering rides to drive Brianna and Brian to their various activities, now that Becky had determined that it was better that she just didn't drive at all. She herself had been making some preliminary phone calls to determine how much it would cost to buy Becky a seeing-eye dog when the time came.

But Judy knew from personal experience that there probably wasn't a more powerful or effective or immediate treatment for an emotionally traumatized Becky than a glorious two-week trip to Europe.

"In fact," Monique added, "I was going to ask Becky today. This very morning." She swiped her sweat-beaded forehead with the back of her sleeve. "But after that spat with Kiera, I guess that's done. I may as well just shove the whole idea of doing that bucket list out of my mind."

Judy shook her head sharply. "Bad idea."

"Yeah, maybe it was a bad idea. Maybe Kiera was right to refuse. It's a difficult year, with the applications and es-says—"

"No, I mean it's a bad idea to axe the trip." Judy pivoted on one foot as they rounded the playground end of the park, the dogs leaping and straining at the sight of the kids climbing the jungle gym. "Next year, Monie, there'll just be another excuse."

Monique's pace slacked. "Excuse me?"

Judy surrendered to the tug of the dogs, wishing they'd drag her so quickly away that she'd save herself from her own foolishness. She eyed the canopy of leaves that turned the path into an emerald green tunnel and told herself she should keep her mouth shut. But the words were expanding against her sternum, an unrelenting pressure. Over the past few months, it was becoming more and more difficult for her to resist the urge to just say exactly what was on her mind.

Like when people came up to her and asked how she was enjoying her "new freedom," now that her last child had flown the nest. Or opined on how they couldn't wait until their teenage son took his smelly socks and his growling, wolfman attitude off somewhere far, far away. Or worse, gazed deeply into her eyes and asked her how she was holding up.

Well, she wasn't holding up. She was in swirling little pieces. She wasn't talking about her wonky knee just starting to twinge, or the excess of gray that was threading through her hair, or the fact that she'd missed another period. She was falling to pieces *inside*. And one of the pieces that was falling away right now was the pleasant social nicety that insisted she hold her tongue.

"The bucket list, Monie." The words tumbled out of her. "You're scared to death of it."

Monie's protest was a stutter of unformed syllables.

"The summer after Lenny died, when Kiera was still in that malleable Junior Girl Scout age, you said you just couldn't bring yourself to do that list."

"I was exhausted. Six months of treatments, two months of at-home hospice—"

"One summer later," she continued, throwing all caution to the wind, "I suggested that filling Lenny's bucket list might be a fabulous way to spend what was probably your last *free* summer with Kiera. Before Facebook and boys and the whole generational social scene sucked that girl into the inevitable teenage void."

"I'd just started at the neonatal ICU." Monique gesticulated with a two-pound weight. "That's the summer when I hadn't accumulated enough hours to justify taking off for two or three weeks of vacation."

"You had enough hours last summer."

A puff of air expelled violently. "Kiera was working for that producer."

"Kiera will be working next year too. And probably every summer through college, and every year through the rest of her life."

Monique opened her mouth, closed it, and opened it again, but no sound emerged.

"Monie, hanging around in Munich sounds like a great time for you and Lenny, but think about this. Why would you want a teenager around? What makes you think Lenny wrote that list for Kiera anyway?"

Monique stopped dead in her tracks. She blinked as if she had something in her eye, and then squeezed her eyes shut altogether. Her reaction told Judy what she'd always suspected. Lenny hadn't said anything about bringing Kiera along.

Judy stumbled forward with the dogs and then pulled mightily on the leash, digging the heels of her walking sneakers into the gravel to try to stop their forward motion. She was halfway to the corner of the park before the mutts finally relented, panting and sniffing around the large granite stone that marked the park entrance.

Monie followed more slowly, scraping the path before her.

"Tell me this," Monie said, a ribbon of annoyance in her voice, "how can I *not* bring my daughter on the last trip her father and I ever planned?"

Judy noticed with a twinge of guilt the tightness of Monie's long, slender neck. "Your daughter doesn't want to go."

"She's not thinking straight."

"She's behaving just like any other teenage girl facing the prospect of going to college. She's pulling away from you."

Judy saw the white line forming around Monie's lips, and a further tightening of the cords of her throat.

"She's supposed to pull away from you." Judy stepped onto the side of the path as two joggers approached from beyond Monique, sweaty and gripping iPods and not really paying attention. "It's what she's hard-wired to do. That's why she hit you with UCLA last night. She's warning you she's growing up. Going away."

"Believe me," Monie said darkly, "I know she's going away."

"And by hitting her with that bucket list, she knows *you're* going away. And not just to Europe. She's thinking 'If Mom is doing that bucket list, then Mom is moving on.'"

"I hate that expression."

Monie dropped the weights on the ground and then sank into a crouch, dragging her fingers through her braids. The dogs rumbled over and sniffed at her, nudging their noses against her forearm to try to get a lick upon her face. Judy reeled up the leashes and then finally pulled on the collars until the dogs sat back, heads cocked, tongues lolling, wondering when the crouching Monie was going to uncover her face and give them the vigorous ear-rubs they deserved.

Monie opened one palm and peeked up at her. "I hate you, you know."

A muscle spasmed in Judy's chest, a tightening pull of regret. "I suppose I could have been more diplomatic."

"You're right."

"There's something about turning fifty that severed the link between my tongue and discretion."

"No, I mean you're right about Kiera." Monique planted her hands on her knees and pushed herself up to her full height. "Damn it."

"Honey, I'm five teenagers ahead of you. Wisdom or insanity, that's the choice." Judy glanced at her watch and then toward the street, searching among the strolling moms, skateboarders, and joggers. "Becky's late. She should have been here by now."

Monique dusted off the seat of her yoga pants, and then started shaking her legs to loosen them up after their brisk walk. "She's probably shampooing another rug."

"Are you going to ask her?"

Weary, pleading brown eyes looked up at her. "I don't know, Judy."

"Personally, I think you should."

"It's complicated."

"I can look after Kiera while you're gone."

"That's not it. My mother would love to move in for the two weeks." Monique bent over to retrieve her hand weights, rolling them over in her palms. "Kiera would love the home cooking. My mother would spoil her rotten as usual. The thing is, Kiera is not my only worry."

Judy shifted her attention to the dogs who were now doing their best to water every sapling in the area, thinking with irritated resignation that Monique was determined to find an excuse—any excuse—to put off what the woman most feared.

"It's the logistics," Monique said. "They have me in knots."

With a grunt Judy backhanded that lame excuse. Before working the NICU Monique had been an emergency room nurse, juggling patients, handling crises, coordinating care, as efficient and quick-on-her-feet as anyone Judy had ever known. "This from you, the woman who raised enough money to fund the entire crew team during school budget cuts? The woman who has juggled a full-time job and an ultra-needy brainiac like Kiera all by herself? The woman who—"

"I've never been to Europe." Monique appeared to be counting the stitches in the pleather ends of the weights. "The only trips out of the country I've ever taken have been to family in Trinidad."

Judy rolled her eyes. Judy had traveled through Europe as a twenty-two-year-old with nothing but a rucksack, a train pass, and ignorant bliss.

"The truth is," Monique said, "I've never had to do anything but check that my passport was up to date, make a reservation, and let family know I was coming. I've been online trying to work things out with hotels and airline tickets but it's so complicated. So many languages."

"This is the twenty-first century, babe. When I was living in Strasbourg, I'd be practicing French or nailing down the verbs with a native German, and everyone I spoke to would immediately switch to English." A memory hit her with a startling vividness of the painted, half-timbered, steep-roofed buildings of the old city, with their "sitting dog" windows and jutting dormers. "It was months before I realized that it wasn't that they couldn't bear an American butchering their language—they just wanted to practice English."

"Well, there's also the issue that this wouldn't be a chartered bus tour." Monique rolled kinks out of her shoulders. "It'd be hectic and draining in an *If-It's-Tuesday-This-Must-Be-Belgium* kind of way. To save time, I considered sleeping on an overnight train."

Air hitched in Judy's throat as she remembered the time she'd taken an overnight train from Paris to Amsterdam. She'd slept on the top bunk, rocked in the berth, and dozed to the sound of rattling wheels. The scent of a clove cigarette had drifted up from the lower bunk. Whenever they passed through little towns, the train had sounded its long, mournful whistle.

Monique continued, "It's all so problematic. I'm going to have to figure out how to read complicated train schedules in multiple languages, and decipher taxi fares and learn the tipping customs—"

"Oh, cry me a freakin' river." The dogs lunged, catching sight of another squirrel. Judy righted herself while they tried valiantly to pull her arm out of its socket. She reminded herself that the young girl who had tripped lightly through Europe had subsequently vaulted herself back home to marry Bob and birth five children and plant her feet firmly in suburban American soil.

That girl was dead.

Judy shook herself out of her odd reverie. "That's the whole fun of travel, Monique. Learning new customs. Screwing up along the way. You'll figure it out."

"And then there's Becky and her disability."

"Becky's not blind yet."

"Yeah, but Lenny's got some hairy things on the list for a blind woman. Walking through the catacombs of Paris, for one. She is already night blind."

"So she can shop on the Champs-Élysées while you look at old bones."

"In a city she's never been to? Come on, you've seen how she's been behaving. She hardly leaves the house." Monie straightened from touching her toes to fix Judy with her sharp hazel gaze. "I could use a second hand."

"You mean helping you convince Becky to go along with you? If she has any sense, she'll jump at the opportunity."

"I'm asking if you'll come with us."

Judy heard Monique's words but she wasn't sure she'd heard them right, and her mind did somersaults as she struggled to understand what was just offered. The dogs took advantage of her inattention and broke from her inertia, dragging her in skittering steps farther down the path. She stumbled after them, yanked just as fiercely into memory.

She'd had long hair that fell to her waist. She'd had flexible knees and no marriage or mortgage or children. She'd had an internship at the European Parliament, as a translator and coffee-fetcher, briskly walking through the echoing halls, shifting papers from one office to another, filled with a sense of international purpose. And after the internship was done, she had money in her pocket and a crew of Belgian and French buddies who were thinking of tripping off to Marseilles. The world had unfurled before her, one winding cobblestoned street at a time. She'd wandered across the continent, sleeping in hostels and on park benches, working the grape harvests, eating from street vendors, basking in the sunshine.

It flooded over her, the hot, hungry, swift-footed joy of it.

"Wow," Monique said, stretching her arms over her head, "I didn't think it was possible to shock you into silence. But it's not a joke, Judy. You can even choose a destination or two, as long as it's not too far off the path—"

"This is crazy." Judy yanked sharply on the leash, dragging herself and her dogs and her senses back to Monique's side. "I'm not going to be a cliché, Monie."

Monique paused in her stretching, cocking her head in confusion.

"It's in all the books. Middle-aged guys in crisis buy little red sports cars and take up marathon running. But middle-aged women trot off to Europe to 'find themselves' and end up shacking up on the Adriatic coast with Italian lovers."

Monique sputtered.

"Besides, to fund this new level of midlife crisis, I'd have to dig into Audrey's tuition money."

"No, no." She waved a finger. "You're not going to spend a single penny. This is all-expenses-paid. Lenny left me enough, and it's been in high-interest CDs ever since."

"You can't have that much."

"Wasn't I prepared to take both Kiera and Becky? Now Kiera's out." Her face was a sudden rictus of pain. "There's enough money for three. Maybe not for an Italian lover though. That's all on you."

Judy opened her mouth but no words formed. She mustn't think of the young woman she once was. She'd cast that girl aside when she'd returned to New York, giving up wanderlust to tumble into Bob's welcoming arms.

No. She must think logically.

She thought about the mums she was going to plant in the side garden. She thought about the shutter on the front of the house that was peeling and needed to be taken down, scraped, and repainted. She thought about her mother's antique vanity made out of bird's-eye maple that she wanted to sand down and refinish. She thought about the attic paint job that had been "waiting" for approximately thirteen years, since she and Bob had renovated the attic themselves, as a room for their oldest boy to live in. Back then they'd finished the Sheetrock and laid a rug over the old attic boards, but Robert couldn't wait so he moved in. The next thing they knew he was moving to college.

A family now scattered, like so many dandelion seeds to the wind.

"Look, there's Becky." Monique glanced over to where the tall, slim mother emerged from around the railroad tracks. The blonde kept sure to the path, her head lowered, her special sunglasses with the amber lenses covering half her face. "I'd like to ask her about the trip today. That is, if you'd join us, Judy."

And in that moment, standing in the dappled sunshine under the broad branches of a sycamore tree, Judy felt the swirling energies that had bedeviled her for months coalesce in one singularly fierce idea.

Europe.

"Oh, God," she said, sucking in a breath so fast that the cool autumn air braised the base of her lungs. "Oh, God, Monie, *yes.*"

chapter four

Becky felt vaguely foolish as she stood in her room with the suitcase open on the bed before her. Through the closed door, she could hear the last sleepy, read-me-another-story mutterings of her children as her mother-in-law, who'd be helping Marco out in the two weeks Becky would be gone, put them to bed. The muted roar of a football game slipped up the stairs from the den, where Marco watched TV. Becky fingered her passport, six months away from expiration, last used on a driving trip to Quebec City before Brianna was born.

Monique's offer for a trip to Europe had been a shock. It was as if it had emerged out of one of those foggy places in Becky's vision. She'd run full-speed into it, only to come out stunned and seeing stars, wondering what the hell she'd just hit. She'd said yes, of course. Everyone in the neighborhood had been trying to help her, all in their own lovable, awkward ways. She'd become "That Neighbor" now, the one the whole coven whispered about, shared concern for, fussed over, like when Mrs. McCarthy down the street had breast cancer.

Becky appreciated Monique's offer. She really did, even

now, as she slipped her passport in the purse at her feet and for the fifth time pulled out the clothes and toiletries and shoes she knew she could more artfully puzzle into the carry-on suitcase. But the feeling she couldn't shake was that Monique's crazy, heartfelt, unbelievable offer to show her the castles of Europe was a mildly reprehensible distraction from what she *should* be doing. Like learning the exact number of stairs in her house from one landing to another. Or studying Braille. Or memorizing the milky shade of cappuccino that formed the inner ring of Brianna's eyes.

She heard heavy footsteps on the stairs. Her spine tightened, and she bent over her suitcase, refolding the yoga pants and sports bras with increased intent. The door squealed open, and Marco came in, swinging it closed behind him.

She didn't look at him, but she was aware of him anyway. His dark mess of crisp Italian hair. His broad longshoreman's shoulders.

He said, "I thought you'd be asleep by now."

She sensed the surprise in his pause. "Everything is harder to fit than I expected." She reached for the compact tin of her wax oil crayons and tried to wedge them upright against the side of the suitcase. "I can't overpack. We have to be mobile."

He flicked his watch off his wrist and set it on the bureau. "The car for the airport is coming at five a.m."

"I can sleep on the plane."

"You'd better. I've seen Monique's ten-page itinerary. You're not getting much sleep once your feet hit the ground."

"I'm almost done."

She felt a tingling at the back of her neck, a certainty that came of twelve long, difficult years of marriage. Marco had something on his mind. It would have been better if she had finished packing earlier, if she'd been asleep when he came upstairs—or at least in bed feigning sleep. She could have avoided that awkward moment when Marco would look at her under the brooding ridge of his brow, a question in his dark eyes. Right now, sex was the last thing on her mind.

Marco seized his T-shirt by the back of his neck, dragged it off his shoulders, and then balled it into his hands. He opened the closet door and tossed it into the laundry. She busied herself rolling a slinky, deep blue rayon dress, her one choice for evening wear, a dress she'd last worn on her and Marco's ten-year wedding anniversary.

"I heard your mother reading to Brian and Brianna," she said, casting about for anything to fill the tense silence. "She must have been at it for a good hour. She's likely to coddle and feed them so well that they won't want me to come home."

"That's Mom's way of showing you that you don't have to worry about the kids. All you have to worry about is enjoying the vacation." He pulled his cell phone out of the pocket of his jeans and glanced at the face. "This was incredibly generous of Monique."

Becky heard the undercurrent of meaning, the vague discomfort that Monique was gifting Becky something luxurious and much-needed, something he, as a man temporarily out of work, could not provide.

"She is as big-hearted as always," Becky said, "bringing both Judy and me along."

His gaze flickered to the notebook lying next to the open suitcase. "You'll get to sketch. That's good."

"Castles, castles, castles."

Unwittingly, her gaze slipped to the drawing hanging on the wall near the closet, a framed sketch Marco had playfully drawn of this old house, just after they'd committed to buy it. Upon Marco's rendering with all its sharp corners and straight lines, she'd made a few fanciful renovations with his wry approval—adding two turrets, topped with flags.

"I'm glad she talked you into this, Beck."

She paused at the use of her nickname, at the low timbre of Marco's voice. That sound always rippled through her, like a low mournful note of a cello in a darkened room. She hardly ever heard it anymore.

She spoke in careful, even tones. "I'm glad too."

"Last week I thought you were going to back out."

"It was a moment of panic." Nudged by the knowledge that someday she'd be a blind mother in a kitchen full of pots of boiling water and hot grease and sharp knives and small children. "I'm fine now."

Then with a sliding drop of her stomach it overwhelmed her all over again, the explanations the doctors had repeated while she struggled to understand. How the photoreceptors of her eyes were slowly deteriorating. How they had been failing for perhaps all her life. How the rods—sensitive to low light—were the first to go, which is why night blindness was her first symptom. She had argued with the specialist. She'd told him that she'd always had perfect vision in the right light, able to read up close and see the whole landscape in the distance. But in his flat, unarguable voice, the doctor informed her that her vision was tunneling, and within that good sphere, there were spots already deteriorating. She wouldn't necessarily notice it, he'd said, because her brain struggled to fill in the information. But those watery little rings of spaces would eventually grow and merge, and eventually her brain would no longer be able to fill in the blanks.

Right now those blanks in between were big enough to eclipse the sight of a small fawn, running in front of her car.

No, this trip wouldn't help anything. As far as she knew, only Jesus was on record curing the blind.

"Beck, maybe we should reconsider the phone situation."

She glanced up. Marco stood by his bedside table, his attention fixed on his phone as he scrolled through email.

"There's no reason."

"I could call tomorrow, add international service."

"It's an unnecessary expense." She wiggled a pair of flats between her cosmetic case and her sneakers. "I agreed to this trip only because it won't cost us anything."

He went silent for a moment, the only sound in the room the nudge of his finger on the face of his phone. Since the furlough from his job began, mentioning "expenses" or "costs" or "money" was a fresh new way to bring tension between them.

"Bring your phone," he said. "I may do it anyway."

"Monique and Judy both have cell phones with international service. Their phone numbers are tacked up on the bulletin board downstairs."

"So we can play international phone tag if there's an emergency?"

She raised her head to look straight at his classic, proud

Roman profile. "If there's an emergency, Marco, there's not a hell of a lot I can do about it from Munich or Paris or Monaco."

"It'd be nice to be able to communicate easily."

With a spasm of irritation, Becky thought, oh, yes, it would be nice to be able to talk easily to her husband again. But the bed that stretched between them may as well have been a moat without a drawbridge. It had been so long since she and Marco had engaged in an easy conversation that even these lame efforts only made her nerves tighten.

She could pinpoint the day the troubles began. It wasn't the day he'd asked her to take in Gina, his twelve-year-old daughter from a failed teenage relationship. During that time they'd had conversations that lasted for days about the logistics of bringing into their growing family a brooding, emotionally wounded girl whose mother had just been jailed on drug-trafficking charges. Marco had confessed his long-simmering guilt about leaving his daughter to be raised with someone who showed increasing signs of instability and bad behavior. He'd frankly admitted his failings and asked her with great feeling and deference to try opening her heart and their home to this troubled fledgling.

She'd agreed, wholeheartedly.

The real trouble began a few years later, when Gina was brought home in a police cruiser, stinking of vodka and vomit, after she'd disappeared for three days into the Bowery with her nineteen-year-old slacker of a boyfriend. That night, Becky and Marco had been at one another's throats, arguing about the appropriate response, the need for discipline, for changes in expectations. She'd accused him of behaving like the guilty, absent dad who indulged his child in the hopes of establishing friendship rather than standards of appropriate conduct. He'd accused her of hardening her heart against his daughter; he accused her of not even trying to understand Gina's temperament. That accusation pinched, because she *did* understand Gina's craving for independence. But for a few twists in their respective fates, Becky could have been Gina.

Since then, the hurts and misunderstandings and differences in opinion had just accumulated, leaving nicks and scars where no nerve endings grew anymore. Long, deep carapaces of hard tissue streaked their relationship, ridges of separation neither one of them dared to approach, whole swaths of emotional real estate now bereft of feeling.

"You know what, forget your phone." Marco tugged on the blankets, flipping them aside so he sat on the sheets. "Just don't bring it at all."

Becky paused mid-zip, glancing across the bed at Marco's back as he fiddled with his bedside clock to set the alarm.

"It's a good idea to take a couple of weeks apart." The muscles on his shoulders flexed as he clicked through the numbers on the clock. "We both could use a breather."

She felt a whole new chill in the room, as if the vent above her had blasted Arctic air. Marco didn't move. She fixed her attention on the nape of his neck, the short hair that grew there. The doctor had warned her that the cones in her eyes would deteriorate too, stealing the ability to see color. Like the little dark mark like a fleck of fresh cinnamon on his swarthy skin, just where the slope of his shoulder muscle met the curve of his neck.

"Let's look at it as an opportunity," he continued. "It's a chance to think about our new situation."

The chill shivered through her. She'd heard those words before. Thrown at her with the same controlled anger after they'd found out that Gina had taken the car without permission. Becky had been at the end of her rope then, a rope that she felt was tied around her hands, preventing her from addressing the root of Gina's problems. So he'd taken his daughter to his mother's and stayed there for a week.

Imagine. She'd once thought things would get better, after Gina moved away to a dorm at Rutgers.

"There are going to be a lot of changes going forward, Beck." He shifted toward her, and with great effort he met her eyes. "This trip will give both of us a chance to think about how we're going to manage."

The word was like a blow to the solar plexus. She zipped the suitcase, pulled it off the bed, and turned away from him to shove it against the wall. She'd always managed just fine by herself. Now she supposed Marco couldn't wait to get her out of the kitchen, away from the car, and far from the kids. He had to prepare Brian and Brianna for the sightless mom she would soon be. He had to prepare himself for a lifetime with a disabled wife.

She couldn't seem to breathe. The last time he abandoned her, he came back out of duty. Now he'd stay with her out of pity.

Pity.

Becky walked into the master bath, clicking the door closed behind her.

The morning couldn't come quickly enough.

chapter five

Monique's experience with travel was defined by two trips: Louisiana, where she and Lenny had luxuriated in the balmy breezes of his mother's riverside veranda; and Trinidad, where after Lenny's death, she and Kiera had indulged in island time, swimming in warm salt waters. Because of this Monique was used to stepping off stuffy planes into the caress of humid breezes, usually coming from a blinding blue sky. Not, as the automatic doors at Heathrow airport swooshed open, to the cold slap of an English fog.

She raised her face to the sky. Moisture prickled her cheeks. Lenny had always been a hothouse flower, staying inside in the depths of the New Jersey winter, eschewing air conditioning in the ripeness of summer. He would have taken one suspicious look at this gray English sky and pulled his overcoat against his shuddering body.

"Cheeky London weather." Judy paused just long enough to completely block pedestrian traffic. "Great for ducks and sherry and tweed and mystery novels. When I was last here, it rained for a full week."

Judy made this comment with a grin—a huge grin that set the skin crinkling at the corners of her clear, gray eyes. Her cheek still sported a groove where the piping of the airplane seat had dug into her face while she slept. The woman could barely contain herself, bouncing on the balls of her feet as she flexed her fingers over the handle of her luggage.

Monique led her away from the automatic doors and scanned the area for a taxi stand. "I can put up with a little rain. We're here for only twenty-four hours anyway. Look—there's the line for the cabs."

"It's a queue," Judy corrected. "It's a *queue* for the *hackneys*."

"Right." Monique headed toward the line where travelers waited their turn for a black taxi. With her luggage clicking over the pavement behind her, she slung her daypack onto one shoulder and tugged out the sheaf of papers rolled up in a side pocket. "We need to be in London by noon, and Heathrow is an hour out, so I think we'll make it. You exchanged that cash while I was tied up in customs, right?"

"Right-o. Pounds and pence."

"I can't believe I forgot to get English pounds back home. Euros aren't going to do us any good in pubs."

"Pubs! Fish and chips." Judy made a strangled little sound. "Crisps. Pints of ale. This is so much better than crew-team trips to south Jersey."

"Hey," Monique said, glancing behind Judy as she took a place in the cab line. "What happened to Becky?"

"She stopped at the loo while I was changing money. Did you hear that bloke?" Judy swung around and gestured to a man in a suit striding past them while talking into his cell phone. "It's like the place is crawling with a thousand Hugh Grants."

"You didn't wait?"

"For Becky to come out of the bog? No."

"Judy!"

"Hey, don't get your knickers in a twist."

Monique tamped down her irritation. It appeared that Judy was determined to use every one of the Unique British Expressions on the list she'd printed out before she left the States. "How do you know she isn't lost?"

"She told me she'd meet us by the hackney stand."

"If she can *find* it."

"Listen, last night she nearly went barmy when I offered to help her to the airplane restroom. So bugger it. She'll find her way here."

Monique sighed. She couldn't be angry with Judy—or Becky. Becky had been all but mute from the moment she'd climbed into the sleek black limo Monique had ordered for their trip to the airport. Becky had slid into the car and waved good-bye to Marco and the kids. She hadn't touched the glass of champagne they'd thrust into her hands. The girl looked like she was going to an execution rather than on a two-week vacation with friends, but she just closed up when they tried to get her to talk about it. With a look of abject apology, Becky had wrapped herself in a blanket and turned a shoulder as soon as they'd found their seats on the plane.

Just then Monique glimpsed Becky, head down, striding through the automatic doors. Becky paused, blinking and scanning the area, and Monique couldn't help but notice how anxiously she stood, so thin and uncertain in the frame of the open doors. Monique waved her arm over her head in big sweeping movements, hoping to capture her attention.

Then, with the power of lungs that had been screaming five urchins down to dinner for twenty-five years, Judy shouted, "BECKY!"

Monique shook the ringing from her ears as Becky turned in their direction. With a quick wave, she strode to join them. Becky moved arrow-straight, her gaze fixed on her destination. So when a young woman in a suit, swinging a briefcase as she spoke on a wireless ear set, crossed Becky's path, Becky reared back a fraction. Her action, unexpected by the other travelers, threw off the whole tenuous commuter equilibrium, and Becky's progress for the last ten feet was an awkward series of shuffled steps and cringed shoulders, of muffled apologies and rolled eyes.

"Freakin' Londoners," Becky said as she joined them.

"Bunch of wankers," Judy added.

Becky grunted. "Worse than walking down Fifth Avenue in December."

At the sight of the dark blue challenge in Becky's gaze, Monique let the incident go. Everyone was cranky and off-kilter. Right now the cloudy sky said it was mid-morning, but her body screamed that it was four thirty a.m. and why the hell wasn't she lying under warm blankets, serenely asleep? Her eyeballs were itchy. She couldn't even think of resting. The three of them had too much to accomplish before she could consider a nap.

She moved up in the cab line and bent over the first page of the itinerary to protect the paper from the drizzle. So many details. She'd tried to take care of everything in the two weeks they'd had before their flights—the international driver's license, the money exchange, the reservations for the Paris-to-Zurich flight as well as nailing down reservations at various international hotels—all while checking the bucket list to make sure everything she needed to do was actually *open* and *available* during the short window of time she'd be in each country. There was only so much she could do while working full-time, especially when two weeks ago an abandoned preemie landed in the NICU. Monique had taken an extra shift after she'd been handed the curled-up little boy, whose body nearly fit in her palm.

And then there was Kiera at home, just as tightly curled-up. Her daughter had only grudgingly given her a dry peck good-bye last night. The girl had been closed-off and moody and uncommunicative, her dark chocolate eyes flashing accusations whenever Monique tried to broach the subject of this trip. The arrival of *Grand-mère* yesterday—with her bags from a Caribbean grocer—had sent Kiera into theatrical paroxysms of joy and affection. The very affection, Monique figured, that Kiera had so intentionally been holding back from her.

Monique pulled out her phone. It was the wee hours of the morning on the East Coast so she chose to send a text.

Arrived safely at Heathrow. Miss you already, baby girl.

"Look sharp, Monie." Judy stepped off the curb as they reached the front of the line, and the hackney driver came around to open the trunk. "Time to put your luggage in the boot."

Monique rolled her eyes as she slung her rolling luggage

into the trunk. "King's Cross," she murmured to the cabbie. She slipped into the backseat after the other women then rattled off the address of the hotel.

"So," Judy asked, "when we get to the hotel, do you think our room will have a loo?"

Monique frowned as the cab rumbled into traffic. "Why wouldn't it?"

"Well, at some of the finer places I stayed when I was last in London, the loo was down the hall, shared by at least twenty smelly backpackers."

"As long as it has a bed," Becky muttered, sinking down in the wide leather seat. "A nice, soft, comfortable bed."

"The hostel I stayed at had a thin mattress and no sheets." Judy sat in the middle of the wide seat, with her belly pack loose on her thighs. "I shared the room with a twenty-six-year-old busker and a group of flamenco dancers from Salamanca." Judy's smile was slow and wicked. "The hookah was smoking all night."

"There's a story," Monique murmured, "that you never told during the last overnight Girl Scout camp."

"Tell me later. I'm so tired right now," Becky said, as she fished her special amber sunglasses out of the depths of her purse, "that I'd sleep right on the sidewalk."

"That's pavement in London."

"No one is sleeping for hours." Monique rattled the papers on her lap. "We've got to do the London Eye today. It's the first thing on the list."

"Look! There's a lorry." Judy leaned over Monique, pointing to a truck on the road. "And it's about to go on a roundabout."

Monique frowned at her. "Are you going to be doing this all day?"

"It's bleeding likely! We're on holiday."

Becky groaned. And Monique thought, as the black cab headed toward London, that it was true what they said about travel: There was no better way to really get to know your friends.

The London Eye was a one-hundred-and-thirty-five-meter Ferris wheel sitting on the south bank of the Thames River between Hungerford and Westminster Bridge, opposite the Houses of Parliament. As Monique glimpsed it, as she emerged from the tube at Waterloo, she was amazed that it had originally been built as a temporary structure for the sole purpose of ringing in the twenty-first century. The enormous, spindly, once-doomed wheel now towered over the city buildings. It had become such a favored landmark that it had made the travel section of one of the newspapers she and Lenny had perused during those last weeks of his life.

"I'd like to go to the top of that someday," Lenny had said, tapping the paper with the corner of his glasses. "I bet from all the way up there you could see the whole wide world."

She craned her neck to take in the sight, his words ringing in her ears. She wished she could will Lenny back to life for just this one moment, to stand beside her and experience the same rush of excitement and expectation.

Instead it was Becky who stumbled against her, letting her head fall onto Monique's shoulder as they walked. "Sleeeeeep."

Monique gave her a squeeze. Once they'd all dumped their luggage at their hotel near King's Cross Station and ordered up strong coffee and a full bangers-and-mash English breakfast in the hotel restaurant, Becky's mood had improved.

"We'll see castles from up there," Monique promised. "I read that, from the top, you can see all the way to Windsor."

"Bloody unlikely." Judy tipped her head toward Becky and gave Monique a wide-eyed look. "Windsor's got to be twenty-five miles away."

Becky intercepted the look with a sigh and a roll of her eyes.

"You do know that Buckingham Palace is only a Tube ride from here," Judy added brightly. "We missed the changing of the guard, but we could go and torment a Beefeater before dinner."

"First things first." Monique reached back and gave her daypack, with its rolled-up itinerary, a little pat. "We've got to stick with the plan."

The crowds were thin, due to the weather, so they didn't have to wait long at the ticket counter to purchase three passes. Soon after they were waiting in the line for the Eye itself. Each of the closed-in, climate-controlled "pods" could carry twenty-eight people, and the wheel moved slowly enough that people embarked and disembarked as it was moving. As they neared the front of the line, Monique glimpsed one pod full of wedding revelers with waiters pouring champagne and another empty but for a single rider, sitting alone on the center bench.

She watched that solo rider's bent back for a long time.

Maybe she should have reserved a pod for herself. Away from the crowds and the noise, she might have been able to summon Lenny to sit beside her. She needed to feel Lenny close, now that she'd started the list. An uneasy feeling had crept over her these past weeks, sparked in part by Kiera's angry outburst, but also by something else, some long-suppressed resistance now elbowing its way into her consciousness. She'd only just begun to understand why she'd avoided doing this bucket list for four long years.

She didn't want to lose any more of Lenny.

"Hey," Judy said, her head buried in the London Eye mini-guide, "what time is our train to Amsterdam in the morning?"

"Noon," Monique said, shaking off her gloom. She clutched her arms as a chill breeze swept off the Thames. "We're taking the Eurostar through the Chunnel, going straight to Brussels, and then we're hopping some inter-city train from Brussels to Amsterdam."

"Maybe we can slip in a trip to the Tower of London tomorrow morning before the train."

Becky perked up a bit. "That's a castle."

Monique said, "Is it even open on Sundays?"

Judy shrugged. "I'll call when we pop back to the flat. Those yeoman warders that work as guides tell the goriest stories. They lick their lips as they talk about medieval torture devices. I love the British."

The doors swept open, and the attendant guided them into the glass pod along with about fifteen other people. Monique took up a position standing by the glass, gripping the rail as the door whooshed closed and the pod began its

steady rise. As they escalated above the surrounding buildings, the great Dickensian sweep of the London roof-scape
stretched before them. Judy, with the guidebook open on
the rail, looked through her reading glasses and then over
them, seeking landmarks. She pointed out St. Paul's Cathedral, and a bunch of other spires built by Christopher
Wren, nudging Becky in the ribs with each discovery.
Becky squinted into the distance to ask the identity of a
particular tall, strange building, and Judy read from the
guidebook that it was called the "Gherkin," for its resemblance to a pickle. Becky dug out her camera to take a
photo.

Well it's begun, Lenny.

Monique's heart began that strange, dizzying pitter-patter,
like something soft and small racing in her chest. She'd
rushed all of them to the London Eye for more than one reason. Sometimes, it was best to just *do* something. Like when
you vaccinate a young child. Don't warn them, don't give
them a reason to doubt, just brandish the needle and then
plunge it in. The pain wouldn't even be noticed until the
shot was already done.

Then Monique became aware of Becky standing beside
her, settling a warm hand on the middle of her back. Becky
wore the amber-tinted sunglasses that the ophthalmologist
had recommended. Standing here limned by hazy English
light, Becky looked like a Swedish rock star trying to go
incognito. Though Monique couldn't fully see her expression, she felt the strength of her concern.

"Hey, guys, Charing Cross Station is right there." Judy
pointed down to the buildings and the trains slithering in

and out on the rails. "Beck, over there you should be able to see Westminster Abbey."

Becky made a vaguely irritated, noncommittal noise then tilted her head against the glass as the pod crept its way higher. "This is sort of an odd thing for Lenny to want to do, isn't it, Monie?"

Monique winced, like she always did, whenever someone said his name out loud. "This is the place that triggered the whole list."

He'd still been getting chemo then, even though his oncologist had already been making noise about hospice. At the time Monique wasn't ready to hear it. She'd still been in that stubborn, determined phase when she was convinced the doctors she trusted and knew so well could help her husband beat the disease.

"I mean, of all the things in London we could be seeing today," Becky said, "the Tower of London, the British Museum, Buckingham Palace . . . it's strange that he'd pick this."

"Can you really see Lenny wandering through dusty old museums?"

"I suppose that's true. But still I remember when he was honorary Team Mom for the girls' soccer team and we went on that trip to Six Flags." Becky tilted her head against the glass, strands of her hair standing upright with static electricity. "Lenny took the role of minding cameras and backpacks while the rest of us rode on Kingda Ka."

"We're not exactly moving at a hundred twenty-eight miles per hour right now."

"No, but we're pretty darn high."

"Honestly, I think this choice was pure coincidence."

Those still-hopeful early weeks hurt to remember. "He'd had to hang out for hours for IV chemo then. On my breaks, I'd come down and bring him newspapers. Those were long hours. He read every single word of those papers, leaving newsprint fingerprints all over the arms of the hospital chair." Monique paused, remembering the light that had gleamed in Lenny's eyes when he first got the idea. "One day, he tapped the paper and said we ought to take a ride on this thing someday. He said we should write it down, make a list."

Becky didn't respond right away. She rubbed a little more vigorously against Monique's back, as if she'd felt a sudden chill in Monique's spine.

"Well," Becky said, "it is one hell of a view."

"Look, there's Big Ben," Judy said, leaning in close as she pointed to the west. "Can you see it, Becky?"

"For goodness sake, Judy, I'm not blind yet."

Monique mentally winced.

"In fact," Becky continued, "on a day like today, when the light is strong but not glaring, I can pretty much see the whole wide world. Same as about a month ago, when everyone just believed I was Becky, the lovable neighborhood klutz."

Judy fumbled the guidebook closed. "You know what? I'm getting vertigo leaning up against this glass. I'm going to go sit down for a minute."

Judy left to find space on the bench in the center of the pod. Monique gave Becky a gentle elbow in the side. "That wasn't very nice."

Her pale jaw hardened.

"For what it's worth," Monique added, "when Judy said, 'Can you see it?' she just meant it as an expression. Judy might as well have asked me too."

Becky crossed her arms. "I hate those damn expressions. 'See you later.' 'I'll keep an eye on it.' 'She's got a great eye.' 'I'll keep my eyes peeled.' 'Keep your eye on the ball.'" Becky shook her head. "You know what? I am turning into Ms. Bloody Cranky Pants. I think I'll sit down too."

Monique kept her place by the window and took solace in the momentary solitude. She gazed upon the iconic British clock tower and Westminster Abbey as well. As the pod began its westerly descent, she noted the surprisingly green, wooded areas of central London, a long chain of parks whose names she probably should remember from her college days, when she was obsessed with British lit. She wondered which of the green spaces were St. James's Park, Hyde Park, Kensington Gardens. How wonderful it would have been if she and Lenny could have walked those green spaces, as they'd once walked in the little manicured park behind the oncology building.

She bent forward and let her forehead rest against the glass, looking down through the spindly white scaffolding to the silver ribbon of the Thames. She knew she shouldn't summon Lenny. This place was too busy, too public, and too full of pattering children's feet and the loud chatter of nearby German tourists. She might embarrass herself. She might say something out loud.

She closed her eyes nonetheless, mentally casting about in search of that soft, warm, oh-so-familiar-glow. She ached to sense him standing just behind her, lingering.

Are you here with me, Lenny?

An image bloomed in her mind of Lenny in that hospital bed, crinkling the newspaper as he lowered it. He gazed at her over the edge of a pair of reading glasses. Monique suppressed a bubble of amusement. Lenny never did admit he needed those glasses. But he'd never had any qualms about borrowing hers, perching them on the end of his nose though the frames were studded with rhinestones.

Sometime later the sensation of a hand on her arm brought Monique back to the present. Judy stood beside her, silently drawing Monique's attention to the sinking landscape. The pod had dropped below the level of the rooftops. A crowd waited by the doors as it slowed to the landing. The doors whooshed opened. The ride was over.

Usually Monique loved checking things off lists. Usually, she loved the sense of accomplishment that followed. Now she ushered her friends ahead of her down the ramp so they would not glimpse the worry on her face. She skimmed her fingers along the railing, prepared to grip it should she sense a sudden, deep-bodied chill or should her knees completely fail her. Then she forced herself to imagine the list as she mentally inked a checkmark by the first item.

She exhaled a long, slow breath and waited. She monitored her vitals, seeking aches, soreness, a sudden drop in blood pressure. But her breathing remained calm, her pulse strong. Her heart did not grow leaden in her chest. In fact her heart felt oddly feather-light, and not because some part of it had just cracked and broken away. She felt weightless…unburdened. A breeze swept off the Thames as she mentally searched for the source of this unexpected buoyancy. The sudden gust swept her braids off her shoulders and brushed the nape of her neck.

The sensation was not unlike a kiss.

Monique stopped in her tracks. Tourists elbowed by her, forcing her against the rail. She ran her fingers across the back of her neck.

Across her face crept a soft, slow smile.

∞ chapter six

*W*anderlust.

The word—straight from the German—bubbled up inside Judy. It churned along with hundreds of other foreign words and expressions that had sputtered in her head since she'd boarded the London-Brussels train amid the business class of Europe.

Becky sat across from her, closing her eyes behind the amber sunglasses as the French country sunshine poured in through the window. Monique perched in the seat beside Becky, her face buried in an Amsterdam guidebook, making occasional grunting noises as a line of concentration deepened between her brows. Judy sat still, ignoring the e-book reader open to a Dutch-English dictionary on her lap. Despite the continuing effects of jet lag and a painfully stiffening knee, she existed right now in a state of heightened awareness, her blood thrumming and her brain alight, gulping the passing scenery as the Eurostar train zoomed toward Brussels.

She read the signs at each station as they zipped by. Calais, Lille. The little villages of Nieppes, Bois-Grenier,

La Chapelle d'Armentières. She rolled the names over her tongue, like plump champagne grapes.

The young girl she'd once been—that light-footed fearless creature she'd abandoned long ago—shifted from a long slumber deep within her, stretching with slowly opening eyes into her roomier, older skin.

Oh, yeah, Judy thought. *I remember you.*

"So, Judy," Monique said, as she turned another page of the guidebook, "are we going to Amsterdam to see the Anne Frank house? Or the Van Gogh museum?"

The corners of Judy's lips twitched. Monique and her itinerary and her pencil and her plans. "Frankly, Monie, I hadn't thought that far ahead."

That had been her favorite way to travel. Just slip on a train with a small rucksack and go wherever the train takes you. Step out into a city and disorient yourself in the warren of ancient streets.

"We're going to arrive around five in the afternoon." Monique flicked her wrist to glance at her watch. "We should have plans."

"We could just wander." Judy remembered the canals at nighttime, the smear of the neon lights on the water, the gentle swish of small boats sliding under the bridges. "The old city is full of great architecture, exotic boats."

"We don't have much time. We're heading off to Cologne tomorrow night."

"It's not a big city."

"How about a boat ride on the canals? Or there's the Rembrandt House museum."

"I'm game for anything."

"Judy, honey, you picked this city." Monique closed the guidebook on her lap. "You were *quick* to pick it too. And after perusing this curiously detailed guidebook for the last hour, I'm just hoping we're not going to Amsterdam to buy Moroccan hash or Nepal bud."

Becky snorted, straightening from the window in sudden attention. "What kind of trip are we taking?"

Monique tossed the guidebook onto Becky's lap. "There's actually a smart shop listed in there—address and all—that sells Ecuadorian mushrooms so fierce that one bite can cause a psychotic breakdown."

"Oh," Judy said, shaking her head, "I'd stay away from the mushrooms."

Monique raised a brow. "You think?"

"Yeah." Judy nodded. "But I might consider going to the Pool Dog coffee shop and rolling up some White Widow."

That was the first thing she and Thierry did, all those years ago, when they skipped off the train from Strasbourg. He'd taken her hand and led her down the narrow, cobbled streets to a coffee shop. She'd followed him with a light heart, watching the way the Dutch sunlight turned the delicate hairs on the nape of his neck a fragile gold. In the smoky café, they'd nervously perused the menu of weed and hash and prerolled joints, then struck up a conversation with a couple of French university students giggling at the table beside them. The four of them had pushed together their rickety tables and, with increasing hilarity, dared to share a fatty over strong Dutch coffee at eleven-thirty in the morning.

The gentle rattle of the swift-moving train seemed suddenly loud, and with a glance at her seat mates, Judy realized she'd shocked them into silence. She felt vaguely uneasy. They hadn't seen this girl before. Until the moment she'd stepped off the plane in London yesterday, she'd made a point to pretend this young woman had never existed.

"Oh, for goodness sake." Judy straightened one leg, trying to stretch out a kink in her knee. "Are you two going to look me in the eye and tell me you never inhaled?"

"I haven't." Becky blinked and cast a quick glance Monique's way. "I *haven't*. Weed wasn't so easy to get in my tiny corner of Minnesota. Our poison was blackberry brandy and peppermint schnapps."

"Well, well," Judy said, "we've found that rare creature. A mom who didn't lie to her stepdaughter during the drug talk."

Monique's lashes flickered. A muscle moved along the edge of her jaw as she raised her hand. "Liar, liar, sitting right here."

"We're all liars," Judy said. "We told them about Santa Claus and the Easter Bunny too."

Monique murmured, "I believe that still makes me a hypocrite."

"You're no hypocrite. You're a *realist*. Rule number sixty-two: Avoid giving teenagers ammo. You can regale them about the adventures of your misspent youth when their brains have developed enough to correctly weigh risk and reward."

"In any case, I didn't like the stuff," Monique said. "It made me paranoid."

"Then avoid the space cakes in Amsterdam." Judy grimaced. "You can't gauge the strength of those until after you've eaten one."

"Please tell me you're not serious, Judy."

"About the space cakes? I'm absolutely serious."

"No, about rolling a joint and smoking it in some Dutch coffee shop."

Judy paused, remembering what it was like to sit in those rattling chairs with the haze of blue smoke above their heads. She remembered how she and Thierry laughed every time the bell over the door rang, how once they were done, their group—and there was always a motley, ever-changing group—would tumble out into the darkness of a Dutch evening and into the crowd. She remembered how they'd stand in front of a head shop just to admire the colors of the lights. They'd find a park, throw themselves under a tree, feel the prickle of grass on their faces as they made stories out of the stars.

Judy shrugged and avoided Monique's eye. "It *is* legal here."

Monie muttered, "Oh my God."

"But I have to admit, there's been so much genetic engineering in the last twenty-seven years that the idea makes me anxious."

"So *this* is why you chose Amsterdam?"

"No, no. It was never about the drugs. That was just a little . . . rebellious experimentation. The last time I was here, all I really wanted to do was roll around in bed with my French lover."

Thierry had a gentle smile, the kind that made one eye crinkle more than the other. She'd first met him on a city train in Strasbourg. She'd been dressed for work—neat skirt, sleeveless top, and flat shoes. He was tall and lanky, and the warmth of his body released a loamy, aromatic fragrance from the wear-softened cotton of his T-shirt. The sway of the train thrust him against her as they held on to straps through the tunnels. He'd apologized for bumping into her. He told her he was just back from picking grapes at a vineyard in Champagne. Would she like to go for a coffee?

Judy became aware, again, of the sway of the train, the rhythmic clatter of metal against metal, and her friends' gaping silence.

"My, my, my." Monique's voice was a low rumble, her eyes alight. "You've been holding back on us, girl."

Oh, dear.

"All those Friday afternoon barbecues," Monique continued, "and never once did you mention a French lover."

"Did you really expect me to bring up my ex-lovers while the whole neighborhood is sitting on the McCarthys' deck?"

Monique raised a brow. "Under the influence of pinot grigio, you usually overshare."

Judy looked away, hesitating. There was a certain kind of man a girl met when she traveled far and wide. They flooded the continent during the summer months, breezily attractive, easygoing, and adaptable. They knew multiple languages and switched between them effortlessly. They were charming to a fault and, for the most part, really skilled lovers. Thierry just happened to be her last.

"Wow." Becky shifted in her seat, curving one leg under her in a way only a skinny woman can do. "And here I thought you and Bob had grown up together. You know, like in a big green pod or something."

"Bob and I didn't meet until after I came home from Europe." The thought of Bob gave her an unexpected twinge. "Woodstock was way before my time," Judy said. "But I suppose Amsterdam was like my Burning Man."

Monique gave her an incredulous once-over. "You mean that nudity-filled, crazy-men-in-chicken-suits music festival in the desert?"

"I was young." Judy patted her sleek, chin-length cut, newly trimmed for the vacation. "I had hair down to my knees. My thin, flexible, twenty-one-year-old knees."

Monique shook her head. "I can't picture it. I spent too much time watching you march your boys in military formation while cleaning up the backyard."

"Voice like a drill sergeant," Becky added. "You could slice carrots with it."

"Well," Judy murmured, "that woman you saw whipping her kids into shape spent six months backpacking solo through Europe."

Becky paused, a water bottle halfway to her lips. "I thought you got your packing skills from Cub Scout leader training. Or Girl Scout preparedness badges. Or herding five kids on camping trips to the Adirondacks."

"When you're spending three bucks a night at a place like the Flying Pig youth hostel, in a warehouse of bunk beds crawling with backpackers, you learn to keep what few valuables you have right next to your skin."

Monique said, "Please tell me you have photos of those years."

Judy tapped her temple. "It's all in here."

Back then she'd wanted to freeze time. They'd all discussed it—she and the young Austrians and Italians, French and Germans who'd became instant friends. How could they preserve this phase of life that held no plans, no responsibilities, and yet millions of possibilities? In Amsterdam life just *happened*. They met a Senegalese man who knew all the best coffee shops in the city and the back door into every techno club. He was like a supernatural wizard who opened the doors to the kingdom. They spent hours lolling in the sun on the grass of Vondelpark, enjoying one another's company, learning more in one international conversation than in hours of classes in the university at Strasbourg. They listened to music at the Paradisio. They slept together on random roofs. They were a tame wolf pack, roaming territory. After a while they stopped trying to speak each other's languages, and they all spoke their own. Here's the strange thing—they all understood each other.

"And yet all the places you saw," Monique murmured, "all the cities you visited while you were backpacking, you chose, after twenty-seven years, to come back to Amsterdam."

Judy smiled and she felt the young girl within her smile, too, a wistful dreamy little smile that lingered.

"In Amsterdam," Judy murmured, "I was happy."

"It's *Broodje haring*." Judy held out three sandwiches, bought at Stubbe's Haring kiosk outside Amsterdam Centraal train station. "It's a national delicacy. The Dutch version of a hot dog."

"I'm so hungry I'd eat a dead horse." Becky reached for the sandwich, thumbed the bun open, and paused. "Um... what is it?"

"It's better than a dead horse."

"Yeah, but—"

"Live a little, Beck. Take a bite."

Judy sank her teeth into the soft roll, closing her eyes as she felt the give of the flesh, the pickled taste, the burst of the onions. Stubbe's Haring kiosk was geared toward tourists coming or going from the international train station, so buying these sandwiches here was like buying hot pretzels just outside Grand Central Terminal in New York City—they were a bit dry and wildly overpriced. But she and the girls had just arrived and checked into the hotel, and dusk was already falling. They'd have a proper dinner later. This nip of street food would tide them over as they wandered the city before daylight faded.

The taste burst in her mouth, fresh clean fish and diced onion and pickles.

Becky choked and held the sandwich away from her, the bite a bulge in her cheek. "Judy—what is this?"

Monique's chewing slowed as her brow rippled. She gave her sandwich a good, long sniff.

"You can't guess?" Judy asked. "It's pickled herring."

Becky turned toward the railing by the canal. She dislodged the chewed-up wad of sandwich from her cheek and launched it into the water. Becky tossed the rest of the sandwich in the garbage nearby, missing the opening entirely.

Then she unscrewed her water bottle and took a long, wincing gulp. "Well," Becky said, "I've now publicly vomited in a
river. We can check that off the list."

"It's not that bad," Monique said, swallowing a tentative
second bite. "Vinegary. Kind of squishy. But in a weird-good-
sushi kind of way."

"We'll find you something else, Beck." Judy popped the
last of her sandwich in her mouth and hoped they ran into
a vendor who sold cones of greasy frites or spicy *bitterballen*,
breaded, deep-fried meatballs. "Come on, ladies, let's walk."

She headed out of the main square. She knew exactly
where she was going. She remembered the salt-smell of the
air, the worn wobble of the cobblestones, and the clatter of
boats bobbing up against the walls of the canal. She remembered the rows and rows of three-window-wide brick buildings. She made her way to a main canal street, Oudezijds
Voorburgwal, glanced at the old familiar unpronounceable
street signs—Bethlehemsteeg, Monnikenstraat. Passing one
side street, she glanced longingly down its shadowed length,
knowing that the Flying Pig youth hostel still lay down
there. The sky was dimming quickly in this northern lati-
tude, darkening the silver of the canals.

"Um, Judy," Becky said. "Where are you taking us?"

"Old stomping grounds."

"Well I'd just like to note that we just passed a store with
a sign that said 'condomerie.'"

"It won't be the first."

"Also," Becky added, glancing over her shoulder, "I believe we're being followed by multiple clones of Gina's ex-
boyfriend."

Judy followed Becky's gaze and noticed the two guys following them, men who'd just stumbled out of a nearby coffee shop. They were laughing and swaggering, cigarettes hanging out of their mouths. One had a tattoo up the side of his face. The other peered at Monique through swollen, red eyes, cataloging her attributes from her sensible flats to the jean jacket she pulled closed over her dress.

"Just ignore them, they're harmless stoners." Judy pulled Monique closer, giving her a little squeeze. "And you two call yourselves New Yorkers."

"I'm no New Yorker," Monique said. "I'm a suburbanite from New Jersey. I don't walk red light districts in strange cities at night."

"Maybe we ought to plan a trip to Flatbush."

"Right," Becky scoffed, "because Gina doesn't bring enough 'harmless stoners' into my house."

"Think about it," Judy said. "What kept us, back in Jersey, from taking a bus just to wander around some new part of New York City?"

Monique made a scoffing noise. "Common sense?"

"Expectations. When we're home we have those we put on ourselves, and those imposed on us by others. So we avoid adventure altogether. Come on, let's cut down here."

Monique resisted. "That's a narrow street."

Judy grinned. "Winding and mysterious."

"I think," Monie said, "that we should stay by the main canal."

Judy blew out a breath. "Honestly, is this how it's going to be for the next two weeks?"

"Do you want to get mugged in a foreign country?"

"Look at that crowd." Judy gestured to the milling throng. "We'll be just fine."

Monique frowned. "I'm getting danger vibes."

"So you're going to spend this whole vacation sticking to the main canal, the tourist stores, and the well-worn routes?"

Monique nodded. "Sounds good to me."

Judy felt a rumbling irritation, the frustration of the newly reborn girl inside her. "Listen, we're thousands of miles away from home. Don't you feel it, Monie? The urge to try something different? To stumble heedless," she said, waving down the crowded street, "into another culture, another whole world?"

Becky breathed. "Who are you, and what did you do with our Judy?"

"The old Judy's back home, painting the walls of the spare bedroom and dealing with a midlife crisis. But the young Judy is right here, primed for fun. Believe me, you'd rather take this trip with her."

Judy plunged them into one of the busier areas. She breathed in the perfume of Amsterdam, the familiar scent of hash that lingered. The neon glowed brighter than she remembered it, the shouts of the crowd more boisterous.

Becky stumbled on the cobblestones. Judy tried to curl her hand under Becky's arm, but Becky made a point of swaying out of her range.

"Cobblestones are a bitch," Judy said. "You'd think they'd be worn smooth after so many centuries."

"Maybe I'm just getting stoned." Becky took an exaggerated sniff. "All you have to do is breathe in this place."

"Oh, look, a sex supermarket." Monique made a tight smile. "I think I'll just drop in and pick up some incredibly huge dildos. That ought to be fun getting through customs. And how about—wait." She slowed down, cocking her head. "Is that a gas mask?"

Becky squinted at something on the opposite side of the street. "Judy, what does that sign say?"

"It's a theater," Judy said.

"A gas mask?" Monique repeated. "What the hell would you do with that?"

"Is that some kind of tropical sex show?" Becky asked. "That neon sign is in the shape of a banana."

"Hey, this gas mask place is right next to a shop called Sadomasochisme. How convenient! I bet they sell a lot of those cat-o'-nine-tails."

"Wait," Becky said, "wait—the banana thing. Is that what I think? Is that when a woman puts a banana—"

"Bingo." Judy tugged them both through the crowd. "I'm told the middle of the banana gets shot clear across the stage."

"How is that even possible?"

"As our kids would say, epic skills."

A man suddenly stepped directly into their path, startling all of them. His unfocused gaze shifted everywhere at once. "Coca? Eh, you want coca?"

Monique glared at him as she hiked her hands on her hips. "Should I explain to you what a preemie looks like, born to a mother addicted to cocaine?"

Judy tugged Monie away. Judy's heart pounded a little, in a good-bad way, excitement skittering with fear. A group of young people stumbled by like zombies, giggling uncontrollably. Judy grinned at the sight of them because, a few decades ago, she'd have been bouncing around right in the middle of them.

Then Monique came to a jarring stop.

Judy followed Monique's gaze. They stared up at one of the famous red-lit windows that gave the area its name. A young woman gyrated behind the glass. She was dressed in a silver G-string and a strap of some sort that stretched across her back and covered just enough of her breasts to keep some mystery. The girl's eyes were closed as she swiveled her hips to music only she could hear. In the corner of the window lay a little placard.

Fifty euros.

Judy felt the same cold jolt she'd felt the first time she'd seen one of these prostitutes, caged in glass. The sight caught her by the throat, filling her with revulsion, disbelief, and an inability to look away.

She'd talked to Thierry. She'd said it was terrible what those girls did for money. Thierry had argued with her. He said that their work was legal, that these women weren't coerced. They made enough money to support their families, that at least here they were protected by the law. His explanation unhinged her. It filled her with confusion. Her mind had been cracking open to so many new possibilities. This bit of caustic reality had flummoxed her. So she'd shrugged it away, unwilling to dwell.

Now Judy stared at this girl gyrating in the window and wondered why she'd ever believed that deceptive crap.

This girl was Audrey's age.

She resisted a violent urge to pull her belly pack from around her waist and hurl it at the glass, crack it to slivers, and set the poor girl free.

Monique's voice was flat. "I want to leave now, Judy."

Judy swiveled on a heel, the brightness of her mood snuffed and smoking. Mindlessly she led her friends down the street past smart shops and coffee shops, sex shows, loiterers, and buskers playing reggae. Slowly she noticed the creatures in the shadows of the doorways, poking up from the underground entrances, loitering on the stairs, all the lurking silhouettes. The homeless sprawled in nooks and under awnings. She looked at her old stomping grounds not with the eyes of the young girl she'd been, but with her fifty-year-old eyes, and it was like a veil had been torn from her vision. She saw all that she'd once blithely ignored— the danger and the fear, the crime and the addictions, the poverty and the stink of desperation.

Monique took a deep, sucking breath as they tumbled out into the open air of a canal. "Please tell me there are better parts of Amsterdam than this."

"I know a restaurant," Becky suggested. "I read about it in the guidebook while we were on the train."

Monique asked, "Is it far from here?"

Becky nodded. "We'll have to hail a cab."

Judy leaned over the railing by the bridge while Monique flagged down a taxi. Her knee twanged, her legs felt leaden, her mind raced. The herring sandwich turned acid in her stomach. And suddenly she felt the weight of every single one of her last twenty-seven years. Twenty-seven years of a happy marriage, made meaningful with the all-absorbing work of raising five kids. Twenty-seven years of worthy life lessons. In the blind excitement of being back in her old stomping grounds, Judy had forgotten why she'd abandoned that former life altogether.

Yes, she'd been happy, as that young girl.

But that girl had been a fool.

∞ chapter seven

Back at home, Becky could be walking up the neighborhood street on a pitch-black Halloween night and know—with one lift of her head—whether she was up by Judy's house or down by the Holts'. The glow of the Holts' single yellow bulb followed by the Reeses' flanked lanterns was a familiar pattern, as was the solar-powered trail of low lights that edged the winding pathway to the McCarthys'. All up and down the street, the lights had a particular sequence, a visual Braille. She was hardly conscious of noticing this. She'd just assumed this was the way everyone made their way through the darkness.

Her doctor said that the deterioration of her night vision must have occurred over years, in such slow increments as to be almost imperceptible. She'd long ceded night driving to Marco, and that hadn't seemed unreasonable. Whenever she'd complained of the blinding glare of oncoming headlights and the terrors of badly lit roads, people bobbed their heads and commiserated. See? Everybody else had these problems too.

Now Becky clambered out of the silver taxi into the Jordaan section of Amsterdam, into a dizzying world of smeared lights disengaged from any sense of structure. She could assume that the dim square glow ahead of her was the entrance to In Het Donker, the Dutch restaurant she'd read about in the guidebook, but until she approached she couldn't be sure it wasn't just a light cast on a wall from a store window across the street. Beyond the cab car headlights loomed, brightened, and then cut away in odd directions. She turned her back on their unpredictable configurations. She took one hesitant step away from the cab and then waited as casually as she could for Monique or Judy to come around and join her on the sidewalk.

She started as a couple passed right by her, her hand freezing in her purse as she pretended she was searching for a lipstick. The couple had passed close enough for her to smell a faint aroma of men's cologne. They were young. She could tell by the laughter and the bouncy way they walked.

"Dutch hipsters," Monique said, coming around to her side. "Good call, Becky. I think we've taken a significant step in the right direction."

With a rustle of movement, Monique headed away. Becky stepped swiftly into her wake. Resisting the urge to touch her friend, Becky watched for any sudden changes in Monique's walking cadence or height that might indicate stairs or a rising slope or a sudden step downward or any one of the hundreds of things that had been tripping Becky up since she'd stepped off the plane in London. Fire hydrants. Little fences around the plots of sidewalk trees. Uneven pavement. Curled welcome mats in hotel lobbies.

Inside the restaurant a gentle light bathed them. Her eyes

strained to adjust. She could just make out a few shapes in the small anteroom—tables, high café chairs, a milling of merged silhouettes. Monique wandered off to talk to the maître d', and Judy made a beeline for something. Becky fell into Judy's wake and soon found herself in an eclectic, language-bending crowd by the bar. Judy ordered three glasses of white wine. She thrust one in Becky's hands just as Monique returned.

"Good news," Monique said, raising her voice to be heard above the crowd. "We made it in time for the next seating. They'll be letting us all in in a few minutes."

"Excellent." Becky took a sip of the wine and then clutched her stomach, growling since the disaster with the herring sandwiches. "I'm going to pass out if I don't eat soon."

"Here's the catch. We have to lock everything up." Monique's face was bathed in blue light as she checked her cell phone, not for the first time this evening. "I mean *every-thing*. Cell phones, watches, anything that might possibly give out light."

Becky didn't actually see the glance that Judy and Monique exchanged. Some things didn't need to be seen in order to be sensed. She'd been getting the nervous vibe from them all during the cab ride, from the moment just outside the red light district when she'd suggested they eat at this particular—and very peculiar—specialty-themed restaurant.

"So," Becky said, as she followed Monique toward what was shaping up to be a wall of lockers, "what worries you two more? Eating in absolute darkness? Or being served by a fleet of blind waiters?"

"Blind waiters," Judy responded. "It's dangerous. Like I'll get the tip of a steak knife driven into my hand."

"I assume they won't be juggling the knives," Becky said drily.

Monique shoved her purse into the locker and held out her hand for Becky's. "The whole concept is unnerving. Not knowing what we're going to eat. Not seeing what we're eating. Trying to manipulate cutlery in the dark."

"They're feeding us meat, fish, or chicken, not bull testicles," Becky said. "The place wouldn't last long if it were some grand prank on the sighted."

"Down, girl." Monique shut the locker and pulled out the key. "How did you find out about this place, anyway?"

"I've got a knack for noticing things with the words 'blind' and 'darkness.'"

She'd first heard about this restaurant weeks ago, back in New Jersey. It showed up in one of her Google searches, for "tips for blind travelers" or "How long does it take to go completely blind?" The restaurant she'd read about was actually in London. Like this one, it featured legally blind waiters serving a mystery meal in total darkness. If she'd had the nerve last night in London, she might have suggested they'd go to the trendy section of Clerkenwell and give it a try. But they'd all been so exhausted she'd let the moment pass. Noting, even as she did so, that there were similarly themed restaurants in Florence, in Paris . . . and in Amsterdam.

"Don't worry, ladies." Becky lifted her glass, making it a target for easy clinking. "We'll all manage just fine. You're dining with a professional."

A waiter emerged from across the room and asked for

attention in a voice that carried. He introduced himself as Hans and then repeated, in three languages, the instructions to form two lines of twelve and put their hand on the shoulder of the person in front of them. He then led both lines through a curtain into an antechamber, and then through another room into utter darkness.

Becky didn't squeal, like some of the other patrons did, as they encountered the thickness of the gloom. The blackness washed over her with a peculiar sort of comfort. Here there were no confusing, darting blobs of light. Here there were no problems of depth perception or mistaken identity. She heard the voices of the other diners, felt, once, the brush of a chair against her thigh. She smelled sautéed garlic and the slight wood-chip scent of char-grilled meat. As they filed deeper in a room of indeterminate size, she heard the clatter of a utensil, the squeak of something against the floor, and the undeniable sound of a glass tumbling off a table and shattering.

Becky muttered, "Greenhorns."

Monique snickered.

The waiter guided them to what seemed like a very long single table but, as they were directed to take the seat in front of them, they realized they were sitting at a series of smaller tables, pressed so close together that they may as well have been sitting on the laps of the Germans beside them.

"Wow," Monique murmured. "This is cozy."

Judy muttered, "I've got my wine right in front of my face, and I can't see a thing. These waiters could be naked for all I know."

Becky snorted. "That might make things interesting."

"After the red light district," Monique murmured, "I'd believe anything. Becky, you sure this isn't some kind of twisted strip club?"

"Right. Like I'm into oiled, hairless, gyrating men."

"Well, if it were," Judy said, "at least nobody would be staring."

In the silence she knew their thoughts had turned back to that window in the red light district, to the young girl dancing inside. Becky had only seen a swaying silhouette in a pool of pink light, but her imagination had filled in the rest. It might be the first time she'd ever be grateful for partial night blindness.

A waiter announced his arrival. He asked them to sit back as he slipped the appetizers on the table in front of them. Becky could smell onions and something vaguely fishy, which made her remember the raw herring sandwich Judy had fed her. Her stomach turned a little, and she told herself it was because she was so hungry. He took their orders for the main meal—chicken, fish, or beef—and then slipped away.

"What the hell is on these plates?" Judy made an exaggerated sniff. "I smell the onions, and maybe some peppers. I think I'm touching an olive but I can't be sure. It's slick. For all I know, it could be a cow eyeball."

"I think I've got a sausage." Monique sounded as if she were facedown in the china. "Or maybe a pickle."

"Sausage." Judy breathed deeply. Even in the darkness, Becky could sense her nodding and leaning back in her chair. "Nice. A little spicy. You'll love it, Monique."

"The garlic smell is coming from shrimp." Monique tip-tapped her way through the plate with a knife or a fork, and Becky held her hand back until Monique was done explor-ing. "And there's some kind of...I don't know. I guess it's chutney? It's got a sweet-onion sort of flavor."

Judy murmured, "I think this is an olive. I never really knew how much olives felt like slimy little eyeballs."

"Yup. They're definitely olives," Becky said, popping a slimy orb into her mouth. "I'd guess green ones, Judy, pitted with pimento."

Monique spoke around a mouthful of something. "When you can't see it, it even *tastes* different."

Becky then bit into a plump, greasy bit of shrimp, listen-ing to her friends chatter. She didn't need light or eyesight to know what her girlfriends looked like right now. She'd eaten so many meals with them that she knew Judy was digging in with gusto, using her fingers without hesitation. She'd be chewing with enthusiasm and finishing everything on her plate. Monique, on the other hand, was struggling to use her silverware. Monique would prefer to slice up the shrimp and then spear each individual piece, chewing thoroughly before picking up the next, and Becky suspected it might take a course or two before Monique finally gave it up to eat with her fingers.

Becky's throat grew taut. When her eyesight faded to nothing, this feast of sound and smell was what dinner would always be like. The three of them would be old ladies catching the early bird special at the local diner, but in her mind's eye Monique and Judy would always be the vibrant middle-aged women they were right now.

Only their voices would age.

"So," Monique said, as she did something with her fork, a low, scraping sound. "How are you managing, Becky?"

Becky forced words out of her throat. "Just peachy."

"This isn't freaking you out?"

"No." She winced. In the dark she could hear the wobble in the word. She hoped her friends couldn't. "This place is just like a romantic Saturday night dinner at Epernay."

Monique laughed. Epernay was a fi-fi little French bistro in their hometown. "At Epernay there are candles on the tables. You can see what you're eating."

"Well, *you* can see what you're eating." She rolled the wineglass under her nose, breathing in the perfume of the fruity white, as an excuse to take a long, deep breath. "I should tip extra every time Marco and I go there, just to cover the cost of cleaning those lovely linen tablecloths."

"So is that what this is all about? You're evening the odds?"

"At least here I'm not the only one making an ass of myself." As if to punctuate her comment, somewhere deep in the room a glass clattered over. "And maybe, after an evening in mutual darkness, you'll see how well I manage. Then you'll both stop treating me like I'm going to stride off a bridge and drown in some canal."

Monique sputtered, the sound echoing, as if she did it from within the bowl of her wineglass. "That's a little harsh."

Becky set her glass on the table. "Truth hurts."

"Listen." Monique shifted in her seat. Becky knew because the action made the table shake. "I know we've been a little overprotective."

"You've both been smothering me."

"Well, frankly, in the past thirty-six hours I've seen you trip over more things than I've seen you trip over in the last four years."

A slow heat prickled across her skin. Becky had a new reason to be grateful for the darkness. Her fingertips grazed the point on her thigh where she'd bumped into the sharp edge of a planter at Heathrow. A throbbing began on her foot, where she'd miscalculated the size of a man's trailing luggage. Her shoulder ached from where she'd taken two full-body blows into commuters rushing across her path. And she'd already broken into her pack of emergency Band-Aids to hide the cut on the shin she'd received as she hurried to dress in the hotel room, sliced by the edge of the lower bureau drawer.

"You know what, Monie?" Becky said. "You're right."

The scrape of utensils on Monique's plate stopped. Judy's noisy chewing slowed. Becky pressed her spine against the back of the chair until the wood squeaked. It was always easier to speak frankly in the dark. This was why she'd brought them here, after all. She was freaked out enough by her diagnosis, but each time they coddled her, they drove a sharp spike through her pride. She didn't need to be reminded that someday she would be completely and hopelessly dependent.

"Look," Becky began, "this is the situation. Back home, on the third stair to the second floor in my house, there's a crack in the riser that I've been nagging Marco to fix, but we'd have to rip up the carpet to do it right." Ripping the carpet up meant spending money to have it repaired or replaced.

And all nonessential repairs had been put off until Marco was no longer on furlough. "That riser always gives under my feet, especially if I'm racing up the stairs. It's a slight difference. Marco doesn't even notice it. But when Brian was sick with the flu last winter, and I heard him cry out, I took the stairs too fast. I didn't compensate for the change in the rise. I stumbled and bruised my knee up good."

Becky felt a rush of air against her cheek, like Judy was waving her comment away. "Beck, do you know how many times I've skipped a step running up the stairs in my house? After all the knocks I've taken, I've now got shins of iron. *Anyone* could have done that."

"That's my point." Becky quite carefully, quite deliberately, placed her fork down, fingering the linen tablecloth until she found the spot for it right next to her plate. "Back home I just know these things. I know to walk carefully on the sidewalk by the old Norway maple halfway to town because the roots of that tree have pushed up the pavement. I also know that the Reeses never trim that ash tree in front of their house so I have to remember to dip my head not to get a branch in the eye." Neighborhood memory, a map she'd sketched in her head. "But here, in strange places, I know none of this detail. Plus it feels like the whole European world is proportioned differently."

The risers on the hotel stairs were lower than she expected. The step to get into a taxi was higher. The ratio of the seat in a pub in relation to the table was different, somehow, so that in London she'd knocked her pint hard against the wood and sent ale sloshing. Walking on cobblestones made her feel like she was stumbling over a loosely packed ball pit. Amsterdam swarmed with bicycles, zooming without warning across her path.

"I'm tripping up so much because everything is new," she said. "It's *not* because my eyesight is getting any worse."

Monique's voice, flat and straight. "Beck, we don't think your eyesight is getting any worse."

"Good. Then you both can stop seizing my elbow every time we approach a curb and warning me of every little obstacle. I have to figure this out by myself." Becky patted the table in search of her wine until her fingers came in contact with the round bottom of the stemmed glass. "As long as the light is good, and the day is bright, then treat me like clumsy Becky Lorenzini, who's run whitewater on the Lehigh River, climbed the high ropes in the park, and is currently in charge of a somewhat successful household. Just like the two of you."

Monique was doing something with her fork upon her plate, the little tines making scratching noises. "The rules change at night, though, don't they?"

Becky suppressed a ripple of helpless frustration. She really didn't want to talk about this anymore. Hadn't she already told them what they needed to know? She didn't want to tell them about the dark puddle she'd seen on the floor of their hotel room last night, only realizing afterward that what looked like motor oil was actually Judy's slick new raincoat.

But Becky knew she wouldn't win a face-off with Monique, not on this subject. "It's true that my night vision is not so great," she conceded. "I see lights, but I have questionable depth perception. My doctor compared it to looking at the night sky. You see a flat layer of stars. The truth is, those stars are hundreds of thousands of light years away from one another."

Monique murmured, "Did you and Marco talk about all this?"

"Of course."

"All of it? Like you just told Judy and me?"

"Verbatim? No."

One beat between the words, and in the darkness, that hesitation revealed itself as too obvious a lie.

"You want to talk about that, Beck?" Monique asked. "Because though I'm glad to finally hear some detail about exactly how this disease is affecting you, I get the sense that there's something even more serious going on. Something you've been hesitant to share with us, maybe?"

Becky's insides went liquid. She hoped the chatter from the Germans and the clinking of dishes and the whole ambient noise of the place covered up the swift hitch of her breath. Becky knew that Monique understood a lot about her disease. Monique knew the medical jargon that filled those websites. And Monique had friends at the hospital— doctor friends—who could fill her in on all the terrible details.

One particular detail Becky kept pushing out of her mind. It was unspeakable, inconceivable. It could not be true.

So she swiftly changed the subject. "Marco and I," she stuttered, "had a very bad parting."

Despite the Germans chattering just beside them, Becky felt the intensity of Monique's and Judy's attention, their magnetic concentration on her words. Without seeing their faces she didn't know if they caught on that she'd dodged the real question.

"I bet he feels like a shit," Judy said into the pause, "for blaming you for the fender benders and the lost keys and the misplaced mail—"

"Judy," Monie interrupted, "why don't you let Becky tell us exactly what's on her mind?"

Becky heard the pat of Monique's fingers on the table, searching amid the dishes, tugging the tablecloth in search of Becky's hand. Becky pulled her hands away and clutched them in her lap. She did not want comfort. She did not want to speak aloud the unthinkable. Nor did she want to wade too deeply into the sucking, bottomless mess of her relationship with Marco.

So she condensed her fears into something simpler, something pithy, something that nonetheless cut to the bone.

"I used to dream," she said, "that after Gina left for college, things might get better between Marco and me. You know I always wanted a home like yours, Judy."

"Filthy?" Judy chirped. "Broken-down and creaky?"

"Crawling with kids."

In the awkward pause Monique made a choking sound while Judy drew in a slow, uneven breath.

"For a mother who is soon to go blind," Becky said, "there can be no more little Lorenzinis."

∽ chapter eight

Are we having fun yet?

Monique pulled the hood of her raincoat over her hair as she handed her ticket to the man at the pier in Cologne. It was a grim, foggy sort of northern German day, not exactly perfect weather for a pleasure cruise down the Rhine River.

Becky, wrapped in a thin windbreaker, followed Monique over the worn pier to the ramp. Judy brought up the rear, grimacing against the needles of rain and clutching her hood as her luggage bumped behind her. As soon as they ducked into the low-ceilinged center of the boat, Judy spied the restaurant. "Coffee," she groaned. Judy scraped her luggage around and planted it beside Monique. "Check my luggage for me. I'll save us a table by the window."

Monique agreed and headed toward baggage check, Becky in tow. They'd had to check out at 8:30 a.m. from their hotel in a rather grubby part of Cologne before taking a taxi to the pier. She wished she could blame their attitudes on the overcast day, or the three-hour train ride from Amsterdam last night, or the heavy dinner they'd eaten—thick on the potatoes and the schnitzel. She'd even like to blame it on the difficulty they'd had sleeping in a room that smelled like vinegary, fermenting sauerkraut.

But this trip shouldn't feel like drudgery. She was German on her father's side, through a line of Pennsylvania farmers that stretched back to the Revolution. She should be soaking this up, even though all that remained of that heritage was a tendency to enjoy scalloped potatoes and micro-brewed beer. Yesterday she, Becky, and Judy had gaped at the soaring nave of Cologne's famous medieval cathedral. Today this pleasure cruise promised a visual feast of castles, ruins, and little postcard-perfect Rhine towns.

As she checked their luggage and wound her way back to the restaurant, she told herself to be happy. They were firmly on track with the itinerary. She was checking another item off Lenny's bucket list. That was, after all, what she'd come to Europe to do.

They found Judy in the restaurant, nursing a cup of coffee. Two more cups steamed by a plate of pastries.

"*Apfel,*" Judy said, pointing to what looked like an apple pastry. "*Schnecken.*" She nudged what looked like a bear claw and then pointed to a donut. "And a *Berliner.* My German language skills are rusty but I remember good pastry."

Monique sank into the booth and glanced out the window. On the deck were two rows of tables, one up against the railing and another closer to the wall. Though some hardy souls were walking the deck, no one sat out in the rain. Even inside she could smell the iron-tang of it, and feel the seeping cold. She curled her fingers around the coffee cup, wondering what Lenny would have had to say about this soggy adventure, as the boat wobbled off the pier and chugged into the choppy current of the Rhine.

"So," Judy said, "last night on the phone I had the pleasure of a stern lecture from Maddy."

Monique lifted her mug in a vague toast. "Welcome to the teenagers-know-best club. Kiera's a founding member."

"Maddy's no teenager anymore, but she spent her junior year abroad in Mainz. So apparently that means she's an 'expert' in foreign travel."

"Oh, boy." Becky bit into a donut.

"I told her about Amsterdam," Judy said. "Does she ask me about the herring sandwiches, about the canals, the museums? No. She screams at me that I'm crazy for walking the red light district. She says I may as well be walking the Patpong Road in Bangkok."

"If that's some Asian red light district," Monique said, "then I'll just note that Maddy's got a point. We did wander through a pretty dangerous area last night."

"Come on." Judy flung out her arms. "Who's going to sell *this* into sexual slavery?"

Behind the rim of her coffee cup Monique suppressed a smile. If she looked like Judy did in five years, she'd be one happy woman. Judy was a smidge soft in the middle in the way Monique felt herself getting lately, despite the regular exercise, but Judy's light brown hair was thick and shiny. Judy's best feature was the gathering of lines at the corners of her eyes—proof that she'd spent a good part of her life laughing.

Becky wiped the crumbs from her mouth. "I'm surprised at you. You should have told Maddy you were just trying to find a reputable smart shop to buy some weed."

"But you had trouble," Monique added, "and decided to opt for mushrooms."

Judy shook her head. "It wouldn't work."

"Why not?" Monique reached for the strudel. "Are you telling me Maddy doesn't know about your sex-drugs-and-rock-and-roll past?"

"Absolutely not. She thinks I'm completely naive. If I'd had my wits about me, I would have told her I was stocking up on sex toys for myself and her father."

Becky nearly spit her coffee across the table. Monique thrust a fresh napkin at her before she stained her shirt.

"Now you've heard my tale of woe," Judy said, "so spill, Monique. How did Kiera correct *you* last night?"

Monique didn't answer right away. She pulled another napkin and soaked a few drops of coffee off the battered tabletop. She had called home late last night while standing in the dim hotel corridor, near an interior window so her service could roam and find a signal. There'd been particularly long, awkward pauses between her intentionally upbeat questions and Kiera's curt responses. She couldn't even blame the disconnect between them on the delay or the terrible static. It had been a relief when the call finally dropped.

"As expected, Kiera still hasn't forgiven me," she said, tucking the wadded napkin aside, "for the unspeakable act of abandoning her in the middle of her senior year."

"Drama queen." Judy raised her palm in humble defense. "And I mean that in the fondest of ways."

"She is milking it. Like a true director, she has decided to cast me in the role of the Bad Mommy."

Becky said, "You know she'll come around."

"Maybe after my mother has softened her up with fried cod and shark and bake and *katchouri*."

"Ohhhh." Becky gave herself a little shake. "I love those vegetable fritters. You think there'll be leftovers?"

"See? I'm doomed. My mother's got sweet hands and I don't. When I get back, Kiera will move in with her."

"You know this is emotional blackmail." Judy stretched her arm across the back of the booth. "Kiera's reacting in that knee-jerk, thoughtlessly hurtful way teenagers do. You can't allow her to do that."

In a cold-blooded intellectual way Monique understood what Judy was saying. But she was emotionally attached to her daughter by deep hooks. After Lenny's death Monique had dug them even deeper, mooring Kiera even closer to her, so the grief of her father's death wouldn't sweep the sensitive young girl away. "I'm here, aren't I?" Still feeling guilty as sin. "No law says I can't feel bad about making that decision."

"Wow." Becky picked at her apple strudel. "I guess I ought to be grateful I didn't get international calling on my cell phone."

"That is ironic, because of the three of us," Judy said, tapping the table in front of Becky, "you should definitely call. Your kids are young and malleable. They won't lecture you or chide you or make you feel guilty. They'll slather you with love and transatlantic air kisses on demand."

"You're welcome to use my phone." Monie nudged the daypack she'd hung on the spindle of the chair. "Just say the word."

Becky turned her dark blue gaze to the window, to some fixed but indeterminate spot. In the stretching silence, Monique noticed a muscle twitch at the corner of Becky's eye and the sudden tightness of her jaw. Monique couldn't help but remember the whole difficult conversation they'd had the other night in Amsterdam. Becky was holding back secrets upon secrets. Monique wondered how long it would be before the woman finally broke down.

So Monique unzipped her hoodie and deliberately changed the subject. "Ugly river, isn't it? I can't see a darn thing out there."

"You know what? I need some air." Becky shot up, knocking the chair back. "I'll be back in a little while."

Monique sat with Judy for as long as she could, worrying over their mutual friend, while a distracted Judy tried to parse out the slangy conversation of the young Germans at the next table. Finally, swinging her leg onto Becky's chair in order to massage her knee, Judy ordered Monie to stop squirming and just chase Becky down. Monique leapt up, pulled on her damp raincoat, tugged the hood over her head, and set off to search the boat.

She caught up with Becky twenty minutes later, doing brisk-walking laps on the mostly empty upper deck.

Monique fell into step beside her. "Old habits die hard, huh?"

"That Wiener schnitzel is still expanding in my stomach."

"It's already taking up residence on my hips. I'll join you. It'll feel good to work off some of those calories."

"I'd be happy to work off the damn black cloud hanging over me. The one that I've thrown over this whole vacation."

Huh, Monique thought, so she wasn't alone in that feeling. "I'm holding up my end of the wet blanket too."

"Why did Lenny want to do this, anyway? You told me he hated boats."

"That's true. My uncle in Trinidad once took him trolling for bait fish in Las Cuevas Bay, and Lenny spent the whole time vomiting off the side of the dinghy." Monique remembered how Lenny looked that night as he stumbled in, his skin as gray as a dead fish. "He called it 'chumming the waters.'"

"I guess this is a big, lumbering engine-driven boat," Becky conceded, "and on a river rather than the open ocean...but still. It seems so un-Lenny."

"Lenny's list was a collection of dreams. In dreams no one gets seasickness."

"Ah."

"Besides he was lured by the promise of German beer." Monique glanced toward a cluster of Germans at the bow, seemingly oblivious to the needles of rain, raising steins as they belted out a drinking song.

"Didn't Lenny know he could get German beer onshore?"

"The Rhine cruise he'd read about involved stopping at various cities and touring breweries. I told him while he hit the breweries I'd do the churches and castles."

She remembered him sitting with a hospital blanket over his lap giving her a full-cheeked grin and a rumble of approving laughter as he'd murmured, *that's why I married you.*

"Well, this is one butt-ugly industrial stretch of river."

Becky nodded to the enormous smokestack-like structures looming up on the bank.

"I believe that's a nuclear power plant."

"I hope it's reactive. Mutate away, oh nuclear power plant." Becky found interest in the gray froth of the boat's wake. "Maybe I should drink this river water. It's not like I'm going to breed anymore."

Monique didn't look at Becky. Instead she tugged her hood farther over her hair as the drizzle persisted. Becky must have been that kind of teenager—the kind that only really talked about serious things in the dark, or while power-walking, or riding in the car, eyes facing forward. Kiera wasn't like that at all—she was the oversharing kind—so Monique's experience was limited. But Judy once confessed that all three of her boys had been uncommunicative. Judy would abandon dinner while it was frying in the pan, just so she was available for any drop off or pick up, in order to seize an opportunity for ten minutes of real conversation.

And so Monique waited in stillness, her breath coming in little cold puffs. Her professors never taught this while she was studying nursing in school. It was a technique she'd learned over years of coping with grieving patients and devastated families in the ER. Hard news sometimes took weeks or even months to fully sink in. There was simply no substitute for time. So Monique did what she'd been doing since the day she found out about her friend's diagnosis. She gave Becky all the time and space and silence the woman might need to gather her courage. And she made sure Becky knew by her constant presence that she was available whenever Becky was ready to talk.

It took one circuit of the boat deck.

"Monie," Becky said. "Why didn't you and Lenny have more children?"

Monique kept walking briskly but her mind had come to a complete stop. So, apparently, had her breathing, because halfway across the deck she found herself choking in deep gulps of air that smelled of damp ink and moldering paper, rising up from the discarded newspapers on the scattered tables.

Her mind hurled back to her first date with Lenny, casual over coffee in the hospital cafeteria. It had been raining then too, fat droplets hitting the glass window by their seat. He'd talked about what he aimed on doing with his life.

She'd expected him to say what the young doctors always chattered about: Choosing their specialty, how many more years of training they had, how little they slept, how they couldn't wait until they made a real salary. But the first thing out of Lenny's mouth, Louisiana-slow in that rumbling baritone of his, was his insistence on having a sane life. He didn't want to get torn away from his wife in the middle of the night to deliver babies. He didn't want to travel the world teaching one special, specific surgical technique. He was happily bumping from one department to another right now, he'd told her, doing six-week rotations to see what's what, but he already knew he was going into radiology. He wanted to stay married, buy a decent house, work in a solid practice, and coach his kids in soccer.

She'd all but melted into the molded plastic seat.

"You don't have to answer, Monie." Becky reached out to trail her cold-pinked fingers along the boat railing. "It's none of my business. It's just that a year after he died, you were training for the NICU. We all wondered why the change. Why *that* change."

This question had an easier answer than the first. Monique grasped it so she wouldn't have to respond to the earlier one. "The ER is a crazy place to work, Beck. When I came back after taking family leave, I'd forgotten how frenetic it could be."

"You used to thrive on that."

"I guess I'd spent too much of my leave with the hospice nurses." She shrugged her hands into the sleeves of her hoodie, warming them in the thick cotton. "They were wonderful. They were *wise*. And they got to spend a lot of time with only a few patients. Which is the whole reason I chose nursing over medical school in the first place."

"Why NICU over hospice then?"

She shook her head sharply. "I couldn't do hospice. Too soon. I couldn't watch another man die."

Becky hesitated only a beat. "But preemies die all the time, don't they?"

Every day she held those little lives in her gloved hands, wizened creatures she could splay upon her forearm, their bellies distended, and their little immature lungs flexing for air. Tiny sparks of life. It was her job to spend weeks, and often months, blowing gently on those embers. Nurturing their undeveloped bodies and stimulating their emergent minds until they could be released to the parents who would love them. Those preemies developed personalities, too, while they were in the NICU. There was one there right now, one she'd left behind with trailing regret, a skinny-legged boy who instead of crying, tightened and loosened his fists and crumpled his face when he needed something, as if holding on to life by sheer will.

But preemies never lingered. At least not long enough. Some died, fading before they'd really sparked. But others she got to release to the world, like butterflies.

Monique let the thought go and gathered her wits. "You sure are asking a lot of questions about babies, Beck."

"I know. After my experience with Gina, you'd think I'd have had my tubes tied."

"You can't blame yourself for that. You didn't raise Gina from infancy."

"But I welcomed the idea of bringing Gina into my house. I couldn't wait, in fact. The more the merrier, I thought."

"Confess: You thought—instant babysitter."

"Guilty as charged. But can you imagine? She'd be sitting them in front of R-rated movies and dosing them with cough syrup."

"That's harsh, Beck. And absolutely not true. You know she adores them."

"I know, I know. I'm being sarcastic. Just like I was when she stumbled into the house stoned, and I told her that she was a *fabulous* role model for her little brother and sister. That might have been the only thing I ever said to her that had any effect on her behavior."

"Brilliant strategy," Monie conceded.

"Props go to Judy."

"Mother of five to the rescue again."

"Still it turns out I prefer kids when they're young. Not snarky and hormone-crazed and vomiting fruity vodka drinks."

"You know there's no guessing what'll happen to Brian and Brianna once the hormones kick in," Monique warned. "Maybe Brian will crash cars. Maybe Brianna will sneak away to get a belly-button piercing."

Becky raised her head, blinked up at the gray sky, and slowed to a stop. "It doesn't matter, Monie. I'll take whatever comes." She turned toward the water and sagged against the railing. "If it weren't for my diagnosis, I'd do it again in a heartbeat."

Monique sank her elbows on the rail. Mothers always talked about the rush of love they felt for their newborn children, yet when Kiera was born, Monique hadn't been prepared for the all-consuming nature of the feeling. She drowned in it willingly. She threw herself into the raising of her daughter, almost to the exclusion of all else. When Lenny started hinting about having a second baby, she'd put him off, put him off, and put him off…until he just stopped hinting altogether.

Of the two of us, Monique thought, *Becky is the braver.*

"I was afraid." Monique forced the words out before she could change her mind. "I was terrified to have another baby, Beck."

Becky shook her head dismissively. "No, no, no, no. Monique Franke-Reed is not afraid of anything."

"You have been sorely misinformed."

"I once saw you yank a splinter the size of a number two pencil out of Kiera's foot."

"You're mistaking a nurse's training for courage."

"I saw you bury your husband."

Monique blinked. She didn't remember much about those days after Lenny died. It was a blur of service arrangements and choosing a casket and too many casserole dishes left on the dining room table.

"I told myself I couldn't handle the schedule with two kids," Monique said. "I didn't want to quit my job because we needed the money to pay off all our school loans." She gazed at the German river, from the boat she was cruising on, with the bank account full, those concerns long gone. "I worried about the dangers of getting pregnant at my age. I worried whether Lenny and I could put away enough for two college tuitions."

Excuses. Every last one of them. Excuses she'd told Lenny and herself, so she wouldn't have to admit what she was really afraid of: That she'd never be able to love a second child as fully as she loved Kiera.

"There you two are." Judy arrived, walking across the deck as she raised three bottles in her hands. "I thought you might like some good cheer."

Monique raised a brow. "It's ten thirty in the morning."

"It's cocktail hour somewhere." Judy held out a bottle. "Besides these beers are already opened. Lenny would strike you dead if you finished this cruise without drinking German ale in his memory."

Monique wrinkled her nose as she took a swallow. The beer was warm, yeasty, and strong. "There, now I've had a beer in Lenny's honor. But I haven't seen a single castle yet."

Judy rolled her eyes. "I guess you guys were too busy

wallowing in gloom to notice that we just passed the Ehren-breitstein fortress."

"An unpronounceable pile of rocks," Becky muttered, hunkered against the rail.

"In English it means the 'Broadstone of Honor,'" Judy retorted. "And it's got a rocking youth hostel."

Monique sighed. "Let's just get off at the next stop, what do you say?"

Becky, with the beer to her lips, muttered agreement.

"Geez, this is like babysitting two cranky toddlers."

"Judy," Monique said, "it's gray, it's cold, it's boring, and if Lenny were here, he'd agree while vomiting up his motion-sickness pills."

"I used to sing to make my kids laugh when they were cranky." Judy cast a gaze toward the cluster of German revelers singing at the stern of the boat. "You know, I recognize that drinking song. A couple of rugby-playing Austrians taught it to me in a *biergarten* in Salzburg. Should I sing it to cheer you up?"

Monique shook her head. "Please don't."

"Maybe I'll just join their party. Torture them with my rusty German. They look like they're having fun. Want to come along?"

"Judy!"

"I'll do it, you know. Somebody's got to do *something*. I know Lenny didn't send you on this cruise, Monique, so that you could spend it weeping into a German beer." Then Judy's gaze shifted. A sudden break in the clouds cast sunshine upon the smile that broke across her face. "Ah, Lenny. Impeccable timing."

Monique turned to follow Judy's gaze. The boat had just rounded a jut of land that had, until now, obscured the view upstream.

Against the sky stood a castle, perched alone on a windswept hill. Not a crumbling ruin or a set of stone walls, but a fanciful creation that looked like it had been plucked from some children's book of fairy tales. It had conical turrets, shaped like the princess hats that Monique used to make out of cardboard for Kiera with scarves cascading from their pointed tips. A central keep was topped by neat crenellations, and the top of each window was perfectly arched. It was a cliché of a castle, the kind of building a little boy would draw for his knights to play upon.

Drawing in a sharp breath, Becky pushed up from the railing. "Judy, is that real, or did you spike my beer?"

Then, with a start, Monique realized that a little boy *had* dreamt this up, or at least, a scarily similar version of it. On Brian's seventh birthday, Becky had concocted one of her fantasy specialties, covered in white fondant. By Brian's precise instructions, she'd topped several towers with pointy, slate-gray roofs. Then she'd constructed an inner keep complete with crenellations through which Brian put his miniature knights, aiming their arrows toward a horde of invaders beyond the wall.

Becky fumbled with her daypack. "Can we get off here? Can we tour it?"

Judy grinned like the Cheshire cat. "Marksburg Castle is the boat's next stop. If I understood the German right, I was told that we can leave our luggage at the Braubach tourist office, walk up, take a tour, and be back on the boat in a couple of hours."

Becky stared at the castle as if she feared that, if she looked away, it might disappear as abruptly as it had appeared. Watching her friend's amazement, Monique felt a loosening sensation in the middle of her chest, an odd unfurling of tension. She'd come to Europe for lots of reasons. For herself, for Lenny, for Judy. But one of the most important was to see Becky just like this—startled, amazed, and completely distracted from her troubles.

Monique blinked up at the breaking clouds. The sunshine warmed her face as Judy leaned in close.

"I'd say Lenny knew what he was doing when he wrote that list, Monie. Maybe better than we'll ever know."

chapter nine

Y ou guys are out of your freakin' minds."
Judy leaned against the wrought-iron railing on the
stairs just outside the third German hotel they'd occupied in
as many days: First in Cologne, then in Koblenz after touring the Marksburg Castle, and now in tiny Cochem on the
banks of the Moselle river. She watched in growing conster-
nation as Monique and Becky snapped on rented bike
helmets. The air was soft and warm, washed clean by a recent rain. Sun glittered on the river just across the street
from the hotel, and the blue sky stretched over the wooded
hills on the opposite bank.

It spited her to admit it, but it was a beautiful day for a
bike ride.

"Judy, it's not going to be that rigorous." Monique pulled
off the helmet to adjust the straps. "It's going to be an incredible trip along the banks of this loopy river, and it's all
flat biking to Moselkern."

"Eleven-effing-miles."

Monique made a *pffft*. "I've seen you walk Goldie and
Chocolate. That makes you a suburban warrior."

"Just because I allow myself to be dragged along a park path by two dogs doesn't mean I'm willing to sit on one of those rented torture devices."

Judy eyeballed the two paint-chipped, battered old bikes. *Fahrrad.* She'd nearly forgotten the German word for bicycle. She'd biked all over Strasbourg when she'd been employed there. She'd used that word nearly every day, telling coworkers that she'd biked to school, or that her bike was locked up just over there, or querying friends if they had a *Fahrrad.* Her mind had erased the word from her brain. Just like she'd fumbled *Fahrradverleih* when trying to ask the *Portiersfrau* at the hotel desk where her crazy, hyper-athletic friends could rent bikes.

To think she'd once been fluent in German.

"You'd do fine, Judy." Monique slipped the helmet carefully over her cascade of braids. "I know you would."

"Says the woman who does kickboxing twice a week."

"Says the woman who used to do fifteen loads of laundry a week."

"Give it up, Monie. I'd be like gum on your sneakers, holding you both back."

"Then take the train." Becky wrestled her arms through the straps of her daypack. "It's a sixteen-minute train ride from here to Moselkern, and the train runs on the half hour. You told me that yourself."

"Yeah, before you guys ate too many sausages and cheese at brunch, had some kind of protein seizure, and committed to this bike ride marathon."

Monique said, "It's on the itinerary."

Ah, yes, the word of God. "Lenny's list mentioned a bike

ride, darling," Judy said, "it didn't specify the Tour de France."

"Then skip the bikes and meet us there." Becky shrugged until the pack lay comfortably against her spine. "You can't miss the most beautiful castle in all of Europe. Burg Eltz is my fantasy castle squared. When are you ever going to be able to do this again?"

Judy felt her will waver. Becky looked so very happy today. Yesterday, as they'd explored Marksburg Castle, Becky had been as excited as a teenager touring a rock star's crib. Gone was the gray aura of impending doom. For the first time since they'd stepped off the plane at Heathrow, Becky was honestly enjoying herself.

But there was still an ugly reality that could not be completely, or safely, ignored. "Becky, how's this bright sunlight going to work for you? It's a busy road."

"I'll be fine." Becky crouched to tug at the laces of her sneaker. "If I stay right behind Monique, following close in her wake, then I won't be surprised by anything rushing up in my peripheral vision. I can do this."

Judy thought that there might be an element of plain, stubborn determination overwhelming Becky's common sense, but she wasn't going to be the one to squash it. "So here's another question. Once you guys park your bikes at Moselkern, it's another three miles to Burg Eltz. Uphill. Are you going to catch a cab? "

"It's a beautiful hike through the woods." Monique unscrewed the cap from a bottle of water. "You read the raves in the guidebook about the view as you approach from the hiking trail."

"I stopped reading at the words 'hiking trail.' You both know I'm not the hike-bike-climb-the-rock-wall type."

She waited for Monique to catch her in that lie. After all Judy had hiked part of the Appalachian Trail with Audrey, Kiera, and Gina's Girl Scout troop. She'd done an all-night-walk-around-the-park to raise money when a classmate of Michael's was diagnosed with leukemia. That was at least six years ago, before her knee started going wonky.

She was saved by Becky, who pinched a thin roll of skin at her waist. "I ate Mosel toast for brunch. Ham and peach on toast slathered in melted cheese. It's going to take lots of miles of biking and hiking to burn it off."

Monique took a quick swig of her water. "If I eat any more bratwurst, roasted potatoes, or goulash, I'll have to buy new clothes in Paris."

Judy snorted. "Oh, horrors."

"Ha. Ha."

"Eleven miles of biking and three freakin' miles of hiking uphill," Judy sang. "Ladies, I rest my case."

Monique tucked the bottle into the holder on the bike. "You liked touring Marksburg Castle yesterday, yes?"

"My knees doth still protest."

Monique glanced at Judy's knees and frowned. "I should have insisted you ice them last night."

"My knees are fine. Achy, but they'll recover. Can you tell me what's wrong with wanting to sit on a couch and read a book for a couple of hours? Or linger in a café, nursing a glass of some sweet Moselle wine until you guys get back?"

"Sounds like a good idea," Monique agreed, "for *after*."

"Burg Eltz, Judy." Becky leaned forward, quivering in excitement. "*Burg Eltz.*"

Monique swung a leg over the bike. "And we're only here for one day."

Judy stewed, sensing the prickling discomfort and sudden flush that usually preceded a full-blown hot flash. She didn't like to disappoint people. Her urge was always to accommodate—to attend that ballet recital and then zoom off to the karate test, to help at the bake sale and also run the craft table at the school fund-raiser, to gussy up for a dinner with Bob's colleagues even though a migraine pounded behind her right eye socket.

She wondered if that urge were a mother thing or just a woman thing. She wondered, too, why these days she felt more and more like a grumpy contrarian, someone less and less inclined to say yes.

"We're in every city for only a day." Judy stepped back into the shade of the awning, climbing up one stair to the hotel. "This is the fifth city we've been to in as many days. So today I'm going to sit for a little while. Soak it in for a change."

"I know it has been tight," Monique said, "but in Paris we'll be doing a lot of nice, calm—"

"Monie, darling." Judy felt the words rise up her throat before she could even attempt to tamp them down. "I'm a mother of five who's just shepherded the last bird out of the nest. Can I sit down now?"

Becky froze where she crouched, retying her shoes. Monique straddled the bike, balanced taut on her toes. Judy avoided their eyes by glancing down the Moselpromenade to the riverside stretch of colorful hotels and shops. She knew one block away from the river lay the real Cochem, a little medieval town with winding streets and quaint half-timbered buildings that she could probably tour in a leisurely hour. If she had a yen to see a castle, she could lean forward and look up a bit down the road to see Reichs-burg, an ancient stronghold that had been rebuilt in the Neo-Gothic style on a bluff. And all through the area there were plenty of native-speaking Germans she could eaves-drop on, trying to hone her old skills.

The heat that had started in her cheeks now spread all over, making little beads of sweat start to pop up on her neck and her upper lip. She looked at both of them, so bright-eyed, so fit, so eager. Monique looked livelier than she had for a while, less grimly determined now that she wasn't working to check something off Lenny's list. Both of them had come off the Rhine with new energy.

But in Amsterdam Judy had discovered that she was no longer the twenty-two-year-old girl who'd tripped so easily across the continent. She'd outgrown that silly little pip both mentally and emotionally, and that was a very *good* thing. But after five straight days of ceaseless travel, and after la-boring up the steep stairs to Marksburg Castle, an uglier, less palatable truth had emerged: She no longer had twenty-two-year-old stamina—or knees.

"Oh, go, both of you." She waved her hands at them, as if she were shooing her children off to school. "Have a great time and take lots of photos. You can tell me all about it later over a nice bottle of Riesling."

Monique hesitantly put her feet in the pedals. "Only if you're sure."

"I'm sure."

They climbed on the bikes and slipped between the cars into the bike lane. Her heart did a little stutter as Becky risked a collision by glancing once, over her shoulder, to give her a last wave. Judy stood on the stoop of the hotel, watching them weave through the traffic until she could no longer see them.

Then she leaned against the wrought-iron railing. She winced at the sharp stab of pain in the back of her knee. She let her weight bring her down, until she all but bounced on the cold stone step. A chill seeped through her jeans. The pressure of the hard surface threatened to put her legs to sleep.

Well, she got what she wanted.

But, damn, it hurt to wave her youth good-bye.

Judy emerged from the Paris Metro to the ringing of the bells of Notre Dame.

She glanced across the bridge at the front of the church. Behind her Becky tripped up the Metro stairs. Monique seized the post that arched over the exit and stood beside Judy, taking in all of old Paris, all at once.

"Flying buttresses." Becky stepped dangerously into the stream of pedestrian traffic, blinking as if the light glared through the amber lenses of her glasses. "The rose window and gargoyles. Can we tour Notre Dame first?"

"Definitely." Judy looked both ways and headed across the street. "I'll even lead the charge."

Small cars zipped along the road. Boatloads of tourists on the river's *bateaux mouches* waved and shouted and raised glasses of wine to their fellow tourists hanging over the edge of Pont Saint-Michel. The October sun beat down warmly, washing the island in sunshine. Judy soaked in the ambiance, moving amid a flood of natives speaking French, some of it vaguely comprehensible to her ears.

"Brianna and Brian are going to *love* this." Becky dug in the outer pocket of her backpack for her camera. "They adore the movie *The Hunchback of Notre Dame*. They have no idea that this is a real church."

"I'll buy them gargoyles from the gift shop," Judy said.

"I've got dibs on the most hideous one." Monique swung her arm over Judy's shoulders and struck a pose as Becky focused. "It'll loom over Kiera while she's in college. She'll probably call it 'Mom.'"

"Hey, back up a little, you two. I want to get both towers in the picture."

Judy smiled but her gaze was everywhere but at the camera. It was on the glimmer of the Seine River on either side of the island. It was on the little artist tables lined up against the stone walls by the bridge. It was on the sharp-cut little hedges in the front courtyard and the stone edging that served as benches. Nothing had really changed. If she thought long and hard enough, she could pinpoint the exact spot where her heart had once been broken.

"So what's on the agenda first?" Becky slipped the camera in the pocket of her khakis and shrugged her backpack into place. "Guided tour?"

"Let's do the towers," Monique suggested. "The guide-book said there's a gallery where we can see the gargoyles and a great view of the whole city if we climb to the belfry."

"Perfect," Judy quipped. "We'll be three bats in the belfry."

"How are those knees?"

"Functional."

Monique frowned. "You've got to go easy on them, Judy. There are four-hundred-odd stairs involved in this little tour."

"These knees have done this climb before. They can damn well do it again."

"I don't know. There are a couple of tough physical things coming up on the list. When we get to Interlaken—"

"Let's worry about Switzerland when we get there, okay?"

"I'm getting the sense that you don't want to talk about this, Judy."

"Ding-ding-ding."

"Okay, then, can we talk about your midlife crisis instead?"

Judy answered by swiveling on a heel and leading them to the tower entrance on the Rue de Cloître Notre Dame. This was not the first sharp comment Monique had made since she and Becky had returned from Burg Eltz yesterday. Their bike ride had left the two of them limp and exhausted, but Judy could tell by the way they looked at her that the ladies had spent a good amount of time on that hike talking about *her*. They made a point to spend dinner showing her the photos on their digital cameras, Becky's charcoal sketches of the fabulous castle, and telling funny little anecdotes about the other hikers they came across in the woods.

But they'd increased the pressure this morning. Monique had been full of prickling, provocative questions. Sensing the increasing attention, Judy had made a point on the train from Cochem to Trier to chat with the nice British woman who sat next to her, on holiday with her daughter. And then, on the train from Trier to Luxembourg, and later on the TGV to Paris, Judy had pointedly directed the conversation to their guidebooks and the question of how to best spend their few precious days in the City of Light. She figured if she showed some indication she was getting back into the spirit of the holiday, then her oh-so-energetic, irritatingly youthful friends would stop asking questions she had no intention of answering.

And why should they focus a single ounce of concern on her? She hadn't lost a husband—her relationship with Bob was solid and sexy and wonderful. She wasn't going blind—she could see quite well that she had five grown, successful children, a razor-thin but strengthening financial security, and a sturdy if somewhat life-battered house. The embarrassing truth was that it was her internal scaffolding that was collapsing, the foundations of her identity cracked and surging in an inner upheaval that flummoxed and embarrassed her. She hadn't summoned this, she didn't trust it, and she was only marginally beginning to understand it herself.

The last thing she wanted from her two grieving friends was pity.

"Eight euros a head," Judy said, as they approached the entrance to the tower. "Buck up, you two. Me and my aging knees are going first."

She would regret this later, she knew she would. She creaked up the narrow, circular steps to La Galerie des Chimères, every step causing new pressure on what she'd decided to label her "sports injury." Fortunately, Becky lagged a bit behind because the tower was dim and the ancient worn stairs uneven. After the first misstep Becky seized Monique by the waistband and proceeded with exaggerated care. The delay gave Judy a moment to catch her breath in the open air while she waited for Monique and Becky to finish the climb to the gallery.

She leaned on the stone edge, supposedly to better see the gargoyle glaring down at the front courtyard, the one with the face like a dog, a beard like a goat, and a single horn sticking out of his forehead. Monique and Becky came up behind her. It gave Judy some comfort to hear them breathing hard from the effort too.

"Wow." Monique took in the whole sweeping view of one of the most beautiful cities in the world. "Lenny should have put *this* on the list."

"Instead of Le Jules Verne? No way." Judy's gaze drifted to the Left Bank of the Seine, to the most iconic structure in Paris. Lenny had chosen two Parisian experiences for his bucket list: One was below ground at the famously creepy catacombs. The other was well above: At a Michelin-starred restaurant on the second level of the Eiffel Tower. "I can't believe you snagged reservations to that place. When I was here last all I saw getting into that elevator were women in pearls and furs."

"Well they'll have to make allowances for three women who've been living out of their suitcases." Monique grimaced a little. "And did I mention that our reservations are at nine thirty p.m.? That was all I could get when I emailed three and a half weeks ago."

"How fashionable," Judy said. "I'll try not to faint in my consommé."

Monique added, "At least we'll get an eagle's-eye view of the nighttime City of Light."

"Well," Becky said with a laugh, "I hope the food is awesome too."

With a little start Judy remembered that nighttime Paris would be nothing but streaks and blobs of light for Becky. And then Judy wondered how long it would be before realities like that stopped taking her by surprise.

"Would you guys mind?" Becky pulled the top of her sketch pad out of her daypack. "The stonework is fabulous here. I want to get it all down in pencil now so I can create it with fondant later."

"Sketch away," Monique said. "Judy and I will linger and have a little chat."

Judy kept her gaze fixed on the horizon. Becky, with a hasty clearing of her throat, skittered away very quickly for a vision-impaired woman. Judy suddenly felt like one of her dogs at the vet, backed up and quivering in a corner.

Judy said, "I thought you worked in the NICU, Monie. Not in the psych ward."

"Relax. I just want your advice."

Judy didn't believe that for a minute. Monique was using the back-door technique, asking one innocuous question so that Judy would drop her guard. Judy recognized the technique because she was the one who taught it to Monique for use against a certain guilty, unsuspecting teenager. Judy cast about for a work-around and then remembered the awkward, truncated phone conversation Monique and Kiera had

had while they waited to switch trains in Luxembourg. "If you want my advice, Monie, it's this: Just stop calling Kiera. Text her instead."

"That's not the advice I was looking for."

"Text works like an emotional filter. It gives a sense of safe distance."

"Duly noted. But Kiera will be leaving in a year—"

"All the more reason to perfect the technique. If you text her, she doesn't have to dread the look on your face, or the tone of your voice, and she'll be more likely to—"

"I'll be an empty nester when she leaves," Monique interrupted, her eyes narrowed as she gazed at the hazy horizon. "And I thought, with you experiencing this situation right now, maybe you could give me a tip or two on how to prepare for it."

"And you're asking me this because I'm handling this life transition with such grace and aplomb?"

"Listen." Monique sighed. "If your choice was between complete mental collapse or obsessive landscaping, well, I suppose you chose well."

"There's nothing wrong with mums on the front porch. Or a nice circle of begonias at the base of that cherry tree."

"Keeping up with the Merrills has become a very expensive sport."

"The truth is, having an empty nest sucks."

"This from you, who once told me that when the kids were finally out of the house, you and Bob were going to have sex on the kitchen table."

Judy blushed, thinking of what she and Bob had done after coming home from dropping Audrey off at the airport.

"I cannot be held responsible for what I say under the influence of multiple eggnogs at the Hendersons' Christmas party."

"Judy, it's not like all your kids have moved out permanently." Monique leaned against one of the stone pillars that framed their view of Paris. "Audrey and Maddy are going to come back every vacation. They'll be back in the summer. It seems like kids live in their parents' house through their twenties these days."

"Have you seen any of my boys lately?"

Jake was living in Dubai, working at the embassy, practicing his Arabic. He'd already told her he planned to stay there over the summer—depending on the overall political situation—and she couldn't stop her heart from racing at the news. Robert now lived in Omaha, working for an insurance company. He was so grateful for the employment after an eleven-month job search that he refused to take a vacation day to come see his parents on Thanksgiving. And Michael lived happily in Seattle working for Microsoft, already talking about spending Christmas there with his growing group of new friends.

"Boys are different," Monique said. "Even Becky says so. And after Maddy graduated, she came home and lived with you last summer."

"For four weeks and two days. As soon as her apartment became available in Boston, she was off to 'settle in.'" Judy tightened her jaw. She would not unload her issues on a widow who was about to send off to college her one and only daughter. "Kids grow up, become independent, and they leave home, Monie. It's that simple. They leave mothers behind to stand dazed and wonder what the hell just happened."

Mothers who'd dedicated their lives to wrangling popsicle sticks and toilet paper rolls into Native American wigwams, herding entire muddy teams of ten-year-olds from sports to Dairy Queen, and pacing the kitchen praying for the curfew-breaking teenager they are convinced is bleeding to death in a ditch somewhere.

Mothers who didn't yet realize that a parent's last duty was to stand and wave as those children skip away to their own lives, taking with them a hefty chunk of her own.

"You know, when Bob left the newspaper," Judy found herself saying, "the company threw a big party for him. There was champagne and the usual rubber chicken dish. There were long, loopy speeches and a pile of gifts. The company celebrated his time there and then sent him off into unemployment."

"It was still terrible they let him go."

"The newspaper business is volatile these days. It happens. At least they gave him a good send-off and a gold watch." She felt a heat prickle through her, the onset of the sweaty discomfort. How she hated the new unpredictability of her own body. "Like Bob I've worked myself right out of a job, too. I've been forced into unemployment. Except with no party and no gold watch."

Judy scraped the toe of her shoe against the leaf litter gathered by the edge of the wall, frustrated and embarrassed by that overly simple explanation. A party wouldn't unravel the complicated knot of her emotions. It wouldn't ease the creaking of her knees. It wouldn't bring back her period, which, as of last week, she'd skipped for the second month in a row. But it would have served as a demarcation of some sort: A ritual to separate before and after.

She'd hoped this vacation would be that marker. But she'd yet to feel the seismic shifting within her, the emotional sign of change.

"You know," Monique said, "if you work this analogy to its natural end, you'd realize that after he was let go from the newspaper, Bob soon found a new job."

"Lucky bastard."

"There's nothing stopping you from looking."

"Eighteen effing applications."

Monique started.

"Every single potential employer turned me down cold."

Monique stuttered. "When did you start this?"

"January." She managed an airy little shrug and took some comfort in Monique's surprise. "Hey, with professionals like Marco given furloughs, I can hardly complain. It took Bob eight months to find his new job, and it pays less than the other. And I made ridiculous limitations when I started my search. I didn't want to work retail because that meant working weekends and holidays and summers, which are the only times my kids might possibly visit."

"What a sneaky thing you are. I didn't even suspect."

"I started local, searching for nine-to-five office work. Everyone kept asking me if I knew all kinds of word processing programs, and spreadsheets and databases and PowerPoint, and all those things that my kids did for me."

"You're looking in the wrong places. You should teach preschool."

"Not without a degree in education. And I can't possibly add another tuition bill to the ones Bob and I are already staggering under."

"A teacher's aide, then—"

"Requires training too. The ability to handle kids and a clean criminal record are apparently not enough these days. So here I am, still unemployed. Apparently no one wants to hire an unskilled, dried-up, washed-out homemaker."

Monique made a tsking noise. "The market has spoken, Judy: You're utterly useless."

"Just kick me to the curb."

"Bundle you up like old newspapers."

"Right up on the old garbage heap."

She'd spoken fluent French and German when she was young. She'd worked for the Children's Fund at the United Nations. She had a job she had to wear heels to, a boss who liked the proposals she wrote up, and skills that were valuable to a greater cause. The job had been a singular bright light during a difficult transition in her life. Now standing in this gallery watching the tourists swarm below, Judy struggled to parse out the French.

Voilà, les chimères.

Après vous, je t'en prie.

Ça va bien?

"You've raised five amazing kids," Monique said. "They're in school, employed, self-sufficient. You should be proud. I forbid you to take this so deeply to heart."

"Don't do that."

"Do what?"

"Tell me how I'm supposed to feel."

A sudden rush of emotion overwhelmed her—frustration and helplessness and something else, some rippling anger she was sure was hormonally induced. Of course she was proud of her kids. She'd be proud of her kids no matter what they did. Any mother would. Even the mothers of serial killers must have something they were proud about, because a mother was a mother and thus loved unconditionally.

"I should come with a warning." Judy pushed away from the wall. "Beware the Bitch. She's Menopausal."

"My fault," Monique conceded. "I should know better than to spout platitudes. Some of the meanest things people said to me were platitudes, and they made me furious."

"You, furious? In what blue moon was this?"

"Lenny's funeral."

"Monie, at the funeral you were practically catatonic."

"Numb," she corrected. "I was *numb*. But I was taking hits by the dozens. Someone would say, 'he's in a better place,' or 'at least he's not suffering anymore,' or—the worst—'you're young, you'll fall in love again.' People would actually look me in the eye and say things like that while my husband lay dead in a coffin right beside me."

Judy felt vaguely unsettled as she searched her memory, sure that she'd mouthed one if not all of those same platitudes. With growing guilt she turned back to the view, sinking her elbows on the stone. Her gaze drifted to the benches by the hedge.

"See that long stone bench right there?" Judy pointed to the left side of the courtyard. "It was in that exact spot that I was dumped by Thierry."

She remembered every detail of the moment. The slant of

the sun cutting across the courtyard. The air that smelled so strongly of lilies. The strap of one of her sandals had broken, and it had made a sore spot on her foot where she'd hastily sewn the strap together. Thierry's hair was pulled back and tied with a little piece of shoelace. She loved that neck, the little hairs, the vulnerable paleness of it. She'd resisted the urge to touch it, to nuzzle it, as he smoked a filterless cigarette.

He'd hunched over, breathing the smoke deep, avoiding her eye.

Monique nudged her over so she could plant her elbows on the stone sill right by Judy's side, their shoulders touching. "We could have gone anywhere in Paris today," Monique murmured. "We didn't have to come to a place that held bad memories."

"You misunderstand. I chose this place intentionally."

"Masochist."

"The memory isn't all bad. I was ass-over-tit in love with that man. Helplessly giddy about him. We'd been traveling for a couple of weeks together, keeping each other very warm at night. I'd just assumed he loved me too."

By the time she'd met Thierry, she'd perfected the act of tumbling heedlessly in love. Traveling had a way of shucking the expectations that tended to build around a settled life. Travel became a goal in itself, wanderlust the passion that fed it, and any man with the same sentiment in his heart, an easy target for affection. She'd fallen in love with Thierry not just because he had liquid brown eyes and a way of smiling that made one eye squint more than the other. She'd fallen in love with him because he, too, wanted to work his way across Europe, and if the money held, into Greece and maybe Turkey. He understood her urge to follow the road far, far from where she was, to some exotic destination that would then turn into a jumping point to yet another.

"The truth was that Thierry was just like the others I'd hooked up with," Judy said. "He was a common *goujat.*"

The word came to her, surprisingly easily, feathering off her tongue.

"I assume that means 'gigolo'?"

"More of what Audrey would call a 'player.' Thierry never set himself up to be anything but a man of breezy affections, or our relationship to be anything but one of convenience and common interests. We fell in together, as we happened to be on the same road. At the beginning I had no problem with that. I felt the same way."

Monique leaned into her. Her shoulder was warm.

"But by the time Thierry came along," Judy continued, "I'd been traveling for over five months. Some of the glamour had worn off. I'd started to feel as if my feet were losing their grip on the earth. It's difficult to describe." Judy struggled to find a way to explain how it felt to be rootless for so long, to sense the emotional connections to home and old friends and family stretch so thin, almost to the point of dissolution. "Every step I took farther along those cobblestone paths—every loose, easy, carefree relationship I'd thrown myself into—made me lighter and lighter, until I wondered if I'd eventually just float off the face of the earth. And not a single soul would give a damn."

Monique said softly, "And Thierry changed that?"

"No, *I* changed it. By talking to him about the future." Judy glanced at that bench where she'd last seen him. "Within an hour of broaching the subject, he gave me a kiss and took off."

He'd startled a flock of pigeons when he'd stood up. By the time the fat birds settled back down, the man she thought she'd loved was gone.

"Judy...why would you want to remember this?"

"Because I was a brave and reckless young woman back then, but I was also about as shallow as any garden-variety teenager. I had no clue about what really mattered in life. Until I took my broken heart in hand that day and stood up from that bench." She cast her gaze over the mansard roofs and the dome of Sacre Coeur in the distance. "When I stood up from that bench, Monie, I finally knew what mattered. So I booked my flight back to the States. Within two years I found Bob."

Bob, who rooted her in the suburbs with five fat, happy babies and a brace of big messy dogs. One Bob was worth a hundred thousand flighty French Thierrys.

Monique leaned her head on Judy's shoulder. "That man sure did shatter your heart."

"Yes, he did," Judy conceded. "And so did Audrey—unintentionally—when she stepped on that plane to California."

Monique lifted her head and gave her a quizzical look. "Oh, sweetie," she said, "Audrey's not leaving you forever."

"No, she's not. But when she threw me that breezy wave, that's the moment I understood that my life as I knew it was over." In the courtyard a flock of pigeons suddenly rose up and whooshed to higher perches. "You wanted advice about how to handle an empty nest? I can't give it to you, Monie. I'm floundering. I just can't imagine what the hell I'm going to do with the rest of my life."

✺ chapter ten

Becky braced her sketch pad against her ribs as she stood across from the opening to the Metro station. She sketched the metal archway that held the station sign, Denfert-Rochereau. She adored the loopy script, the chipping green paint, the romantic name. But she kept blinking, trying to clear a film in her eye. Paris was sooty like New York City, with all the cars and the exhaust and the wind kicking up debris. Every time she rubbed her eyes to clear her vision, her eyes just watered more.

Right. That's what she needed. Soot in her eyes, interfering with her already shitty vision.

"Hey, we're moving." Monique, standing a little way behind Becky, kept her place with Judy in the line to the Paris Catacombs. She flicked her wrist to look at the face of her watch. "A forty-minute wait. That's going to kill our plans. At this rate, I don't think we're going to make it to Sacré Coeur in Montmartre, Judy."

"Crazy tourists." Judy craned her neck as the group started filing into the little green building. "Who comes to Paris to go wandering underground?"

"Three women on a mission." Monique tapped the increasingly tattered itinerary jutting out of the side pocket of her daypack. "Besides, we could spend a month in Paris and still not see everything."

"But why aren't these folks at the Eiffel Tower or the Louvre?" Judy said. "The l'Arc de Triomphe, the Picasso museum, the Musee D'Orsay—"

"The catacombs would be Gina's first stop." Becky tucked her charcoals in her backpack. "It'd be the first stop for all her neck spike–wearing friends too."

Becky joined them in the line as she flipped the pages of her sketch pad, noticing how few bare pages were left. She should slip into one of the stationary shops near their hotel in the Marais and purchase some overpriced acid-free paper before tomorrow. As she flipped her gaze caught a series of quick line drawings of the Château de Vincennes, which she and the ladies had visited that morning. Then she admired a detail of a mansard roof and a hasty draft she'd made of the famous pyramid in the courtyard of the Louvre. She flipped past a drawing of the rose window of Notre Dame and then paused on a sketch of a hunch-backed gargoyle.

The gargoyle was bug-eyed and snarling, bird-bone thin, the composition of its arm crooked like a dog's leg. The thought passed through her mind that Gina would have loved that gallery of gargoyles. At Gina's age Becky's sketchbooks had been full of pencil drawings of flower fairies and elves. Gina's were filled with gnomes. Where Becky imagined castles in clouds and woodland cottages, Gina portrayed haunted houses and ruined towers. Not for the first time Becky wondered why she hadn't recognized the broken nature of that girl's dreams when she'd first arrived at her home, a gawky and stone-faced twelve-year-old. By the time Becky recognized Gina as a dark kindred spirit, Gina had already dismissed her as the wicked stepmother.

Judy suddenly thrust a hand between the pages so she could flip the gargoyle out of sight and reveal a sketch of the Eiffel Tower.

Judy tapped the page. "This would look really nice, matted and framed, on my wall near the front door. Christmas is coming, you know."

"I hear you, Captain Obvious."

Becky flipped the pages closed. Through the amber filter of her sunglasses, she noticed the lines of hangover weariness around Judy's eyes. Last night the three of them had put on their wrinkle-free party dresses, high-heeled it to the street, and hailed a taxi. They'd arrived at the Champ de Mars and paraded to the elevator of the Eiffel Tower where, on the second tier, they emerged at Le Jules Verne.

While Monique and Judy oohed and ahhed over the panorama of nighttime Paris, she'd taken a seat with her back to what the girls' determined was the best view. Instead of the blur of city lights, Becky had focused on Judy, drinking too many glasses of a really good burgundy as she regaled them with salacious stories about her French lover. Monique, looking lovely and wistful, idly twirled the stem of her glass as the widow did her usual disappearing act, mentally drifting off someplace where she and Judy couldn't follow.

"It looks like we're going to make the next group."

Monique fixed her clear gaze on Becky. "You sure you're up for this? The book says the tunnels are dimly lit."

Becky bent over to hide a spurt of irritation. She unzipped the backpack she'd tucked between her feet, slipped her sketch pad inside. She took her time fitting it in tight.

Monique's voice rose above her. "I'm not mothering, Beck. I'm just making sure you have full information."

She straightened to her full height, a good inch taller than Monique when they were both wearing sneakers. "I did tell you that the ophthalmologist said there wouldn't be any sudden or abrupt changes in my vision, right?"

"Actually no."

"And that most likely I'd lose only about five percent of my visual field over the course of an entire year, right?"

"Daytime vision, I assume."

"And how many weeks has it been since I got the diagnosis?"

Monique made an exaggerated sigh as she pulled out a pile of euros. "All right, all right, maybe I was mothering a little."

"I appreciate the impulse, Monie, but no worries." She hiked her pack over her shoulder as they stepped up to the ticket counter. "I'll just stay close to you guys and try not to knock down any bone pyramids."

Becky regretted her snarkiness the moment they passed through the entranceway and realized they'd be descending into the catacombs by way of a dimly lit spiral staircase. She flattened her fingers against the opposite wall and then gripped the railing as she toed her way down. The risers were uneven. She stumbled on the fourth step. It wasn't so dim that she couldn't see the way Monique paused, her shoulders tightening, clearly resisting the urge to turn around and look up at her. But Becky only gripped the railing with more determination. She wasn't about to grasp Monique's shoulders now, with the taste of snark still lingering on her tongue.

Monique suddenly sucked in a sharp breath. "Don't touch the walls. They're slimy."

Becky pressed her hand harder against the mossy stone. Her palms were soaked but the sliminess didn't bother her. Should she miss a step she would need to grind her fingers into the mortar to keep upright. And the deeper they descended, the less light filtered in from above. The air billowing up from below smelled of mildew and decay.

She cast through her memory for what she'd read about these catacombs. These old stone quarry tunnels had run through Paris since before the revolution. Sometime in the eighteenth century the city grappled with the problem of too little space, too many dead bodies, and too many ill-placed graves infecting the groundwater that people drew from nearby wells. So the powers that be decided to disinter the bones from the cemeteries and transfer them to these unused quarry tunnels. They piled the bones, one on top of another, in ways both bizarre and artful. The bones of six million people lay here.

The bottom of the stairs came abruptly. Becky stumbled against Monique, and then just as quickly righted herself, but not before she noticed that Monique was trembling.

"Ooh," Monique murmured as she moved deeper into the tunnel, "this place is *creepy*."

Becky didn't feel the same quivering excitement. To her

all strange, dark places were full of dangers. These tunnels were dimmer than she expected. This tour was going to take focus and labor, like walking through an unfamiliar neighborhood after emerging from a new restaurant, gripping Marco's arm and using the red haze of a distant stoplight as a marker for where they'd parked the car.

Judy fell in pace beside her as they followed the crowd down the tunnel. "Monie, tell me there's no steep spiral staircase back up to the street level at the end of all this. My knees are screaming."

Monique folded the map closed. "Let's not worry about the route out yet. We've got a bit of a hike to the main area."

Judy said, "Hike?!"

"The actual entrance to the catacombs is a kilometer or two through this tunnel. But it's flat and easy."

Judy groaned. Becky tried to focus on a faint blob of light ahead, but it kept winking in and out of sight behind the heads of the people bobbing in front of them. The deeper through the tunnels they walked, the more the walls seemed to close in, the denser the air seemed to get. It smelled like the air of a wet dryer, except chilly and tinged with the tang of iron. Over the shuffling of footsteps, Becky heard the sound of water gurgling, like the running of an underground stream.

Monique's voice dropped low with delight. "Isn't this something straight out of a Stephen King novel? Kiera would have *loved* this."

"I'm so glad," Judy sang, "that I'm not claustrophobic."

Monique fumbled with something in her pack. "I'm going to pull out my video camera."

"Nope, I'm not claustrophobic at all."

Becky flinched as something splashed on her shoulder. Beside her Judy flinched too.

"Either it's raining in here," Judy said tightly, "or a bat just vacated his bowels on my head."

Monique clicked the video camera on to the sound of a beep. "It's just water. I got hit too. Can you believe this place? Even the walls are weeping."

"There's enough air down here, right?" Judy's voice rose in pitch. "Because they only allow two hundred people at a time in the catacombs, right? Any more than that and we'd use up all the *air*."

Monique said, "Don't hyperventilate."

"You can only hyperventilate if there's *air*."

"Take deep breaths. Just stay calm and keep walking."

"Are you really videotaping me having an anxiety attack?"

"You're not having an anxiety attack. You're perfectly fine, walking right under the streets of Paris—"

"To see skeletons. Why in God's name would Lenny put this on the list?"

Monique made a sound deep in her throat—a soft little hint of a laugh—a light bit of music Becky hadn't heard in a while. "It's just like a horror movie, isn't it? It's something straight out of the mind of Wes Craven. And to think Lenny wouldn't even sit through *The Sixth Sense*."

Becky murmured, "Wait—he didn't like that movie?"

"Oh, he'd never admit that. He was okay through the first part of it. Until the boy ended up in the little closet at the top of the stairs."

Becky shivered, remembering the scene when a young

boy is locked in the darkness and savagely beaten by something only he could see.

"When that part came," Monique continued, "Lenny shot up out of his chair and insisted that we keep watching as he left the room."

Becky muttered, "I'd be right on his heels."

"Oh, he came back after a while. He kept coming and going. First to go to the bathroom. Then to get a glass of water. Always at the point in the movie when things got really creepy. But he would never admit it scared the hell out of him. Not while his eleven-year-old daughter was wide-eyed and squealing in delight."

Monique fiddled with something on the camera—at least that's what Becky thought, from all the clicking. "Monie, are you saying that Lenny didn't like horror movies?"

"He hated them."

"Then why put this on the list?"

Monique didn't say anything right away, and Becky sensed in her pause a brief uncertainty. "Well," Monie said, "I guess it's because he loved the cuddling I insisted on after."

Judy murmured, "Ooh-la-la."

"Come on, Monie." Becky thought that she may be going blind, but there were some things even a blind friend could see. "This is *really* creepy. If Lenny chose to put this on the list, then it was just for you alone."

"No, no. Everything on that list was for the two of us."

"Becky's right," Judy said. "Lenny picked these catacombs because he was throwing you a bone."

Monique groaned. "You didn't just say that."

"I did," Judy said. "A little humor to keep me sane, Monie,

because I see the vestibule up ahead, and you know what comes after that."

The shadowy silhouettes of the tourists abruptly expanded, and Becky got the sense that they'd just entered a larger space, though the only way she had to gauge that was the slight distance—like an exhale—that both Monique and Judy put between them.

"O-kay." Judy's swift intake of breath was followed by a shaky, uneven exhale. "I guess this is what we're here to see."

"I'm channeling Kiera." Monique's excitement was a shiver that rippled through her whole body. "This is so *keeeeeeewl.*"

The video camera whirred on again. Becky strained to see something in the yellow light. It was like looking at a stucco wall, the details entirely lost. Becky knew what was collected down here. She supposed what was spread in front of her, drenched in the sepulchral light, were the artistically stacked bones of people who'd been buried three centuries ago. It might be better if she could move closer, so that she might actually be able to see some detail. But in this relentless dimness she'd probably find herself six inches from something curious before her brain resolved the image into the empty eye sockets of a skull.

"Hey, Monique," Judy said, "it's getting a little close in here, don't you think? Let's go ahead a little farther, get away from the crowds."

"I'm game."

Becky followed on their heels as her friends maneuvered through the crowd. The back of her neck tingled, the hairs standing up, and not just from the cold and the proximity of the dead but also from the heart-stopping half collisions she was avoiding only by a breath. During the walk from the staircase to these tunnels everyone pretty much had been moving forward in the same direction, but here in the caverns themselves, people milled, veering to the left and to the right, noting to one another the names of the galleries, the little niches built into the walls with the urns within, altars made of bones.

"Look, there's another placard." Judy slid away. "I'll translate."

"I want to get a photo of this sepulchral lamp." Monique fiddled with her camera. "But without a flash the only way it's going to work is if I change the exposure time. You know, I should have just taken my digital camera instead of fussing with this."

Monique pressed various buttons, a little tiny bluish glow indicating the brightness of the camera screen. Becky stood halfway between her two friends, feeling slightly unmoored. Judy was only a few steps away, mumbling French under her breath. Monique was still standing on the opposite side, an arm's length away, if Becky was assessing the distance of that blinking little blue blob of light correctly.

Don't be a freakin' wimp.

They were in tunnels, for goodness sake. Yeah, she was standing alone like a cork bobbing in the middle of a dark sea, but her friends could certainly see her. She would just stand here and face a vague yellow smear of light, and pretend as if she could actually *see* what it was illuminating, while waiting patiently.

"*Où est-elle la Mort?*" Judy, to her right, spoke aloud. "Where is Death? *Toujours future ou passée.*"

To her left Monique mumbled, "I have no idea if this is going to work."

"I think that means 'always in the future or in the past,'" Judy mused. *"A peine est-elle presente…"*

Becky closed her eyes. The smear of yellow light winked out and everything was in blackness. It calmed her somehow. It gave her the illusion that if she opened her eyes she'd actually see something more.

"…*que deja elle n'est plus.* Well that's complicated. I think it means 'as soon as death is here, she's gone.' Huh." Judy shifted her weight in the darkness. "Why is death feminine, anyway? I never did understand that."

With her eyes still closed Becky conjured in her mind the castles and cathedrals and beautiful buildings she'd seen since they'd arrived in Paris. She focused for a while on the castle of Vincennes. Brian's birthday was in June. She would make him that castle. She'd leave space between the outer walls and the tall inner keep so he could slip his knights into formation, along with some of Brianna's plastic cows and sheep and goats for the courtyard. Even the knights have to eat. She pondered how she could re-create the ochre color of the stones.

Becky became aware of more tourists flooding into this section of the tunnels. Brisk little eddies of air brushed past her. She smelled the sudden scent of perfume. A backpack bumped against her shoulder. Startled she stumbled forward a little and then froze, balancing on the balls of her feet.

Vertigo, swift and sudden, a mental plunge into an abyss.

Becky blinked her eyes open and forced herself down to the flat of her soles. She told herself to calm down. During the day, if she got knocked by somebody, she'd try to adjust her motion or her stance to avoid any more collisions. But in the darkness her first reaction was paralysis. She knew this place was riddled with underground caverns, hidden aquifers, and a maze of quarry tunnels not officially opened to the public. Tourists milled around her like bees in a small part of the hive. Becky listened for Judy, but there were a lot of folks reading French. She turned her head toward where Monique had been—or, at least, where she thought Monique had been—but saw no glowing blue blob. A bunch of kids suddenly swarmed near her, dissolving into giggling little gasps.

She said, "Monique?"

No response. A German couple slipped up beside her, chatting comfortably. She slid her foot across the floor and sidled away from them. Another group came up behind her. She wondered if she were standing in front of something worthy of notice. She blinked and blinked and blinked, but whatever it was, it was not lit well, not even by the little spotlights that ran along the walls.

She spoke more loudly. "Judy?"

She told herself they couldn't be far. There was a haze of yellow light toward her right. A spotlight like many of the others, so it was likely attached to a wall. If she headed toward it maybe the light would help her orient herself in this room. Maybe she could catch the sight of a unique, long-necked silhouette amid the shadows. Maybe Judy could better see her if she were standing underneath the bulb.

She shuffled, keeping the soles of her sneakers flat on the ground. Shadows flickered past, startling her. Someone tried to get by her, bobbing one way and then another in impatience before sighing and elbowing past. As discretely as she could she stretched her arms out, hoping to find the edges of something—a wall, hopefully—rather than the sleeves of other tourists or the soft hair of a child or the strap of a pocketbook, swiftly jerked back. Her heart started to trip over itself. She widened her stance, dizzy in the dark.

"Monique?" She hated the edge of panic in her own voice. "Judy?"

That light was just ahead. She splayed her hands and jarred the butt of her palm against something smooth and icy, something that tilted back. She flexed her fingers over it to make sure it was balanced and wouldn't fall and shatter into a thousand pieces. Her thumb slipped through a hole to the ridges inside it.

A hush in a child's voice, somewhere behind her. "Mum, is she allowed to touch that?"

She jerked her hand back. She knocked her knuckles on something stony, the edge of a niche in the wall or a pillar, something sharp enough to graze a layer of skin. She stumbled in the opposite direction and slammed into someone who grunted and dropped something that clattered on the ground, a spinning circle of light. She tried to apologize but her words came out garbled as she fought to breathe.

In her chest her heart pounded pounded pounded. She found the flat of a damp slick wall and she pressed herself up against it, cheek to the chill. Her head felt light, so light, like it would rise up from her shoulders and float away.

She had a dim sense of a hand curling over her arm.

"*Madame?*"

"Breathe, Becky."

Becky clutched a fistful of Monique's yoga pants, stumbling in her wake. Her heart still raced in her chest. It didn't help that she was speed-walking through the tunnels on bruised knees and rubbery legs, twisting and turning following a path she couldn't see. She concentrated on lifting her feet with exaggeration so she wouldn't catch the edge of her sneaker on an uneven surface or a random stone. She wanted to stop and suck in a lungful of air, but she wanted to race away from her shame more.

"Beck," Monique repeated, *"breathe."*

"I'm trying." She focused as Monique had ordered, drawing deep breaths as she plowed forward. "I . . . just . . . don't understand . . . what happened to me."

She'd found herself kneeling on the ground, with a guard gripping her upper arm and talking into his walkie-talkie. She didn't understand a word of French but she'd slowly come to understand that people had gathered, staring. She'd dug her fingers into the grit of the floor so she wouldn't lose consciousness.

"You had a panic attack." Monique's pace was unforgiving. "It used to happen all the time in the ER. A guy would come in gray as paste clutching his chest, and everyone thinks it's a heart attack. But if they'd talked to the guy for five minutes, they'd find out he'd just been fired, or his wife asked him for a divorce, or he'd just been diagnosed with something nasty. Like retinitis pigmentosa."

Waves of shame washed over her. She'd been frightened

in the dark before. Tripping over Brianna's bike left in the middle of the driveway as she tried to drag the garbage out to the sidewalk on a Sunday night. Trailing her fingers against the car on the way back to guide her to the back stairs, sixteen steps beyond the end of the azalea bush. This hadn't felt like that. This had felt like she'd been trapped in a tiny closet and seized by the throat until she lost consciousness.

"I thought you were right there, Becky." Judy panted right behind her, half running to keep pace. "I thought you were right beside me. And then you *weren't*, so I thought you went ahead with Monique."

"You were with me." Monique veered to the left and then centered again, and Becky felt the splash of water as she stumbled into a puddle. "You were there, with me, and then the crowd came, and I tried to get that stupid picture of the sepulchral lamp before someone rushed in front of my camera. When I looked up you just weren't there anymore."

"Monie and I were two chambers over," Judy said, for the tenth time, "before we realized we'd lost you."

"I looked for you." Monique's voice was tight. "I scanned the whole room before I went to the next one. I don't know how I didn't see you there."

"For goodness sake," Judy exclaimed. "How many miles is this place? That guard said it was not even a kilometer to the exit."

"And you, Judy." Monique twisted a little; Becky felt the shift of Monique's spine against the knuckles of her hand. "You told us you couldn't speak French anymore."

"I don't."

"What the hell was that, then, you babbling to the guard? Were you speaking in tongues?"

"I just told him she was blind. *Aveugle.* I didn't think I knew that word. It popped right into my head."

"It wasn't one word. You were having a whole conversation."

"He wanted to call in medics. I told him you were a nurse. It was all present tense, French one-o-one."

"You couldn't step in while we were in Luxembourg when I was talking to that guy at the counter, trying to find the platform for our train connection?"

"You did fine."

"Or at the Metro this morning, asking for directions to the Château de Vincennes?"

"The French always answer me back in English."

"So?"

"That's Parisian for 'your French sucks, lady, so please stop torturing my language.'"

"Tonight you're the one calling the airline to make sure our flight to Zurich is on time."

"Sure, if you want me to screw it up. Oh, damn it." Judy groaned as they took another sudden corner. "More freakin' stairs."

Monique didn't pause. She took a little leap up the first step. "How are you doing, Beck? We're almost out."

It couldn't be soon enough. The air was sticky. It was hard to draw in, harder to push out. Becky flailed with her free arm until she felt the slick wall against her fingers. The stairs had high risers. She stumbled on the first, but Judy was right behind her, steadying her with two hands on the small of her back.

"If you fall, Beck, we're all falling together," Judy said. "And it ain't going to be pretty, the three of us a pile of old bats at the bottom."

Monique tugged on the waistband of her yoga pants. "And I'd like to keep my pants on, thank you very much."

They ascended the stairs, brisk but steady. She vaguely remembered something about there being eighty-four steps down or one hundred and sixteen up, she couldn't remember which or whether that memory was from reading about the catacombs or about the stairs to the tower of the Cathedral of Notre Dame. She just wanted to *see*. She wanted to drink with her eyes all the light she could. She wanted to shake this panicky sense of choking, of being locked in darkness.

"Go on ahead." Judy abruptly let go of the tail of Becky's jacket. "I have to rest my knees a minute. I'm right behind you."

When Judy let go, it was like shedding a weight dragging her back into the tomb. Monique was a steady, strong climber leaning forward and Becky put her trust in her. She fought down her irrational anxiety that she'd never find her way out of this place. The sweat coming out on her was hot now, not the cold dank sweat that burst all over her skin but the kind that pooled and fell down her spine, the kind that made wet spots just beneath her breasts.

"Can you see it, Becky?"

She glanced up and saw a little vertical strip of brightness, like a crack in the ceiling of the world.

"Steady," Monique said, as Becky's toe slipped off the edge of the stair. "Almost there now."

Almost there.

Becky sucked in a deep breath. She smelled car exhaust. From above came the muffled rhythm of footsteps, a burble of language, and a muted jingle of a bicycle bell.

"Judy?" Monique called over her shoulder. "You all right down there?"

Judy's voice, from deep below, was pained. "I'm at half speed. Don't worry, I'll see you outside."

Then the stairs ended abruptly. Monique swung the doors open to bright light. Becky blinked and the room came into focus. Monique swung her daypack onto a table, where a guard in a black polo shirt searched it. A pile of bones lay in a box by his side. Becky gave over her own backpack and then, abandoning it, strode through the doors that led to the street.

She stood in the middle of the sidewalk as people streamed around her. She dropped her head back and blinked up to the cloudy sky. She watched the flight of a bird. She blinked and blinked, taking in the soar of a street-lamp, the six stories of building, the wrought-iron railings across every window, the geraniums hanging limp from a few. She took in the tiny cars zipping across the roads. A jingle as a man walked by, playing with the keys in his pocket, a red scarf flapping about his neck. She walked out of the crowd to the edge of the sidewalk, wishing she could get drunk on this light.

"You don't look so good, Beck."

Monique sidled up beside her with both packs in her

hand. Becky didn't want to look at her. Fear pulsed through her whole body. The terror she'd tried to tamp down all these weeks battered in her throat. She couldn't do this anymore. She couldn't pretend everything was going to be all right.

Abruptly she turned to Monique. She watched two lines deepen between her friend's brows. Becky had been a fool, thinking she could keep the truth from Monique. Those hazel eyes knew everything.

The words lurched out of her. "How long have you known?"

The little lines between Monique's eyes softened. Her expression shifted from concern to a deep, green sorrow. She tilted her head on that long, long neck and pressed her lips together in a way that showed she did know, and she had no words.

"Their eyes are brown," Becky retorted, as Judy exited the building and limped toward them. "Both Brianna and Brian have brown eyes, just like Marco's. So that means they must have Marco's eyes."

Monique dropped the packs by her feet. "It doesn't work that way, Beck."

"I have to go home."

"It's not inevitable." Monique gripped her shoulders. "It's very complicated. The disease may be genetic but—"

Becky raised her palm. "I need to go home," she stuttered, "before both my children go blind."

∞ chapter eleven

M onique sat on the edge of the bed. Her cell phone lay on the bedside table, open to her favorite photo. Three-year-old Kiera sat upon Lenny's shoulders, gripping his ears in her little fists. The light shone on Lenny's skin, emphasizing the spray of freckles on his cheeks and forehead, like fresh-cracked pepper.

On her lap lay the crinkled bucket list, now stained with café au lait and sticky in a corner with German apple strudel. Behind her, in the hotel bathroom, came the spitting sound of the shower as a desolate Becky used up what was sure to be the last of the tepid water. Through the window seeped the noises of the Marais neighborhood. High heels clicked lonely on cobblestones. A shopkeeper whisked the first falling leaves off the sidewalk. A Frenchman called *bon soir* from down the street, chatting with familiarity before he continued on.

Monique took a long look at her husband and then let her eyes flutter closed against the late afternoon light. For the moment she was blessedly alone. After the experience at the catacombs, not one of them was up for a fussy, linen-napkin dinner or even a bite in a brasserie, so Judy had gone off to find the makings of dinner since this hotel didn't have room service.

Monique took a deep breath. The room smelled odd, a mix of freshly baked bread from the *boulangerie* across the street and chemicals rising from the hair salon just beside it. She was used to sensing Lenny in the familiar confines of her home bedroom. She was used to smiling at his teasing directions delivered from the backseat of her minivan while she drove alone. She and Lenny hadn't spent a lot of time in hotel rooms, which she supposed made this harder than usual. They'd always been housecats. Purring and comfortable in their den.

She wanted to talk to him about so much. About Becky. About the view of the city from the London Eye and the surprise of the castle on the Rhine boat trip, the beauty of the bike ride along the Moselle, and the pan-seared turbot with crayfish and mushrooms *à la riche* she'd savored at Le Jules Verne. She needed to talk to him about Kiera, to whom she'd texted about the catacomb experience, including a photo of piled bones...and who'd responded with a terse *congrats for crossing it off the list.*

Monique tried to push that worry aside. She waited for that oh-so-familiar whisper. With her eyes closed, she flattened the palm of her hand on the bedspread and anticipated the sag of the mattress. She ached for him to come to her. A breeze filtered in from the window, and with a tingle of excitement, she raised her face to the chill. She perked her ears to the rustle of the sheer curtains. She waited for the smell of him—hungry for the fragrance of cut grass and Brut, of warm flannel and man.

The breeze faded, the curtains settled.

A key rattled in the lock.

Monique jerked at the sound and then quickly shoved the list back into her daypack, open by her feet. *Damn.* Would she ever get a moment alone? It felt like she hadn't connected with Lenny for weeks. She was thrown off by the foreignness of the rooms they stayed in, and the unpredictable interruptions. She glanced at the picture on her phone just as the door opened, only to find that the screen had gone dark.

"Bon! Je reviens!" Judy swung in, a bag in each hand. *"On va manger bien ce soir."*

Monique twisted, lifting a knee onto the mattress. "I assume that's French for we're not having Chicken Mc-Nuggets."

"I've just spent an hour picking through a *boulangerie,* a *charcuterie,* a *caviste,* and a *pâtisserie,* all within two blocks of here." Judy dropped the bags onto the bureau by the TV, and then glanced at the bathroom door as the shower turned off. "Have you and Becky settled everything?"

Monique stood up and smoothed her yoga pants over her thighs. "Not really."

"Uh-oh. Problems getting a flight?" Judy pulled a loaf of French bread out of a bag and slipped it onto the table. "There should be a red-eye to LaGuardia or Kennedy at least. On a Thursday night out of Paris-Orly I wouldn't think it would be full."

Monique pulled out a chair. "Well...I don't really know."

Judy paused, a wine bottle halfway out of the bag. "You didn't call, did you?"

"Nope."

"You were waiting for me to unfurl my suddenly volcanic French?"

"Not exactly."

"I hate to tell you, Monique," she said, placing the bottle on the table and then tapping her watch, "but if we don't get on this soon, there's a possibility Becky won't be able to get on a flight tonight."

"Bingo."

Judy eyed her as she unzipped her belly pack and pulled out her Swiss Army knife. She cast a glance toward the closed bathroom door as she tugged the corkscrew free. "Dangerous move, *mon amie*. Beck's got that look about her. You know, that rigid, tight-faced, don't-even-*breathe* on me look, like when Marco took Gina off to his mother's for a couple of mysterious weeks. One probing question and the poor woman may shatter."

"You don't think she did just that, in the catacombs?"

Judy peeled the casing off the neck of the bottle and dropped it onto the table, her eyes averted and her voice low. "Why the hell didn't you tell me weeks ago?"

"She wasn't ready to talk about it. It's not my terrible news to share. And it didn't feel right to hash it out behind Becky's back."

Judy pinned the cork with the tip of the corkscrew, blinking rapidly. "I won't believe it. It just can't be true."

Monique thought of the two Lorenzini kids, squealing as they swung on her backyard swing set. Brian a blur of energy and motion, a roaring rough-and-tumble boy who loved nothing better than to roll around with Judy's big, gentle dogs. Brianna and her collection of blue jay feathers, the agate marbles she loved so much, the way she gently pinched you, nudged you, made funny faces, always eager for attention.

"It may *not* be true." Monique rubbed the bridge of her nose. "That's just the problem, Judy. When it comes to genetics, there are so many variables."

"She'll know when she gets the results of the genetic tests, I guess."

"Who said she tested them yet? She and Marco don't communicate that well these days. And genetic testing is expensive."

"Marco still has medical coverage—"

"—which may not cover something so exotic. And just think about this: Would you test your kids for a disease that cannot be prevented and has no cure?"

Judy started to argue—Monique could almost hear her thinking of vitamin A supplements, retinal transplants, experimental gene therapy, homeopathic remedies, and all the possibilities of future medical science—but then, mute, Judy dropped into the chair, still gripping the wine bottle.

Monique let her absorb the shock, just as she herself had when she'd first researched the disease and realized the implications for the little boy and the little girl who affectionately called her Aunt Monie.

Judy absently pulled the cork and then planted the bottle on the table. "Just when I thought Becky was starting to get a handle on her situation."

"Becky is a slave to her own stubborn independence. She

wasn't ready to share something so horrible. She'd just been keeping a lid on the boiling pot."

"But she was like a kid at the Château de Vincennes this morning. And yesterday, so absorbed in sketching at Notre Dame."

"Which means we succeeded, a least for a little while, in what we intended to do all along." Monique pulled the little paper caps off three of the room's four water glasses. "We found her plenty of distractions."

"It doesn't help that the woman is neither here nor there. She knows she's going blind, but she's not blind yet."

"Degenerative diseases suck." Monique reached for the wine.

Judy slapped Monique's hand. "Not yet. You have to let it breathe."

"Wow." Monique ceded the bottle. "You remember that you can speak French, and the next thing you know I'm rooming with Julia Child."

"Save the wine for the meal." Judy planted the bottle on the other side of the table. "And for Becky. Because she's got it the worst. You and I, we already know what we've lost. What we loved is already gone—*poof*."

Judy twisted her hand at the wrist, imitating a bird flying away. Monique lifted the glass to her lips and sucked down the teaspoon of wine that had splashed into it. The tannins must be getting to her, because he couldn't figure what else was causing this burning in her chest.

"But that woman," Judy continued, pointing as she lowered her voice to the still-closed door. "She still *has* the thing that, someday, she is going to lose. That maybe her own kids will lose. And every little reminder, like that fiasco in the catacombs, is a fresh new shock."

Monique dropped her gaze and found interest in the flecked particleboard edge of the little table, running a fingernail along the seam between the shiny veneer and the scratched wood. She disagreed with Judy. Loss was *always* delivered in agonizing, unpredictable little shocks. Grief *always* visited unexpectedly, revitalizing the pain just when you thought you might be ready to lay it aside.

Monique's gaze drifted to her phone, now dark on the bedside table.

Just then Becky, dressed in a faded pair of cotton pajama bottoms and a crinkled Creed concert T-shirt, swung the bathroom door open. She tossed her cosmetics bag in the direction of her suitcase and loosened the towel around her head.

"Hey." Her blond hair, darkened by moisture, fell over her shoulders. She rubbed it briskly with the towel. "Any news about flights to New York?"

Monique exchanged a glance with Judy, who with her back to Becky unloaded a wedge of brie and a wax-wrapped rectangle of country pâté, and then, without another word, picked up the wine and filled Monique's glass.

"Actually, Beck," Monie said, "I need to talk to you about the flights."

Becky's brisk rubbing slowed. "Is there a problem?"

"It's just getting so late." Monique took a sip of the wine. She felt the liquid on her tongue but didn't register taste at all. "I'm not even sure we can buy a ticket online or over the phone from here on such short notice. To do this right, we'd have to get you to Orly and then hope you get on a flight stand-by. But we couldn't go to the gate with you. We'd have to leave you there not knowing whether you'd gotten on or not—"

"It's not pitch-dark in an airport." Her voice was as flat as a nail head. "I can manage just fine."

"You'd end up in the States at some ungodly hour of the morning. With Marco not even knowing you're coming home."

At the sound of her husband's name, Becky sank with a bounce to the edge of the bed, giving up all pretext of drying her hair. Monique knew that Becky hadn't been able to get through to Marco. Her calls dropped before the first ring. Both she and Judy were having trouble with their international calling and texting. Monie suspected this hotel was in some sort of triangulated dead zone for their service.

With a grimace Judy disappeared into the bathroom for a moment to wash a cluster of purple grapes.

Monique forged ahead. "I'm just trying to reason this out, Beck."

"I'm being a pain in the ass."

"You're not a pain in the ass."

"I don't want to drag you two to Orly. Besides," Becky added, forestalling her, "you guys can't nanny me tonight. You both have a flight to Zurich in the morning."

"Eight-in-the-freaking-morning," Judy grumbled, emerging with the wet grapes sagging in a facecloth.

"That's just my point," Monique said. "Zurich is one of the busiest airports in Europe, a major hub. Wouldn't it be better for you to get a good night's sleep tonight and do at least one more leg of the trip? Once we're in Switzerland, if you still feel the same way, we can take the time to make a reservation home from Zurich and contact Marco so he knows you're coming."

Judy arranged the grapes on the table and cast an aggrieved look at Monie. "Were you hitting the whiskey when you dreamed up this itinerary?"

Monique ignored her. She focused on Becky, now curling her bare feet underneath her, looking more like a teenager than her own Kiera.

"If you left tonight, you might get lucky," Monique conceded. "You might catch the last red-eye out, and you'd be home by tomorrow. But if you miss that flight, or if all the flights are full, you'll have to spend the whole night sleeping in a molded plastic chair. And you'll spend all of tomorrow trying to talk your way onto a flight. You'll be home in two days." Monique raised her glass. "But if you sleep here and come with us to Zurich tomorrow, you can still be home in two days if you want."

"I need to go home, Monie." Becky hugged her arms. "I want to see their faces. I *need* to see them."

"You'll have plenty of time for that. You reminded me yourself at the catacombs. It's only a five percent loss a year—"

"I don't give a damn about me."

"Then you know their vision is not going dark in a day or two, Beck." Monique paused, balanced on the fulcrum, trying to decide what to say. She was no expert, and she knew better than to give false hope. But this, at least, seemed clear.

"Your version of RP arrived late in life, relatively speaking. And your night vision was the first thing affected. It might be decades before they show any signs of vision loss. If ever."

"Maybe. Maybe not." Suddenly Becky rolled up the towel and tossed it into a corner of the room. "Tell me how complicated this is."

Monique realized that the time for silence and patience and stillness had finally ended. Still, she hesitated. She thought about everything she'd gleaned from the geneticist at the hospital, from the medical websites, from the case histories she'd studied. The genetics of retinitis pigmentosa were complicated and still being researched. It involved up to thirty-odd genes or locations on genes, but there were three generally dominant patterns of inheritance. Autosomal dominant, autosomal recessive, or X-linked. Monique had already ruled out X-linked for Becky's RP.

Researching all of this had reminded her of how she'd once considered going to medical school. Then she'd spent a couple of summers volunteering in a hospital. She'd watched the doctors juggle blood tests and lab printouts, CAT scans and MRIs, consultations with other physicians about diagnoses, prognosis, drug treatment regimens, surgical intervention. Then she'd watched the nurses talking with the patients, double-checking meds, taking vitals, often harried, but once in a while holding those brittle hands and listening to stories.

Times like these she wished she *had* become a doctor.

"I'm an armchair geneticist," Monique warned. "You'd be better off getting real hard information from an expert.

Someone who'll know what questions to ask about your family history—"

"There's not a soul in my family who's blind." Becky picked at a thread on her pajama bottoms "The doctor told me to call every relative to find that out. He said it would help in determining…probabilities."

Probabilities. What a terrible, terrible word.

"I've grilled everyone," Becky continued. "Even a great-aunt living in Taos that nobody had spoken to in thirty years. No blindness, not a suspicion of it, for at least two generations. On either side."

Monique felt relief like a soft tumbling down a flight of stairs. She hoped it didn't show on her face. "That's… promising."

Becky's sudden stillness held a fragile hope.

"It suggests," Monique continued, "that the method of transition isn't dominant."

"Isn't dominant?"

"If it were dominant, you'd probably see blindness in every generation. You don't. So that suggests that your version of RP is most likely recessive."

"For God's sake, Monie," Judy said, "English."

"If it's recessive, it can skip generations."

With a sharp inhale, Becky's face suffused with color.

"That doesn't mean that they won't carry a copy of the gene, Beck. Carry it, but not manifest it." Monique hesitated, wondering how much Becky could handle. "And when it comes time for them to have their own kids, they'll have to look into genetic counseling."

Monique watched her friend, trying to gauge her mood

as Becky hauled herself back up to a sitting position. Her friend's face was a mask of blank hope and shock and something else, something Monique couldn't identify.

Judy poured a new glass of wine. "That sounds like good news."

Monique felt vaguely nauseous. "I could be wrong."

"It doesn't sound wrong." Judy stretched across the space between table and bed in order to hand the wine to Becky. "It sounds like it makes perfect sense. It sounds like it's worth believing."

Becky lifted the glass to her lips. She sat there with the glass raised, her lips parted, but she made no effort to actually take a sip. Monique wondered if Becky knew how much Monique owed her. Monique wasn't sure she would ever have done this trip if Becky's diagnosis hadn't provided the push she needed. And Monique knew, looking at her old friend, that Becky still needed the distraction of travel. Maybe much, much more than herself.

Monique toed the third chair away from the table. "Come have something to eat, Beck. It's hard to think straight on an empty stomach."

Becky didn't come over right away. She sat for a few minutes, made a halfhearted attempt to drink her wine, and then she unfolded herself from the bed and joined them at the table. She stared at the array—the bread, the brie, the hard sausage, the soft rectangle of pâté, the glistening grapes—but didn't reach for any of it. Not even for the slice of bread smeared with pâté that Judy slipped on a little square of wax paper in front of her.

"This trip," Becky began softly, "has been great, Monie. I

mean, really, really wonderful." Becky braced her hands on either side of the seat, locking her elbows as she rounded her back. "I can't thank you enough for inviting me."

Monique reached for the loaf of bread and pulled the end off, the crust leaving crumbs on the table. "What do you think, Judy? Did you hear a 'but' in there?"

"Sure sounded like a 'but' to me."

"I don't want to cause any trouble," Becky said. "I won't try to catch a flight out of Orly tonight." She shrugged and the stretched-out neckline of her T-shirt fell down over one shoulder. "I'll go with you tomorrow to Switzerland. If it's all right with you, I'll do what you suggested and catch a flight home straight from Zurich."

Monique smiled and tried very hard to mask her disappointment. She'd managed to get Becky to concede to Zurich, yes, but what Monique really wanted was for Becky to stay in Europe and finish the vacation. Becky needed time—probably more time than Monique could give—to come to terms with so many things.

So with a pointed glance at Judy, Monique decided to resort to guilt: A timeless and ruthlessly effective tactic. "So, Judy, I guess it's just you and me abseiling in Interlaken tomorrow."

Judy folded a cheese knife out of her Swiss Army knife and reached for the brie. "If by that fancy European word, you're asking if I'm going to rappel backward down some rocky alpine peak, then the answer is—hmm, let me think—*no*."

Monique shook her head. "Sooooo predictable."

"The twenty-two-year-old backpacker in me is all in, but

my fifty-one-year-old knees aren't complying. Besides you need someone to take video."

Becky toyed with a piece of bread. "Abseiling? What's that?"

"Come on, Beck, didn't you read ahead in Monique's backbreaking itinerary? 'Abseiling' is the next thing on Lenny's list." Judy peeled the paper off the brie and chopped a hunk off with her knife, which she then pointed at Monique. "Amazon woman here won't admit it, but she is terrified."

"Slightly concerned," Monique corrected, slipping two fingers on her wrist. "And showing some physical signs of increased stress."

"It's really physical." Judy took a healthy bite of the bread and cheese and spoke around the wad in her mouth. "You've got to get all geared up, take a lesson, and then just blithely walk over the side of a cliff."

Monique muttered, "All by myself, apparently."

"Have fun with that, kiddo," Judy said. "I'll wave from the top. I've always preferred sitting on the sidelines anyway."

Monique sidled a glance at Becky to see if their little exchange had had any effect. But Becky was just staring at the food in front of her. Clearly Becky's mind was already halfway home.

Monique smeared some spicy pâté across the warmth of a baguette, trying not to feel too grim. She wasn't looking forward to being suspended on the side of a cliff all alone, with the wind cutting through her. But she supposed she shouldn't be surprised that this was just the way it was going to be. Becky had a husband and two children waiting for her at home. Judy still had Bob. Kiera was drifting away long before she actually moved away.

As for Monique Franke-Reed...she'd always be alone.

"Interlaken, huh?" Becky poked at her untouched bread. "Now I remember. That's the hardest thing on the list."

"Lenny and I read a long article about it in *National Geographic*. There were lots of pretty summertime pictures of the Alps." Monique shrugged. "I think he had an urge to be someplace high so he could yodel."

Monique looked up into Becky's blue eyes. The girl was so pale. The long shower hadn't washed away the dark circles, or the fear.

Suddenly, Becky reached across the table and laid her hand on Monique's forearm. "What's a day or two, right? I just can't leave you hanging, Monie. Especially off a cliff."

"No way did it look this steep on the website."

Monique stood at the top of a sheer precipice, frozen not from the wind cutting over the edge but by the distance between where she stood a few yards from the brink, and the alpine valley far, far below.

"Cameras can't always pick up depth perception." Becky planted her hands on her hips and dared to lean forward a bit. "But, man, my depth perception is working today. Those are some big pines down there, and we're way above the top of them."

"I specifically told them that we're beginners."

"Lost in translation?" Becky scuffed her feet against the rock, like a runner itchy to get onto the track. "Or maybe they just didn't want to scare the heck out of you before you got here."

Becky grinned. A somewhat crazed, maniacal grin, Monique thought. Becky wore her usual amber sunglasses beneath the climbing helmet strapped onto her head. A harness sagged on her lean hips. The girl should look exhausted, not just from yesterday's drama in the catacombs, but also because the three of them had hauled themselves out of their Parisian hotel before five a.m. to make a flight to Zurich, where they switched to a train that chugged them into Interlaken *Ouest* only so they could load onto a bus that took them to the Hotel Sonne, where, after checking in, they raced to catch the Swiss alpine guide van waiting to pick them up just outside the hotel.

Trains, planes, and buses for six hours straight...and Becky looked wired, and twitchy, and very much awake.

A whir of a camera caught Monique's attention. Judy, wrapped up to her ears in a scarf, aimed the lens of the camera at her. "They're calling you, ladies." Judy poked her head around the viewfinder and tilted her head toward the step-off point. "You're next."

Monique glanced to where the über-fit, ex-Olympic athlete was waving them over. She waved back though she couldn't really hear him over the roar of the motorcycles pulling off the road into the scrubby clearing. There must have been a dozen bikes kicking up alpine dust as the riders parked their hogs. One rider pulled his helmet off and an iron-gray ponytail dropped out, brushing the back of his belt.

With Judy and Becky trailing, Monique headed toward Hans or Henrick or whatever his name was—the guy who'd given them, like, a *ten-minute* lesson on how to rappel. "Sure you don't want to come, Judy? I hear it takes a half hour for the van to bring you down to the landing point. You could rappel in less than that."

"Oh, you're funny."

"It'd be a hell of a photo to show Bob and the kids when you got home."

"They'd say it's Photoshopped."

"You don't know how to Photoshop."

"You do your midlife crisis your way. I'll do mine my way." Judy gestured toward a couple of stone benches under a little copse of trees. "I'm taking a nap on one of those."

Hans greeted them and urged them toward the ropes. He turned Monique so that she was facing him and the flank of motorcycles. If she glanced to the right she could see the distant white-capped tips of the Alps. Hans forced her attention back to him, chattering in his clipped English, his indescribable accent somewhere between Oslo and London. Monique had to keep shaking herself to pay attention to what he had to say.

"Remember what I taught you, yes? Left hand is guide, right hand is brake hand."

He kept repeating the frighteningly simple instructions. He pulled at the rope in the carabineer, a metal loop that she now knew was the piece that attached the rope to the harness now digging into her butt. He tugged on the edges and the straps, checking everything, pulling the rope so it was taut. Then he casually leaned over and glanced down the great sweep to the bottom of the valley, jerking on the free end of the rope so it swayed unimpeded.

"Now, MO-nique," he said, pronouncing it distinctly French, "take three steps back, and then step over the edge."

Her hands gripped so tight that prickles of the fiberglass rope poked through the fabric of the gloves. Her tongue swelled. She couldn't look behind her. She stared into Hans or Henrick's clear and somewhat crazy green eyes.

"You are afraid," he stated.

"Sh-sh-shitless." Her voice, a croak in her throat.

"Of course you are afraid. It is not natural to step off a cliff."

"Definitely not natural."

"You must look at this fear." He pointed two fingers at his own eyes and then turned them to point those fingers at hers. "Look at it in the eye. Then you do what you must to finish what you set out to do. This is how to live."

Monique stared frozen at the insane athlete who'd strapped her into a harness and was urging her to walk backward over a cliff, the Swiss adrenaline junkie probably pumped with steroids as he gave her life lessons.

Becky shouted, "Stop stalling, Monie. Get down here before I have to catch my train back to the airport."

Becky was already leaning back at a forty-five-degree angle with the rope in one hand and her feet braced flat on the cliff face, staring at Monique like she was impatient with her kids for dawdling at the swing set in the park.

Monique flexed her palm, sweaty in the glove. "Do you *see* what you're doing?"

Becky wrinkled her nose as she stared up at the sky. "The light's good. My feet are flat. It's a fine day."

"You're hanging off the edge of a cliff."

"Yeah, and it's pretty awesome. Unless we get dive-bombed by falcons, it's not likely anything is going to come up behind or beside me. All in all this is a good place for an almost-blind woman. It's exactly what I should be doing the day after I find out my kids might just be okay."

Becky lifted her left hand and slid down so that Monique could only see the top of her helmet. Monique forced herself to swallow the lump rising in her throat. Becky's attitude had switched back to casual flippancy, which was probably a hundred times better than yesterday's panic attack. Monique wished she could summon the same levity.

"Grip the rope now, yah," Henrick said, forcing her fingers around the rope. "Hold it tight in your left hand. This is the guide rope."

She flexed her fingers. She should just pretend that she was stepping over the deck in her backyard. In a windstorm, maybe.

One step. Two.

Then came the shock of nothing under her heels anymore. She curled her toes as if she could dig them into the rock. Monique mentally measured the diameter of the rope. Less than two inches held up her one hundred and forty-three pounds over an abyss. *Mustn't think of that.* A breeze eddied up the sheer face to give her a chill where it shouldn't.

Damn it. She had to do this. Every last item was going to be checked off that bucket list or it wouldn't be done right— she might as well not do it at all. She tightened the muscles in her shoulders and blindly felt for the hanging rope, drawing it up to her hip. She leaned her weight back. She lifted the rope like she'd been taught and a half foot of it slid through her left hand, tilting her into the void, her feet skidding a few inches down the wall face.

She stared wildly beyond Henrick, to the safety of the clearing, to the camera trained on her, to Judy behind that camera, trying in vain to keep her face stony as she waved good-bye.

Her guts in knots, she tried it again.

Becky's voice came lively from below. "There you go, Monie. A few more drops and you'll be even with me."

Don't look down.

She stared at the cliff face just above her braced feet. She fixed her gaze on the bits of lichen growing in the cracks and on the infinite shades of the rock striations, while in her mind spun the vision of the valley below. The tips of her fingers went numb from the steady wind that smelled sharp with snow.

She lifted the guide rope, felt the loosening of the carbineer, and did a jerky dip farther down the cliff, stopping so suddenly that the harness dug into her butt.

"Loosen up, Monie." Becky's voice, closer now. "I've never seen your butt so tight, even kickboxing."

"Shut up." She tried the drop more slowly this time.

"Isn't this incredible? The air is so sharp and clear here, I can practically see to Italy."

"It's because it's so freaking *cold.*"

"I can even see the colors of the jackets of those people below. After yesterday in the catacombs, I was convinced I'd never see right ever again."

Monique dared a glance at Becky who was sitting in her harness, idly twisting one ankle, doing a slow spin in midair.

"Put your effing feet on the cliff, Beck."

Becky tapped the cliff with a toe to make another twirl. "I'm glad you and Judy guilt-tripped me into this."

"The rope is going to fray if you keep doing that."

"The rope can hold three of me, even if it's cut halfway through. Hey, weren't you Ms. Hike-and-Mountain-Bike girl out at Colorado U?"

"Yeah, we *avoided* cliffs." The Swiss air did taste a lot like October in Boulder. If she weren't a bundle of nerves, she'd indulge herself in memories of weekend mountain-biking with pals on rough, rocky trails. "There were plenty of crazy, free-climbing nuts at CU. I got to know them only after they cracked their crazy heads open and showed up in my ER."

Becky casually lifted the rope and slid down another few feet. "I just figured that must be why Lenny picked this for the bucket list—to remind you of your Colorado U days."

Monique flexed her fingers and managed another jerky descent. "No, he originally wanted to go canyoning. It was supposed to be a summer thing, shooting through natural rock slides into crystalline pools." She and Lenny had bantered about it while waiting to talk to the oncologist. Knowing that they had to banter because the news they were about to get wasn't going to be good. "I nixed that idea right away. No way I was squeezing into one of those wetsuits and then diving into frigid snowmelt."

"Island girl. So how'd that turn into abseiling?"

"He said it was too beautiful a place to pass up, so if I wasn't going to canyon, then I had to parasail, ice-climb, or abseil." Monique loosened the rope a little to experiment with a slower slide. "Abseiling just looked the least fatal." Her breath hitched as she glimpsed, for a moment, the valley below. "At least it did at the time."

"Once again Lenny baffles me with his choices."

"We were dreaming, Beck."

"It's not just about abseiling, or the catacombs, or the London Eye, either." Becky hung suspended, waiting for Monique to catch up. "I'm talking about the entire bucket list thing."

She was beginning to get the hang of this, beginning to be able to control the rate of her descent by the pressure on the rope in her left hand, if she could just stop sweating long enough to feel like she had a real grip. "It's just a list of wishes, Beck."

"From a man who was dying."

"We weren't sure he was dying, at least not when we started it."

Monique worked her way over a jut in the stone, trying not to think about that day in the office when the oncologist finally told them that there was no more reason for chemo, no more reason to consider any exotic treatments, no more reason, really, to put Lenny through any more diagnostic tests. She remembered feeling an odd sense of relief that they were signing him up for hospice. The days and weeks would no longer be full of long drives to specialized facilities, endless waits for medication or appointments, drawn-out hours in hospital facilities, bouts of terrible nausea, and frustrating phone calls to medical insurance.

"So you're telling me that our salt-of-the-earth Lenny, our beloved and respected *radiologist*," Becky said, as she twirled the guide rope around her hand, "was in complete denial about his condition?"

"No, Lenny knew exactly what the prognosis was, every single step of the way."

"See, that's what makes it twisted." Becky tugged her snagged ponytail until it was fully threaded through the cutout at the back of the helmet. "Why make a list of dreams just at the point when it's no longer possible to reach them?"

Monique wished Becky would stop chattering so she could concentrate on not getting killed. "Dying is a strange thing, Beck. The last thing that dies is hope."

She had held on to it, even while they were signing the papers to have Lenny put in hospice care. She had grasped it when the oncologist told them that should any new treatment come around, should any promising drug trial open up, he would let them know immediately. And even she, who'd been a nurse so long that she probably should have known better, believed right to the end that a medical miracle might intervene.

"Well, Monie, I may be going blind eventually," Becky said, "but clearly, right now, you're the one who can't see straight."

"Stop." Monique loosened her grip too much and slid down too fast. She jerked up on the guide rope and felt the harness cut into her thighs. "Can we focus on this descent? Because your chatter is distracting me and I'd rather not splatter my bones on the valley floor."

Becky, using her toe as a spring, bobbed against the cliff. "Isn't one of the next things on your list something to do with motorcycles?"

"I'm speaking English, right? Or didn't you hear me because of the howling of this alpine wind?"

"I remember you wanted a motorcycle once, while you were living in the city."

"Feel free to go right on ahead of me. I'll catch up."

"I remember Lenny called motorcycles 'donorcycles.'"

"Crazy people drive scooters too."

"And you used to bike the Rockies when you were in college, before you and Lenny got married."

"Will you please stop spinning? You're making me dizzy."

"And you loooove horror movies, and he didn't."

"It's too bad that your panic attack yesterday didn't completely erase your memory."

"And when you were a little girl you used to go fishing with your grandfather in Trinidad."

"Is there a point to this?"

"Open water, open air, open sea. You and your grandfather pulling in the nets, and not a bit of seasickness."

"Oh, for goodness sake."

"Monie, my old friend, I'm honestly surprised you haven't figured this out."

"What's there to figure out, Nancy Drew?" Monique flattened her sneakers against the cliff. "That Lenny loved me and wanted to make both of us happy?"

"Lenny loved you, all right." Becky swung over, stretching her arm out so she could give Monique a gentle punch on the calf. "Lenny made the first half of that list for one reason: To give you back everything that you gave up when you married him."

chapter twelve

J udy leaned over the railing as much as she dared. Risking the camera, she stretched her arm over the chasm in order to film the sight of Becky and Monique descending the cliff. She hazarded a glance to the scruffy valley, fifteen or sixteen stories below. When little black spots swam in her vision she jerked herself away from the rail.

Thank the stars that Becky had agreed not only to come to Zurich, but also to stick around for one more item on the bucket list. When it came to abseiling, Judy would have let Monique down, big time. No way—*no way*—would she have dared trust all one-hundred-and-mumble-mumble-pounds of her pure Jersey cheesecake to one of those filets of Swiss dental floss.

She fixed her concentration on the viewfinder until Monique and Becky disappeared below the slant of a ridge. Then Judy clicked the video camera off and tucked it away. She slipped by two tall, Nordic-looking young men in black Lycra strapping harnesses around their greyhound-lean waists. She marched past the signs—in German, French, and English—prohibiting the untrained and the pregnant, people with bad backs or heart conditions, and anyone who'd been imbibing alcohol, from enjoying the great sport of abseiling.

Then, gently straightening her left knee, she sank onto an empty concrete bench. She would wait here for the shuttle bus that would bring her down to the landing spot so she could meet up with her vacation mates. In the meantime she supposed she'd make herself useful by perusing the guidebook to Interlaken she'd picked up at a kiosk this morning. Since Monique was otherwise occupied, Judy figured she may as well take on the responsibility of determining what they should do with their single day in the picturesque village. Hopefully her friends would be so wired on adrenaline when they reached the valley they'd be ecstatic to spend the rest of the day planted in a bar sampling Swiss winter wine.

But when she dug into her belly pack to fetch the guidebook, her fingers curled around her cell phone instead. She lifted it up. Roaming, roaming...three bars. She raised her brows in surprise and then glanced through the pines to the peaks around her. Somewhere close there must be a cell phone tower.

Thank God for the efficiency of the Swiss. She punched in the international calling code for the States and then her own number.

Bob answered on the second ring. "So did you get arrested yet?"

His voice sounded low and rumbly, like he'd just woken up. Judy felt warmth that had nothing to do with three layers of clothing and a well-wrapped scarf. "Oh, Bob, it's all a terrible misunderstanding."

"I warned you. Never slip a flash drive to a Russian."

"He was Bulgarian. But I'll try to remember that after you bail me out."

The laughter bubbled up inside her. When they first met in New York she worked for the Children's Fund of the United Nations and he was a cub reporter for the *Post*. Twenty-seven years into the marriage and he still persisted on calling her his secret source for international intrigue.

"It's Saturday," he said, "are you still in Paris?"

"Switzerland." Her belly still roiled with bad airline peanuts and a soggy sandwich from a train café. "Try to keep up, big boy."

"Hold on." Beyond the static came the rustling of papers, probably a copy of the itinerary she'd pinned to the kitchen corkboard. "Interlaken?"

"Bingo. Right now I'm sitting in the shadow of the Alps watching a beer-bellied biker get strapped into a climbing harness. He's got two bells plaited in his beard, and he's about to take a step backward over a cliff." As she watched the biker reached over and took a swig of beer out of a friend's bottle before returning it. "So much for prohibiting the drunks from the sport."

"Wait." Bob rustled some more papers. "Abseiling?"

"Here, I'll paint you a picture: Monique and Becky are in helmets, harnesses, and rope, clinging to the sheer side of a cliff. Me, I'm playing the part of the cheering buddy, freezing my ass on the sidelines."

"Sounds safe," he said. "And sensible."

The word plucked at her. Judy winced. The young girl within her shifted in her restless sleep, and Judy willed her still. The truth was, in her mothering years she'd always enjoyed sitting on the sidelines. She liked being the one who cheered others on, perched on a bench pillow, a warm thermos clutched in her mittens, watching Michael play lacrosse or Audrey and Maddy row or Robert play hockey or Jake debate in forensics team competitions. She'd never craved being on the field or the stage. She took joy in egging others to excel and took a heaping dose of pride in their accomplishments.

That's what mothers did, damn it.

"Here's the real news," she said. "Becky's going home early."

"That can't be good."

"She had a panic attack in the Parisian catacombs." Judy still couldn't bring herself to talk about Brian and Brianna. That was a conversation that deserved low voices and a quiet room, not the chaotic scene unfolding before her with a dozen bikers leaning on the leather seats. "Becky's fine but frantic. Tomorrow morning we're all climbing back on the train to Zurich, to put her on an afternoon plane home."

"Poor kid."

"Monique and I will take a train to Munich. It'll just be the two of us. And she still has six more things on Lenny's bucket list."

Judy tucked her chin deeper into the folds of her cotton scarf as Bob filled her in on what was going on with his job. The air was frosty, but here the wind had been broken by a brace of pines. The bikers razzed each other in slangy German. The sound of the language made her perk up because after the Rhine trip and the day in Cochem, her ears were tuning into it more easily, like an old radio fixed on static finally tweaking clear. She understood enough of their ribbing to know there was a bet involved, and someone was losing it today.

It couldn't possibly be that elderly woman in the center of all the talk. She was a skinny thing, whittled down to the gristle, her face drawn with lines. As she strapped a helmet under her wattle, she leaned over to suck on an offered cigarette, drawing the smoke in so hard that her cheeks went hollow. It was then, with a start, that Judy noticed the harness around the woman's hips.

During a pause in Bob's recitation she blurted, "You know, I really hate those commercials for arthritis medicine."

The silence that met her comment was longer than the usual pause, the one due to the length of time it took for the signal to bounce off a satellite and then back to her phone.

"You know the ones I'm talking about?" she asked. "The ones with the grinning grannies power-walking over bridges? The ones with middle-aged women twisting themselves into pretzels on yoga mats?"

"O-kay."

"I mean, who *are* those people? And why should every postmenopausal woman be expected to push her physical limits beyond a point that would make most sensible twenty-five-year-olds balk?"

The rumbling sound of an oncoming bus distracted her. She glanced to the road to see a white vehicle lumbering around the bend. She hoped it was the van to the valley. The sooner she got away from this place and all the overachievers, the better. She was about to stand up from the bench when she realized that the large bus pulling into the clearing wasn't the little blue shuttle she'd been told to expect.

"Jude," Bob said, through a sudden crackle in the line, "are there televisions on all those trains?"

Judy watched as the bus stopped and the doors creaked open. A young woman bounced out and headed toward the abseiling instructor. "No, no, there are no TVs on European trains. Why?"

"Because I can't imagine you've had much time to watch TV unless you're doing it while traveling."

"Bob, what are you talking about?"

"Arthritis commercials?"

Judy didn't answer. Her heart was sinking with slow, drooping dread as she watched a bevy of excited kids pour out of the bus. Average age, she estimated, was ten years old.

She muttered, "You've got to be kidding me."

"I'm just trying to make a connection here, Judy. Help me out."

"This would probably be illegal in the States. I mean, who lets their ten-year-old rappel down sixteen stories?"

Judy breathed a frustrated sigh. She scanned the clearing, seeking sanity. Her gaze settled on a young biker sprawled in a sidecar, his muscular arms hanging over the edge. He looked fit and red-cheeked, probably from riding in the cold. He didn't have a beard like the rest of the bikers. His hair was close-cropped to his head. He was broad in the chest, rounded in the shoulders, and shouting jokes louder than all the rest of them.

There, she thought. Not everyone here was an adrenaline

junkie. That hunk of young man couldn't possibly have a bum knee or a bad back, yet he wasn't spider-dancing down the cliff.

"So," Bob said, a hesitant note in his voice, "what I think is happening is that lots of people of many different ages are abseiling."

"And I'm sitting here letting this stone bench steal the heat from my ass."

"I think I've got this pinned." He spoke as if he were checking things off a list. "Arthritis commercials. Your friends are abseiling. A bunch of kids are getting strapped in. You're feeling pressured by your own and other people's unrealistic expectations. Here's my verdict, hon—don't go down that cliff."

"I already told you there's *no way* I'm going down this cliff."

"The last time I heard that tone in your voice, you threatened to take a sledgehammer to the wall between the kitchen and the dining room."

"It would open up the floor plan. I still think it's a good idea."

"It's a better idea than you risking those lovely knees in the Alps."

Just then another biker approached the young man in the sidecar. The biker seized the boy under the arms and yanked him up. Judy expected the boy to fight but the kid just grinned and let the guy manhandle him. It wasn't until the biker had deposited the young man on the leather seat of the motorcycle that Judy realized why the boy hadn't complained.

The boy didn't have a bum knee...because the boy had no knees.

"Oh, fuck me."

Laughter rumbled over the phone line. "As soon as you get home, Jude. As soon as you get home."

She watched as the biker pulled two prosthetic legs out of the inside of the sidecar and fixed them on the stumps of the boy's legs. The boy wiggled himself off the bicycle to test his balance and then made a jerky walk toward the abseiling instructor.

Judy glared up at the blue, blue Swiss sky. She knew, deep in her heart, that there was nothing wrong with knowing one's limitations. She knew that there was no shame in reaching the point in one's life when one accepts that not all things are physically possible. But Judy also knew that once Becky flew back to the States, Monique would need Judy as a friend more than ever, and Monique would need her willing and absolutely fearless.

Judy wasn't going to disappoint her best friend.

"I have to go, Bob."

"Judy, don't go down that cliff—"

"I'll call you later."

She slipped the cell phone back in her belly pack. She sucked in a lungful of frosty air. She reminded herself that she'd once been a very silly young woman, but she'd had bravado. She'd lived day-by-day on sheer nerve. That same courage had sustained her when she'd taken the plunge with Bob. And if raising five kids had taught her anything, it was that there was more than one way to face one's fears, and not all of them were as loud and flashy and physical as dangling from a rope off some cliff.

Blood coursed to her head, a sudden plunger-rush of adrenaline. She narrowed her eyes on all those bikers.

Then Judy took her heart in her hands and stood up from the bench.

chapter thirteen

There's still hope.

A breeze teased Becky's ponytail. The whole cloud-and-crystalline sky spun above her as she twirled at the end of the rope. When she first heard her diagnosis she'd numbly asked the doctor if she should stop reading altogether and start wearing sunglasses even indoors, hoping she could hold off the deterioration by good behavior for both herself and her children. The doctor had conceded that wearing sunglasses might help. But, he continued—and she still felt the impact of that "but" like a blow to the solar plexus—you need to understand that you're not doing anything to ruin your eyesight. *It's just going to fade away, all on its own.*

So she shut her eyes and then peeled them open again. She twirled to face the cliff. She spied the tufts of yellow-green lichen growing out of the spidery cracks. She eyed the places where the rub of the ropes had worn the stone shiny. The sharp Swiss sunlight and the reedy mountain air must act like a magnifier, for she could even trace the pattern of blue shadows on the peaks that surrounded Interlaken.

It was true. Most people didn't truly appreciate what they had until it slipped away.

"You're wrong, Becky."

Becky hazarded a glance toward her friend. Since Becky had shared her opinion about Lenny's bucket list, Monique had gone stone-cold silent. Monique had worked her way down the cliff at half speed in brooding, inching little jerks. Across the eight feet or so that separated them, Becky could see the whites of her eyes.

"I sat with Lenny," Monique insisted, "and we planned every single thing together. We talked about the Rhine cruise, the catacombs, Munich, Monaco. I know he wanted to take every one of these excursions, just as much as I did. And I can't believe you'd say something crazy like that to me while I'm up on a cliff."

"It's all part of my evil plan."

"I keep my mouth shut for five weeks about Brian and Brianna, and now you just lob grenades at will."

Becky winced. It probably hadn't been the smartest idea to be so frank. Defiance and denial were a grieving woman's last defense mechanism. It was the sort of behavior that Becky had become uncomfortably well-acquainted with over the past month. In fact, when Becky sat in the hospital office listening to the doctor dropping terms like "autosomal" and "digenic" and "mitochondrial," she'd reacted in a similar way. That doctor was *stupid*. The doctor was just so *wrong*.

But yesterday Becky felt like she'd shrugged off a suit of lead armor when Monique forced her to hear the truth. Now Becky wanted Monique to accept the reality of Lenny's list and share the same lightness of being.

"All right, Monie." Becky mentally braced herself as Monique came level with her. "I'm going to ask you some hard questions now."

"Are you *kidding* me?"

"No, I'm not. And you can't duck."

"Monique Franke-Reed does *not* duck."

"Not usually, so you should be okay to answer this. Did Lenny really know he was dying when he made that list?"

"Oh, for goodness sake, of course he knew," she said sharply. Then Monique hesitated longer than she should, fussing with the back end of the rope so it moved in undulating waves to the valley floor. "But there's a world of difference between knowing something like that and talking about it like it's an appointment coming up on the calendar."

"Nice dodge."

"Ever been with someone who's dying, Beck?"

The memory returned like a sharp plunge of a needle. "Yes."

"Someone close?"

"My grandfather."

"How old were you? Six? Seven?"

"Twenty-two."

He'd collapsed in the dairy barn in the middle of the five o'clock milking. She'd found him lying in scattered hay, clawing his chest. She'd gone to the hospital in the ambulance. Once out of the ER, she'd taken a spot at his bedside and held his thick-knuckled hand. All through the night she played connect the liver spots with her thumb, a silent rosary.

Her father was dead and then her grandfather was dying. Men were always dropping out of her life.

Monique's voice softened. "If you've seen someone die, Beck, then you should understand. It's bad luck to talk about that stuff in the sickroom."

"Now you sound like your *grand-mère*."

"Smartest woman I know when it comes to things like this."

"You and Lenny didn't even discuss the funeral arrangements?"

"Please." Monique made a grunting sound that had nothing to do with the way she bounced against the harness. "I might as well just tell the guy he'll be buried in a week."

"I remember how surprised you were after the funeral when that lawyer told you he had an addendum to the will."

"Tell me how you slide down like that so fast. I keep thinking I'm going to get rope burns through these gloves."

"Use your left hand as a brake on the guide rope. And don't change the subject."

Monique looked anywhere but at her, fussing with the rope and trying to adjust the harness and setting and resetting her feet on the cliff, until she finally confessed, "The sneaky fool didn't want me to know he'd set money aside just for the list. Like I hadn't noticed the periodic withdrawals he'd been making online."

"Then there's the answer to my question." Becky lifted the guide rope, walking her feet down in pace. "I didn't think you could fool a radiologist with cancer and certainly not a man as sharp as Lenny. He understood exactly what was happening."

"I never denied that."

"The real question is—did you know?"

Monie's lips tightened so Becky could see the bright white line of pressure around the edges. "I see patients die all the time."

"Neonatal. Those poor little things can't talk."

"I saw plenty of dying in the ER, too."

"Where dying, from what I hear, happens really fast."

"And?"

"That means there isn't a lot of time to deal with that pesky coming-to-terms thing."

"Lenny and I had plenty of time to come to terms. Six weeks of family leave, thanks to my hospital policy. We had nothing to do but read magazines and talk about the things we *both* wanted to do, the places we *both* wanted to see."

Stubborn, stubborn Monique, repeating the same litany. Becky suspected that her friend had memorized Lenny's last words by rote. In the process they'd become no more than a gathering of words, bereft of any sense of deeper meaning. But after a week with that list Lenny's intentions had become as clear to Becky as if they'd been written on a white wall in black Sharpie.

Clearly it was time to change tactics.

"While Lenny was dying, Monie, did you ever get up to fetch something, or make a meal, or get some tea, when you couldn't sit there anymore?"

"Of course. Even a dying man's got to eat something."

"When my grandfather was dying, we drank enough tea to float us to China." Becky could still smell the hospital room, the heavy scent of the freesias one of her father's friends had sent, wilting on the bedside table. "That's be-cause my mother kept finding an excuse to get a drink or make a meal whenever he brought up the fact that he wanted to be cremated. My mother didn't want to hear any-thing about caskets or cemeteries or cremation."

Monie paused, twisting a little as an alpine breeze swept around the edge of the cliff, making their ropes sway.

Becky said gently, "Is there anything you didn't want to hear, Monie? Was there a reason why Lenny arranged that addendum to the will when you weren't around? Or made those money transfers in secret?"

"He was trying to surprise me." Her voice was clipped.

"Or maybe Lenny wanted to talk to you about a whole lot of things. Maybe he knew that you weren't in the right state of mind to hear them." Like her grandfather, struggling to speak, anxiously tugging at the edge of the blanket, beg-ging her to promise. "Or maybe he just couldn't find a way to bring up the subject of all those things you gave up when you married him."

"I didn't give up anything when I married Lenny. He knew that working mothers don't have time for three-hour bike rides through the local preserve. He knew that I cut back on the trips to Trinidad just so we could put a little more money in Kiera's college fund."

"Oh, he definitely knew all those things."

"Life has a way of taking things away simply by the changes it brings, Becky. If you don't believe me about that, just go ask Judy."

Becky didn't need to go ask Judy. Life was going to take away something from her, too, something that had, until yesterday, paralyzed her with terror. Someday, in the not so far future, her eyesight would dim and wink out.

But not here. Not today.

Becky said, "Deny it all you want, but here's the truth. These first six things on his list give back to you what you lost when you married him. And the second six excursions have a special meaning too."

"Stop. You're reading fortunes in tea leaves."

"The second half is a road map, Monie. They're Lenny's hopes for your future."

Ten minutes later Becky landed in the dry, crinkling carpet of pine needles at the base of the cliff. Two guides unleashed her and Monique from the ropes. Becky pulled off her helmet, unbuckled her harness, and walked with her terribly quiet friend to a safe zone to wait for the shuttle. Monique made an excuse and wandered toward one of the portable toilets nestled in the pine woods. The poor woman looked ready to vomit.

Becky suppressed yet another pang of guilt. It was the same kind of regretful distress she felt whenever she grounded Brianna. Becky's heart ached listening to her daughter sob into her pillow, but there wasn't anything she could do. Hard lessons had to be learned.

Hard lessons had to be learned, indeed, and not just by Monie. Becky sought distraction by watching the other climbers. She saw a heavy man in a leather jacket rappelling down the mountain to the faint sound of bells. She watched another man with strange curved appendages for legs—

metallic strapped-on prosthetics that gave his walk down the side of the cliff a certain bounce. She felt a fierce urge to rappel down the cliff again. She took deep breaths as her body trembled from the vestigial effects of adrenaline.

She knew she was trembling from more than just adrenaline. She knew that her urge to repeat the rappel had more to do with avoidance than excitement. After the painful discussion with Monique she'd be a hypocrite if she didn't take a hefty dose of her own bitter medicine and faced what she now most feared.

When she got home tomorrow she'd have to face Marco. They would have to talk about what Monique had told her about the genetics. They'd have to make some decisions about Brian and Brianna. She couldn't shuck responsibility and defer to Marco's judgment in this, as she'd done so many times with Gina. No matter how icy their relationship grew—no matter how fractured their marriage became in the months to come—the two of them had to decide right now what to tell the kids about her diagnosis and whether genetic testing was even a good idea.

A cold wave of dread passed through her. She thought of those medieval maps she'd seen framed in the Château de Vincennes, parchment drawings where, etched on the edges, were words of warning.

Here be dragons.

She heard Monique shuffle up behind her. Becky got hold of herself and turned to find her friend not poised and calm but more wild-eyed than ever.

"You know what, Becky?" Monique walked a few steps in one direction and turned in another, like a runner trying to work off leg cramps. "If I could see Lenny now, I'd shake him. I'd just shake him silly."

"You shouldn't be angry with him."

"Don't tell me how I should feel."

Becky took the hit. Clearly the time had come for empathy, not advice.

"I've made a decision." Monique scuffed in the gravel. "I'm not going to finish Lenny's list. As soon as I get back to the hotel I'm tearing that thing up."

She's just kidding, Becky thought, eyeballing her twitchy friend. She doesn't really mean it. Monique was just shocked and angry and blowing off steam.

"And when we get to the Zurich airport," Monique continued, "I'm going to check if there are any seats available on your plane for me."

Becky blurted, "No, Monie."

"I know Judy will be disappointed." Monique wiped her face on the sleeve of her fleece. "I can't help that. If I fly Bob out to take my place, Judy will at least have a reason to stay."

Becky tried to catch her eye but Monique avoided it. Monique fixed her gaze on the dust rising up on the road as a line of rumbling motorcycles pulled into the clearing. Becky searched for words as she struggled with a sense of growing guilt that she, and her self-righteous honesty, was the exact cause of this about-face.

She had to change Monique's mind. "You're already halfway done, Monie. You *have* to finish it."

"No, actually, I don't have to do anything."

"You always finish what you've started."

"Maybe it's time for a change."

"And what kind of example would that be to Kiera?"

"Kiera will be thrilled. She never wanted me to do this at all."

"You promised Lenny."

"Only because I was too blind to see what that sneaky fool husband of mine was trying to do."

"He was trying to help."

"No. Lenny is trying to make me *forget him*."

No, no, no. Becky ran through their conversation on the cliff, trying to figure out where she'd gone wrong, how she'd made Monique think of the list all wrong. Then she glanced around the clearing to look for Judy. Where was she? Judy would know what to say. She should have been here long before now. Becky peered past the gathered bikers dusting off their leather jackets. She swung around to the group of Japanese tourists chattering to their left, huddled around the screen of a video camera to view the descent they'd just made.

Then Becky became aware of a man approaching. He was big and burly and tall. He pulled off his leather gloves as he looked them both over. The chains on his leather jacket rattled. He had a faded tattoo of a pagan symbol right between his eyebrows.

In German-accented English, he asked, "Becky? Monique?"

Monique answered with a hesitant, "Yes?"

"Judy says wait. She comes."

Becky stared at this guy with his grizzled beard and chained epaulets and a red bandana tied around his probably balding head. Nervously she scanned the road for the shuttle. And then, with growing disbelief, Becky followed Monique's gaze and looked up the cliff face.

Monique murmured, "She wouldn't."

"She *couldn't*."

Becky scanned the ropes. She looked for a healthy female bottom. She saw one older woman, too thin to be Judy. She wondered if Judy were up at the top right now, strapped into the harness. More bikers zoomed up in front of them, kicking up a spray of pine needles as they filled the clearing with the smell of exhaust. The biker closest to them canted his front wheel as he twisted the ignition key. His companion swung her leg off the back of the seat. She pulled off her helmet and tossed her brown hair.

It took a minute before Becky could morph what she was seeing into the woman with whom she manned the Girl Scout cookie booth in front of the local grocery store.

Judy grinned. "You two didn't really think I was going to rappel down that ridiculous cliff, did you? With these wonky knees?"

Words abandoned Becky once again, along with thought and sense. Monique was threatening to throw over the bucket list. And now Judy, the mother of five, was hitching rides with foreign bikers.

Monique stuttered, "I'm glad to see you made friends while we were gone, Judy. But we should—"

"These are the Hahns," Judy interrupted. "They're here for that soldier up there with the metal legs. After he makes his way down, they're going to some techno bar to celebrate his one-year anniversary out of physical therapy." Judy looked oddly different, loose-limbed, bright-eyed and wild. She casually tossed her helmet to one of the men. "You've got something on Lenny's list about motorcycles, don't you, Monie?"

"Um...yeah?"

"Then say hello to our rides back to Interlaken."

∞ chapter fourteen

Beep beep beep beep.

Monique thrashed in the bed. The screeching noise pulsed in rhythm to the needle of pain just above her eye socket. She yanked the pillow from under her head and pressed it over her ears, willing Judy or Becky to do something to *make it stop,* as the noise resolved itself into the distinctive, international, undeniable sound of an alarm clock. Then the part of her that was always on time for work, always ten minutes early for a doctor's appointment, always delivering medicine exactly on the four-hour mark, shuddered into reluctant consciousness.

With a groan she snapped the pillow off her head. She forced herself to peel her lids open. They stuck as if her eyeballs had gone dry. She blinked into utter darkness, then blinked again, confused. Above the wretched alarm clock she could hear the rumble of traffic outside their cheap, off-season Swiss hotel, but she couldn't see light seeping around the edges of the shades. As she rolled up into a sitting position, the pulsing above her eyes intensified, and she pressed her palm against her temple...only to come up against cloth. She seized a fold of it and tugged it over the top of her head.

In the dim light she discerned the shape of the bureau, two beds, table, and two chairs of their hotel room. She held in her hand a folded bandana.

The sight of it triggered a memory of tripping down a narrow staircase to a loud, dim underground bar that smelled of stale beer and mildew, of yanking a bandana off the head of a grizzled biker, exposing the bald spot above the iron-gray of his waist-length braid.

Beep beep beep beep.

It hurt too much to think, especially when that beeping was driving her mad. She glanced around the room until she pinpointed a blur of red numbers. Reaching across a snoring Judy, she fumbled with the thing, pressing buttons and flicking switches until finally in frustration she just yanked at the cord until it jerked out of the wall socket.

Silence buzzed in her ears. Neither one of the motionless lumps of Judy under her arm or Becky on the next bed even budged. And Monique felt the pressure of a full bladder, a pressure she couldn't ignore.

She stood up and hissed as the floor shifted strangely beneath her feet. Pressing a thumb beneath her brow bone, she used the edge of the bed as a guide to head toward the bathroom. At the bottom of the bed, her toe caught under something heavy, sending her stumbling. As she struggled to stay upright she cursed Judy for leaving her pack in the middle of the floor again. She opened the door to the bathroom and walked smack into something.

Monique grunted. She winced an eye open and found

that she'd knocked herself against the metal leg of a fold-up ironing board. She backed out of the closet and shut it before coming to the reasonable conclusion that the hotel hadn't switched the layout of the room overnight. She grudgingly admitted that maybe she'd had too much to drink.

Images of the night flashed through her mind. A motor-cycle vibrating between her thighs. Flashes of bright light, a pounding, ear-shattering beat. The yeasty cold of a fresh beer as the liquid slipped down her throat. Her feet sticky against the floor as she raised her hands into the path of the strobe lights and danced.

Danced?

Her bladder screamed with urgency. She wheeled around and saw the bathroom open just behind her. She stumbled in and took care of business. She sank her head into her hands and tried to remember when she'd last danced pub-licly. Not since her cousin's wedding in Trinidad years ago, under the influence of too much coconut rum. Fortunately Kiera had been too young to notice how "happy" Momma had become. Monique dug her knuckles into her gritty eyes, just hoping there weren't any videos this time.

Aspirin. She needed aspirin. And a tall, cold glass of wa-ter. Some vitamin B and a good breakfast. And to get the hell out of Europe, away from Lenny's nefarious plans, back home where she could finally give Lenny a piece of her mind. All the booze in Interlaken couldn't subsume that de-sire, though she was beginning to suspect that last night she'd tried.

She stumbled to the sink, bracing her hands on either

side. She remembered they all had to catch an eleven-thirty train to Zurich today, to get Becky—and hopefully herself—on that three p.m. flight to New York. Turning the faucet on she pooled water in her hands and splashed it over her face. As she wiped the water from her eyes she noticed something dark lying like a coil at the bottom of the sink.

It moved.

Monique shot back. She hit the wall, the corner of the towel rack bruising her shoulder. She threw out an arm and slapped the peeling wallpaper in search of the switch plate. As fluorescent light exploded in the room, Monique saw whatever it was poke its head over the porcelain edge.

Monique stumbled out of the bathroom backward, backpedaling wildly. Her foot caught on the luggage on the floor which shot her legs right out from under her. Her butt took the brunt of the hit that rattled her vertebrae.

Becky shot up, a blindfold cocked across her face. "What? What?"

"S-S-Snake." Monique kicked away from the luggage. Light poured from the bathroom and limned the lump she'd stumbled over. Monique scuttled back farther, clutching the arms of the desk chair to struggle to her feet, as the "luggage" groaned, lumbered off the floor, and formed itself into the shape of a man. A hefty, bull-chested man. He clambered to his full height and lazily rolled his shoulders with a jangle of chains and creaks of leather, and then with a healthy snort, headed into the bathroom.

Becky wrestled the bandana off her face and then stared in that sightless way she had in the dark. "What the hell are you yelling about, Monie?"

"There's a snake in the bathroom sink." Her heart raced in her chest. "And a man in our hotel room."

On cue came the sound of a man peeing, that loud undeniable splash she hadn't heard in her own house for years, that macho voiding done with the door wide open that went on for so long it was a boast in itself.

Becky's eyes went so wide that, even in the gloom, Monique could see the whites of them from clear across the room. Monique reared back, taking the desk chair with her, falling into it so it careened back into the curtains. She shot her feet up off the floor where there might be more snakes. She dug her toes into the seat and realized by the pressure against her ribs that she'd slept wearing Judy's belly pack. Inside it a cell phone buzzed.

"Judy," Monique whispered hoarsely. "Judy, wake up."

Judy moaned.

"Judy, *wake up*. There's a *man* and a *snake* in our room."

Judy shifted slightly and muttered something unintelligible, something guttural and vaguely German.

Monique glanced around for something to use as a weapon but the room was bare, unless she intended to poke a snake in the eye with the hotel pen or ward it off with a memo pad. She seized a fold of the curtains behind her chair and jerked them open, letting in a sharp wedge of light. Becky whipped away, wincing. Judy flinched where she lay sprawled with her mouth open and a bag of Zweifel Pomy Chips under her cheek. The light stabbed her eyes, but at least when their intruder returned Monique knew now she'd get a good look at his face and either recognize him from last night—or blind him before he could attack.

She tried to remember coming back to the hotel. Was this guy one of the biker crew? Had he passed out here? Why would they let him into their hotel room in the first place?

"For the sweet love of Jesus," Judy mumbled. "Close the effing drapes."

The biker came out of the bathroom, tugging on his fly. A scraggly mane of white-blond hair stuck up in all directions. He cringed and raised one hand against the light. The other hand held a fistful of snake.

Jager.

Monique suddenly remembered him galloping around the bar, whooping as he pretended to be an American cowboy with Judy clinging to his back, hallooing at the top of her lungs.

Jager crouched down to slip the snake into a pouch. He said something in German. Judy mumbled a reply and lifted a hand that looked vaguely like a farewell. Jager stood to his full height, slung his pouch across his chest, and gave them all a gap-toothed grin. With a wave he swaggered out, the door squealing closed behind him.

Becky dared to lower the blanket an inch. "What just happened?"

Monique said, "A biker just left our room."

"You said there was a snake in our bathroom."

"He took it with him."

Another memory of dancing in the heat, of feeling something cold on the back of her neck, of looking down and seeing a snake draped around her.

She'd thought it was rubber.

Becky stood up, weaving. The blanket slipped off her and

fell to the floor. She was fully dressed. A cocktail napkin stuck to the seat of her pants. She minced her way to the bureau and then stared at the floor where Jager had apparently spent the night. "Monie, where's my suitcase?"

The cell phone buzzed in the belly pack again, but Monique ignored it. She looked around the room. Becky's suitcase didn't lie open on the bureau. Judy's dirty clothes didn't lie in a heap by the door. Monique forced herself off the chair to pull out the drawers, one by one. Empty empty empty. She stumbled toward the closet, looked in the bathroom, saw no toiletries on the shelves. Saw no suitcases, no daypacks.

Monique seized the doorjamb. "We've been robbed."

Judy growled into her pillow.

Monique tried to think past her pounding headache while Becky stood in shock by the bed. They'd have to go to the American embassy. Thank God she'd had their passports photocopied and left copies at home. Kiera could fax that stuff over to the embassy and they'd get them replaced. Monique wondered how long that would take. Her head was going to split open if she didn't get coffee soon. They couldn't leave the country without their passports.

Monique looked down and realized she was wearing one sneaker. The other one lay by the side of the bed. She seized it and bounced on the end of the bed trying to pull it on over her sock. Then she slapped Judy hard on the hip.

Judy sprang up. "All right, all right. I'm getting up."

"Everything's *gone*, Judy. Everything."

"Please lower your voice."

"Great freakin' idea you had, going off with those bikers."

"Absinthe is a nasty, nasty thing."

"'It's just a techno bar,' you said. 'Becky only has one more night,' you said. What were you thinking?"

"You two should have stuck to beer."

"Absinthe?" Becky said vaguely, dropping back onto the bed. "I remember that."

Monique sucked in a quick breath, remembering it too. She recalled the neon green liquid in the little glasses. The raucous glee of the crowd as they put a few drops of absinthe on the sugar cube sitting on a spoon, set it on fire, and let the caramelized sugar drip into the green liquid, making it go cloudy. She pressed her swollen tongue against her teeth, tasting the bitterness still.

Becky murmured, "I told everyone that I wanted to see the green fairy."

Monique bent her head between her knees. The pattern in the carpet swam before her eyes. She didn't *do* things like this. She didn't drink to oblivion. It was poison to the liver, poison to the soul. She'd been feeling so upset yesterday, so unhinged. She'd been so…angry. Oh, lord. What would Kiera think if she learned that her mother had been drinking absinthe in a Swiss biker bar?

The cell phone, buzzing again, against her ribs.

It was her own phone she pulled out of Judy's belly pack, her own phone, buzzing to indicate Kiera's latest text.

Haven't heard from u Mom. So what did u die on that cliff?

Monique shoved the phone back into the belly pack and muscled the shame away. "Listen," she said, trying to get a grip on herself, "we've got to call the Swiss police."

Judy's voice sounded tired. "We're not calling the police."

"We've got a crime to report."

Monique strode to the window and flung the curtains wide, flooding the room with light. She winced at the view of a parking lot, edged by an industrial building with corrugated metal siding. Right under their window lay a Dumpster. She looked at it with a mind that had suddenly gone blank. With her heart skipping a beat, she glanced back into the room at the paneled walls, the crooked Alpine prints, the nubby coverlet, the big old television.

"Oh, God," she said. "This isn't even our hotel."

Monique sidled her way down the dim corridor, cringing as she noticed the peeling wallpaper and the water stains on the ceiling, the smell of stale cigarette smoke, and the webbed areas of carpet. Looking around this place and thinking about the bed she'd just slept in had her skin crawling. "We just spent the night in a flophouse."

"Clearly you've never actually spent a night in a flophouse," Judy snorted. "It's a perfectly respectable place. We all stumbled over here from the bar, which was a hell of a lot smarter than taking the bikes. We were lucky we could snag a room."

Monique glanced over her shoulder, catching Becky's eye before zeroing in on Judy, who had a terrible case of bedhead. "Did you look in the mirror this morning, Judy?"

"I avoid that before my first cup of coffee."

"How does your neck feel?"

"Pretty good." Judy ran a hand along the side of her neck, tilting her head with a satisfying crack. "No ache for a change."

"You have a tattoo."

Judy's fingers shot to her neck. "Is that thing still there?"

Monique started. "Still?"

Becky leaned in for a better look and then hissed a breath through her teeth. "Tattoos are permanent, Judy."

"You might want to lift up the right sleeve of your T-shirt, Beck. And Monie, did you check under your shirt this morning?"

Monique's blood went cold. She tried to hone her aching senses, but above a pounding headache and a mouth full of cotton, she felt nothing more than the bite of Judy's belly pack into her tummy, none of the prickly soreness she'd expect from— She fumbled with her shirt, jerking it out of the cinch of the belly pack. She found it on her stomach— the same square mark that Judy had on her neck, the same square mark that Becky revealed as she tugged her sleeve over her shoulder.

Becky breathed a relieved laugh. "It's one of those stick-on tattoos. The kind I won't let Gina use on Brianna and Brian, in case it gives my kids ideas."

Monique suddenly remembered the sight of one of the bikers—not Jager—running his tongue along a piece of paper and then pressing it firmly against her belly while she whooped at the top of her lungs.

"Yup," Judy said. "The Hahns have staked their claim, girls, by planting their Austrian flag."

Monique shook her head and turned into what passed as a lobby, currently occupied by a snoozing, fragrant, tattered old man and a boy behind the counter. At the sight of them the boy perked up and slipped off his stool. His grin stretched apart the rings that pierced his lower lip. Judy stepped up and said something in German. The boy bobbed his head and disappeared momentarily to click a series of locks and chains on the nearby door. He swung the door open and pushed out two backpacks.

Monique nearly cried with relief. She fell to one knee and unzipped her pack, doing a quick inventory. She took out the half-empty bottle of water, drinking it to the dregs even though it was piss-warm. The boy kept grinning. The kid was looking at them like they were three forty-something cougars who'd taken on a whole fleet of bikers. Monique had never been so self-conscious of her frizzed hair, her bloodshot eyes, her rumpled hoodie, and the smell of stale liquor that rose up from her pores.

Judy spoke to the boy briefly and then turned to them. "Jager left a message. He says good-bye and we can keep the blindfolds."

Monique had left hers upstairs, tangled among the sheets, not really keen to keep a kerchief pulled off the head of some strange man, even if he was the devoted husband of that older woman with the crew cut who spent the night sitting demurely in a corner, sipping a glass of merlot and watching all the antics with great amusement. She was mother to three of the six bikers in the room, including the war veteran amputee who'd joked, Monique remembered, that his new legs made him six foot one and that was why he was never without a girlfriend.

"Jager also said that if we're ever in Weerberg, just wave those bandanas in front of anyone and they'll direct us to the best bar in town."

"Great," Monique muttered. "Now we've got gang colors."

Monique slung her daypack across her shoulder and followed Judy and Becky out the door, slipping on her sunglasses. Through a squint she noticed the train station—Interlaken Ouest—and realized the rumbling she'd heard all morning was the passage of incoming and outgoing trains. Judy seemed to know the direction of their hotel so Monique followed her with her head down, feeling dirty and sweaty and rumpled and sore in places she hadn't been sore in years.

"Okay," Monique said, falling into pace beside Becky, wishing the whistling Judy would slow the heck down. "What exactly do *you* remember?"

"I remember we rode on the back of those bikes down the mountain and the steep turns scared the hell out of me."

"They took us to some sketchy place," Monique murmured. "No storefront at all. Just a set of concrete stairs down into a cellar."

"As usual I couldn't see a thing."

"So the amputee—"

"Karl," Judy barked. "He's got a name, guys."

"Yeah, Karl." Handsome kid, Monique remembered. He spoke English fluently. He bounced like a kangaroo on his titanium prosthetics, so full of fun. "I remember Karl," she continued. "Once he heard that you were night blind, Becky, he pulled the kerchief off his throat and tied it around his eyes."

"Didn't last long," Judy said, "He nearly took a header down the last step. I think he was sweet on you, Monie."

Warmth spread through her as she remembered a moment near the bathrooms, bumping into him, the brush of bodies, a fumble of awkwardness, the lowering of his young face toward hers.

She stepped off the sidewalk to allow an older woman pulling a rolling canvas cart of groceries to step by, and to give her girl parts time to stop reacting.

"There were strobe lights," Becky continued, "and neon lasers. It was all a blur except for the long bar and the next thing I knew there was a row of shot glasses swimming in front of me."

Monique pushed away the memory of a young man's kiss. "Edelweiss liquor," she said. "I can still taste it."

Judy stopped abruptly in front of a restaurant. A barrel-chested man with a pipe clenched in his mouth shouldered by them. "Hey, I'm starved. Breakfast?"

Monique gasped, "Coffee."

"You lightweights need more than coffee. You need protein. This place is advertising a 'Big American' breakfast."

Judy plowed in through the front door, chattering in German to the maître d' who obliged quickly by sending all three of them deep, deep into the restaurant, into a little corner table as far away from a window as they could possibly get. Probably, Monique mused, so their stench wouldn't seep through the room and their bedraggled looks scare off other patrons.

A waitress arrived, slipped three menus on the table, and filled their coffee cups. Monique gulped down half the brew and lifted the cup for a refill before the waitress could slip away. Then she added cream and took another sip. She moaned and closed her eyes, feeling the healing effects seep through her system.

"If you girls really want to remember the night," Judy said, sipping her coffee with more grace, "you may want to look at Monie's cell phone."

"Photos?" Becky stiffened. "We have photos?"

Monique's heart did a little lurch.

"Videos too." Judy perused the menu with a cat-in-the-cream look on her face. "Do you think they have bacon like our crispy American bacon? Or that lame fatty stuff we got in Germany?"

Monique dove into the front pocket of her daypack searching for her cell phone. She poked the screen until she saw the small blurry icons of a series of pictures and videos. With hesitation, Monique pressed on the first video.

"You know," Judy said, sinking back in her chair and idly perusing the thin population of the restaurant. "This is definitely the way to do a midlife crisis."

Monique tried to puzzle out what she was seeing as noise blasted from the speakers. "Becky, I think those are your sneakers."

"Oh, God," Becky murmured. "I'm doing Zumba. I remember this. I'm teaching Zumba to a bunch of Belgian backpackers."

"Here I am," Judy continued, "moping around in Europe of all places, trying to figure out who I am—since I'm not twenty-two, or an active mother, or employable anymore. I've been thinking I just have to get through this time, just have to wait it out."

"Oh, God." Monique's eyes widened as she flipped through a series of photos. "We *are* doing shots."

"But you know what?" Judy said. "I should have eaten

a hash brownie in Amsterdam. At Le Jules Verne, I should have ordered another bottle of the Cote d'Or Grand Cru vintage, even if I had to finish it myself."

Monique gasped at the next video. Between the strobe lights and the lasers it was hard to pick out silhouettes, but the longer she looked at the two people gyrating in a cage elevated on some sort of pedestal—like the kind you'd see in a cheesy strip club—the more sure she was that the butt filling up the screen was hers.

"Nice sports bra, Monique," Becky said.

"Judy, did we really dance in a *cage*?"

"Yeah, and your sports bra is pink, Becky," Judy added. "And I didn't just find that out this morning when you were washing up."

Monique pushed the phone into Becky's hands. Monique didn't want to look anymore, but Becky couldn't seem to look away. Becky made little gasping noises as the tinny music continued to play from the camera. Monique sank a little lower in her seat, wishing she could just curl up and hide in a crack somewhere.

"Oh, no." Becky covered her mouth with her free hand. "I guess I should be relieved we're partially dressed."

Judy toasted her with her coffee cup. "I knew you'd thank me for that later."

Becky blinked at Judy. "Did it hurt when the alien took over your body?"

Judy's grin was sly. "You like the new me?"

"Please." Monique gave up trying to squeeze the headache out of her temples. "This isn't a new Judy. This is a *young* Judy."

"Oh, no, foolish young Judy stuck to her own generation. She would *never* have struck up a conversation with a bunch of old guys on Harleys."

Becky muttered, "Neither would the mother of five who ran the PTA for six years."

"That's the point. I'm switching gears."

Becky sputtered, "Right to overdrive."

Judy shook her head. "Have either of you ever driven a manual transmission?"

Monique frowned, having difficulty keeping up with the conversation. "That's all they've got for cheap rentals in Trinidad."

"When you're driving a manual," Judy explained, "you've got to press down on the clutch. And for a moment you're between gears."

Becky shrugged. "Don't get it."

"I get it," Monique said. "When your foot is on the clutch, it's a moment when you have no control. When the car can roll absolutely anywhere."

Judy slapped the table. "Exactly. Next week I'll be home putting up Halloween decorations on my lawn. Right now I'm hungover in a restaurant in Switzerland. Welcome to my clutch moment."

Monique nudged her coffee cup as the waitress came by to refill. She watched the black brew fill the cup nearly to the brim. She went through the motions of adding cream, of stirring it more than she needed to, wincing at each tap of the spoon against the ceramic cup. It was hard to think when her head was pounding so much, when her body felt stretched and drained and ill-used.

"Why didn't you stop us?" Monique gave Judy the evil eye. "Why did you let us make complete asses of ourselves?"

"Because I kept thinking that we three should have drunk ourselves silly the very first night in London."

"So you took videos to memorialize our idiocy."

"Well, yeah." Judy shrugged, smiling at the waitress as she approached. "Now I can post them on my Facebook page."

Monique stilled. Judy started chattering in German to the young girl in an apron, chattering away as easily as if it was a Friday morning stateside at the Cozy End. "I ordered your eggs over easy, Monie," Judy said, her Cheshire-cat grin widening as the waitress left. "And Becky, I figured you'd go for pancakes."

With cold-hearted purpose, Monique seized the phone from Becky and flipped through the rest of the photos and videos until she came to the one she wanted. She pressed play and turned the phone so Judy could see it.

"Here's something Bob might be interested in." Shouts of "*giddy up*" rang through the tinny speaker. "Jager's got quite a wide, comfortable back, don't you think?"

"I sent Bob that one already. We have a full-disclosure kind of marriage." She winked. "Boy, a hangover really sucks the sense of humor right out of you two. Of *course* I'm not going to post anything incriminating on my Facebook page."

Monique narrowed her eyes because Judy ended that sentence in a way that suggested she hadn't quite finished it.

"I won't post them," Judy said, planting the cup back on the table, "as long as Becky stays for the rest of the vacation, and you, Monique, agree to finish Lenny's list."

Judy gave Monique the kind of pinned-butterfly look

that had her shrinking in the little European chair. Monique found interest in the swirl of light cream in her coffee. She must have told Judy last night what she'd decided about the list. She had a vague memory of an intense conversation screamed over the music, with Becky bouncing to the beat in the background. She remembered shaking her head and doing another shot, telling Judy that her mind was made up.

Yes, her mind was made up, but Becky's revelation still stung. On that cliff yesterday Becky had yanked back the curtain to reveal Lenny tugging at levers and gears. Until then Monique had been perfectly happy believing in the illusion. So, yeah, maybe Lenny had meant well. But she'd be damned if she did the things he'd wanted her to do, just to close the door on him forever.

"Well," Becky said, "despite a serious case of cottonmouth, the fact I have bruises I can't account for, and a rather diffuse sense of sheepishness, last night was the most fun I've had in a very long time."

Judy mumbled, "Amen."

"So if you don't mind changing the flight plans one more time, Monie," Becky said, casting a hesitant glance as she searched among the videos on the phone until she found the one she wanted. "There's no way I want to miss any more of this."

Becky tilted the phone, playing a video that appeared to be Judy doing a chicken dance. A smile played around the corners of Becky's mouth. An easy smile that Monique hadn't seen in a long, long time.

Judy didn't bat an eye. "What do you think, Monie? Are you going to finish what you started?"

"It doesn't matter what I want. Clearly we're not making our train today." Monique leaned back and folded her arms tight. "I've still got five more items on that list. Physically it just can't be done."

Judy pursed her lips. "I wouldn't say that."

"It's impossible," Monique insisted. "Not without tightening the itinerary. And I know both of you are sick to death of planes, trains, buses, shuttles—"

"—and motorcycles," Becky added, as she shifted her thighs.

"Open your minds, ladies." Over the rim of her coffee cup Judy's lips stretched in a slow, wicked smile. "Lenny didn't say that all those things on the list were chiseled in stone. He didn't disallow...slight modifications."

Monique frowned. She sensed a trap, long set and utterly unavoidable.

"I have," Judy said, "the most wonderful idea."

∞ chapter fifteen

An itinerary blown to pieces? Judy knew all about those.

There was the time when Bob had finagled a ski trip to a Vermont resort, taking over a coworker's time-share for a five-day holiday for the whole family. In anticipation Santa generously left new snowboards, parkas, ski boots, and insulated gloves under the Christmas tree. Judy had bribed a teenager to care for the dogs, the rabbits, the birds, and the hermit crabs; she'd stopped the papers and the milk delivery; had the car tuned up; bought a storage container for the roof-rack; hounded her children to finish projects and homework well ahead of time; and packed each suitcase so tightly they could be mortared like bricks.

But on the morning she packed the car Audrey and Maddy—who'd been particularly cranky the night before—woke up vomiting.

She'd given Bob a long, sorry look. They'd both known what had to be done. This was not the first time their best-laid plans went awry. So Bob took the boys snowboarding in Vermont just as planned. And she stayed home with two daughters who sobbed and wailed and all but tore their pajamas in distress.

Out of the attic stash Judy then dug out a video game the girls had been anticipating. When they could eat she served chocolate milkshakes and homemade soup on trays in front of the TV. As they started to feel human Judy fetched every pillow, blanket, and cushion to the living room so they could construct a fort in which they spent the nights sleeping, sprawled like pups. She decreed every day "Messy Day," absolving all three of them of house duties and toy pick-up responsibilities and bedtimes. As the "silly French cook" she took orders for hamburgers for breakfast and bananas in cereal for dinner. The dining room table became a staging point for a Risk board game marathon where the girls ganged up on her to take over the world.

When the boys came home the girls rushed to them, scattering toys and game pieces and books and pillows, jumping up and down and shouting that they'd just had the best week *ever.*

Children got sick. Cars broke down. Friends lost their way. When life was unpredictable, Judy embraced the chaos. And that's just what she intended to do as a sporty, European-size taxi pulled up in front of their Interlaken hotel.

Judy hustled out into the chill Swiss evening and shuttled her friends into the cab. "All right, ladies," she said as she told the driver where to take them. "Are you ready for a ritzy night at a European casino?"

Monique shrugged, still moody.

"All I can say is don't expect Atlantic City." Becky's slinky, emerald-green dress had risen up to reveal enviable knees. "I read up about this place during my pedicure this afternoon. The guidebook said that this casino has slots, roulette, blackjack, and Texas hold 'em. That's it."

"No craps tables?" Judy exclaimed. "How disappointing. I was looking forward to blowing on some guy's dice."

Monique sidled a look toward Becky. "You got the first watch, right?"

"Just pray that the light isn't too dim."

Monique raised the flat of her palm. "I'm not waking up in a flophouse with a snake again."

Judy arched a brow. "Hey, it wasn't me calling for belly-button shots at three in the morning."

Becky narrowed her eyes. "You are totally making that up."

Judy barked a little laugh. "Boy, you really don't remember any of your criminal behavior last night."

"Absinthe is legal in Switzerland," Monique said. "I checked."

"Maybe I wasn't talking about the absinthe."

Two heads cocked in suspicion. So, all right, maybe she was teasing them too much. It was just so easy. The poor women had spent the day gasping at odd moments as the fog of the alcohol cleared. Judy had jogged their memories along by dropping little facts. Like when Karl followed Monique to the bathroom, and Monique had returned later than expected with a wild look in her eyes and slightly swollen lips.

"Becky," Monique mused, "I think I liked Judy better when she was a neurotic empty-nester resisting her own midlife crisis."

"I object," Judy said, "to the term 'neurotic.'"

"When a woman's hormones go wild," Monique contin-ued, "it's just like being a reckless teenager again."

"No brakes at all," Becky said. "No consideration of con-sequences."

"If she's not careful," Monique added, "she'll end up shacked up on the Adriatic coast with an Italian lover."

Judy felt that familiar prickly heat rise. So, yeah, maybe she did feel like a wild woman. She was feeling powerfully attractive tonight. Earlier today, after a restorative nap, Judy had hustled Monie and Becky to the Kosmetiksalon Beauty Création for manicures and pedicures. A German-speaking Helga had spent an hour styling her hair into perfection. After, she joined Monique shopping, where for a hundred and seventy Swiss francs Judy bought a new dress at the de-partment store Schild. It was a slimming A-line confection of black lace over a chocolate sheath that fell with thrilling ease over a figure that had lost five or six pounds.

She felt strong and determined in the sexiest of ways— a creature both freshly born yet mature, too, swimming in physical and intellectual confidence. The feeling was elec-trifying. She was determined to hold on to it for as long as possible.

"So," Judy said, moving right along, "the only tables this casino has are blackjack, roulette, and Texas hold 'em. I've always preferred poker and I never understood Texas hold 'em. Either of you know it?"

"Marco plays it with his brothers at their annual poker party. It's easy," Becky said. "I'll teach you."

"That's fine," Judy said. "And we can watch for a while.

No reason to jump right into things. We've got the whole night ahead of us, as long as you lightweights can make it past your ten p.m. bedtime." She nudged Monique. "Lenny did want you to make that stash of yours last for as long as possible."

Judy focused her attention on Monique's little purse. Monique crushed the clutch between her elbow and her side. It currently contained one thousand dollars' worth of crisp Swiss francs.

"I wouldn't hazard to guess what Lenny would want me to do with this stash of his." Monique's lips twitched, and not in a happy way. "That man kept a whole heap of things to himself, didn't he?"

Uh-oh. She'd hit the trigger again. She and Becky had nearly worn that trigger out at breakfast, trying to nudge a stubbornly defiant Monique into re-embracing the list. They'd gently prodded her into thinking about what Lenny had really meant with each item. Sure, number seven specified that they go to a casino in Monaco to see how long a thousand bucks would last...but was it Monaco that formed the heart of that wish? Monaco, which hogged hours and hours of the itinerary in transportation time? Or did Lenny just want his fiscally responsible wife to experience the primal thrill of blowing a thousand bucks?

If that were the case they could honestly check that item off the list right here in Interlaken, at the casino the taxi was now pulling up to.

The casino itself was a large, open room. Slot machines lined the walls, rattling and ringing, crazy with lights. It was not yet seven o'clock in the evening, but the casino hummed with the low chatter of men in business suits with their ties pulled loose. Those who'd shed their jackets sported name tag stickers on their shirt pockets. The usual gambling junkies were fixed in place, reserving the stools on either side of them in order to run three slot machines at once, drinks, chips, and snacks within easy reach. Judy thought that if it weren't for the casino's distinctly European décor that hovered somewhere between decadent Old World and cheesy bordello, they could be gambling in Peoria.

She flicked her wrist to look at her watch and asked, "Do either of you know what time our reservations are for the Swiss folklore dinner theater?"

Becky said, "Seven thirty. Dear God I hope there's no yodeling. I don't think my head can take yodeling."

"We've got some time then." Judy caught sight of the cashier's booth. "Let's get that wad of cash transferred into chips. It might take a whole evening to work through that much money."

The cashier spoke fluent English as Judy exchanged a hundred francs into ten-franc chips. Becky exchanged what remained of her "mad money" into tokens. Then, with Judy and Becky behaving as furtively as Secret Service agents, Monique approached and pulled out her cache.

When Monique finished her business Judy glanced at the small pile of chips with alarm. "Monie, you've only got a handful of tokens."

"They're worth the equivalent of about a hundred bucks each." Monique clinked the plastic disks against one another. "Amazing how light they are. They could fall out of my pocket, and I'd hardly notice."

"You should exchange them for twenty-five-franc or even ten-franc pieces. If you play such high stakes, the fun will be over before it's begun."

Monique breezed by, the long column of her Nefertiti neck corded and taut. "Let's pass by the tables, shall we?"

Judy exchanged a worried glance with Becky as the two of them followed Monique through the room. They passed by a roulette wheel, a blackjack table, and then another for Texas hold 'em, and then they took another circuit. Judy nudged Monique when they reached the blackjack table again. "There are a few open chairs."

"I'm too lucky at love to have any luck at cards," Monique said. "If I try to shuck this thousand here, it'll be like death by pinpricks."

"Watch me for a while." Judy sat down and was dealt in on the next round and Becky joined her.

Monique shifted restlessly behind them as they continued to play. "What's 'boule'?'"

" 'Boule?' It means 'ball' in French," Judy said, "but it usually means a type of bread that looks like a ball. Why do you ask?" As the dealer loaded a new set of cards, Judy followed Monique's glance to the boule table in the middle of the room. "Well, *that* looks like a roulette wheel, so clearly the word has multiple meanings."

"Boule's a little different from American roulette." Becky eyed the card that landed in front of her. "It's an old French type of roulette wheel, harder to win."

Judy tapped to split her two tens. "Do you have a secret gambling problem, Beck? Because I can't think of any other reason why you'd know that."

Becky shrugged, squinting as if she were calculating odds before asking the dealer to hit her again. "There was an Indian casino about forty miles from my grandparents' farm. My boyfriend and I used fake IDs to sneak in there. The room in the back, the half-empty one we hung out in so no one would bother us, had weird games. Faro, baccarat, trente et quarante. One table was called boule, and it looked like that."

"Slow down," Judy said, "I didn't hear anything after 'fake IDs.'"

"There are more things to do in rural Minnesota than just tip cows."

"Did you really tip cows?"

Becky rolled her eyes. "I wouldn't bother with boule, Monie. The odds are bad, and it's all luck, no skill."

Monique twisted on one heel and headed straight toward the boule table. Judy and Becky startled, quickly finished the game, and then swept up their tokens to follow. Monique stood by the boule table with her arms crossed, watching the large rubber ball set loose on the wheel bounce around until it landed on a five. The dealer dragged piles of chips off the board with a little squeegee.

Judy asked, "Have you played?"

"Not yet." Monique clinked her chips, frowning. "How does this work?"

"You put your tokens on any one of those boxes." Becky pointed to various marks on the green baize. "You can bet odds or evens, or red or black, or low or high, and the odds are a bit less than fifty-fifty. You can also bet a specific number on the wheel, but that's a long shot."

"Bet black," Judy muttered. "I read somewhere that that gives the best odds."

Monique waited until everyone else in the circle started slipping tokens onto the baize, and then she set her tokens down with a clatter.

Judy started. "Monie, you don't mean to—"

"Yes I do." Monique shot out an arm to prevent Judy from reaching for the column of tokens. "I'm putting all of it on red number nine."

"Monie," Becky warned, "the odds for winning are less than ten—"

"My wedding anniversary was the ninth of September. The ninth day of the ninth month."

Judy strained against Monique's arm. "Darling, this isn't what Lenny meant."

"I know what Lenny meant. He wanted to loosen me up." Monique's throat flexed as if she were swallowing something whole. "He wanted me to not worry about money so much. He didn't want me to keep stuffing every penny of our disposable income into Kiera's college fund or our retirement account or into our slush fund for house repairs and future car purchases—"

"Monie," Judy interrupted, "just think about this for a minute."

"—He wanted me to blow a good chunk of it doing something crazy, something utterly irresponsible." She gestured to the tokens, teetering on red nine. "Like this."

Becky said softly, "I think he wanted you to have fun."

"Well, that he doesn't get." A muscle twitched by the corner of Monique's eye. "He doesn't get that because he doesn't know what a relief it was, after he died, to have saved so diligently. He doesn't know how many problems were solved by the whole life insurance policy that I insisted we invest in, just after he finished his residency. How could I have done this," she said, raising her palms to the high ceiling, "if I hadn't saved like a madwoman for the fifteen years of our marriage?"

Judy's glance danced over the table and the dealer, knowing that time was running out to pull those tokens off the number. "I'm sliding it over to red."

"Judy—"

"The odds are you're still going to lose. Right, Beck?"

"Fifty-two percent."

"At least give winning a sporting chance."

Monique's lips tightened but she didn't object as Judy reached in and slid the column of tokens into the box for red.

"Rien ne va plus."

Judy moved them just in time. Betting was over. She curled her finely manicured fingers into her sweaty palms. She might have increased the odds but she hadn't staved off a swift, sharp end to the evening, like the fall of a guillotine.

The dealer set the wheel spinning.

Judy couldn't watch the roulette wheel spin like Becky did, with her hand cupping her mouth. Judy watched Monique, observing the table with utter indifference, as all one thousand bucks of Lenny's casino money teetered on red. Staring at her friend's stone-cold face, Judy understood with a new clarity that Monique just wanted to get it over with. This list that Monique had anticipated for so long... now it just brought the widow pain.

Her mind buzzed forward, trying to anticipate how she should deal with the fallout. There'd be no more gambling. They'd enjoy the Swiss folklore show, and she'd make jokes about its corny little skits and oompah music. They'd laugh about the whole thing and make it an early night, which was probably best considering how little sleep all of them had gotten after the previous night's shenanigans. Tomorrow they'd set off for Munich like they'd decided so that Becky could see Neuschwanstein, King Ludwig's fairy-tale castle, and Monique could finally cross Oktoberfest off the list.

It'd be a new adventure. She'd have to make it good.

"*Neuf rouge.*"

Becky's squeal pierced her ears. Judy watched with horror as the dealer clinked on Monique's pile a token of a color that no one else at the table sported. Judy flattened her palm on the edge of the table as the dealer pushed everyone else's chips off the betting green.

"I won?" Monique frowned. "That wasn't supposed to happen."

Becky bounced on the balls of her feet. "You just doubled your money."

Judy didn't know whether she was seeing black spots in front of her eyes or if she was having a seizure from all the blinking slot machine lights. By shoving Monique's money off of red nine, she just cost the woman who took her to Europe nearly the full cost of the trip.

"She would have won seven grand," Judy sputtered, "if I hadn't moved those tokens at the last minute—"

"Thank goodness you did. It'd take me forever to blow seven grand in this place." Monique leaned forward and pushed the pile of tokens back onto red. "It can't happen twice, right? What are the odds of that, Beck?"

"Forty-eight percent. Same as—"

"Rien ne va plus."

Judy twitched at the sound of the wheel spinning. She blinked her eyes open to see Monique's tower of tokens on the baize, again on red, as the wheel made a clatter and the dealer released the rubber ball. Judy opened her mouth to say—*no, no!* But the tokens were committed, all of them— the original thousand and the additional piece, perched on top like a little black hat.

She had a fleeting, wicked thought that, if Monique won again, at least she would be partway to the seven thousand dollar payout that Monique *should have had,* had Judy not at the last minute yanked all of Monique's chips off red nine.

"Deux rouge."

The words didn't register at once, nor did the sight of the red rubber ball sitting in the hole of number two red, as Becky released another dolphin-like squeal.

Monique hiked her fists to her hips as the dealer clicked two more black chips on top of her pile. "Oh, for goodness sake."

Judy seized her arm. "Cash out, Monie."

"How's a girl supposed to lose money in this place?"

"Pull the chips," Judy insisted. "Just take them off the board."

"I mean, what are the odds? Twice in a freakin' row."

"I think," Becky said, "that the odds are about—"

"Pull them now," Judy interrupted. "Take your winnings and be done."

"It's Lenny, Monique." Becky nervously tugged a lock of her hair, blown out in shiny, blond perfection. "He's trying to tell you something."

Monique's gaze shot up to the rafters of the casino. The gleam in her hazel eyes turned bright and sharp.

"He wanted you to be crazy with money, right?" Becky said. "So he's just sending you more."

Judy shot daggers at Becky, but Becky's gaze lay on the piles of chips, one kid's worth of orthodontic bills. Judy had no illusions about the money; Monique *would* lose this money because, well, that's what you did at casinos. It was just a matter of time. Becky was only throwing gasoline on the fire by mentioning the possibility of Lenny's heavenly intervention.

Then Judy heard the scrape of tokens against the baize and saw Monique push all the tokens right smack in the middle of red. Judy couldn't watch. She turned her back.

Four thousand dollars on red. A murmuring began all around them, as the crowd started to take notice.

"You hearing me now, big boy?" Monique stood with her arms crossed, eyeballing the dome of the ceiling as she tapped one foot.

"Rien ne va plus."

The long clatter of the wheel. The release of the ball, the thud as it bounced around in the depression, rebounding off the edges of the holes, cast into the sides, and veering with a spin across the numbers. Becky turned away and seized Judy's arm. Judy slapped her own hand over it, acutely aware of Becky's uneven breathing. Judy *wanted* Monique to lose. Losing four thousand dollars at the boule table might be cathartic, and the only way this widow would finally stop being so angry at her dead husband.

The ball did a few short, lazy bounces along the edge of the slowing wheel until it sank, finally, into a hole.

Monique's gasp was full of frustration.

"You're having a drink." Judy took a seat at the linen-covered table and waved for a waiter. "I don't care if you're still hung over from last night. We've all had a shock. Unless you want to pick your own poison, I'm ordering the best bottle of Chasselas they've got."

Monique collapsed like a bundle of bones into the chair. Becky guided herself around the other side of the table and then sank into the opposite seat. Theirs was one of sixty tables arranged in front of a tiny stage where Judy presumed the Swiss folklore show would begin once they'd ordered their appetizers. The room was quiet enough that Judy could still hear the ringing of slot machines in the casino.

When wine and food was ordered Judy dug into her purse and tossed the tokens worth eight thousand bucks in the middle of the table. The little plastic disks rolled amid the wine and water glasses, bounced off the crystal salt and pepper shakers, and collapsed in a random pattern around a bowl of water with three floating candles.

Becky made a small, choking sound. "They look like oversize game pieces for tiddlywinks."

Judy snorted. "My boys would use them for drinking games."

Judy had rescued the tokens from the baize, taking advantage of Monique's shock to toss them in her purse. She'd dragged both her friends away from the casino as if she were staging an intervention for gambling addicts. By the time Monique caught sight of the exit, she dug in her heels to protest, but Judy had been ready with an excuse. They were nearly late for their dinner reservations. She'd be damned if she'd miss a dancing Heidi in the opening act.

At least Judy didn't have to feel guilty anymore for her initial folly of pulling Monique's chips off nine red.

"When we go back," Monique said darkly, "I'm putting them on nine red, and this time you're not going to stop me, Judy. Let's see if Lenny could pull that one out."

Becky sputtered, "Then we'll be dealing with sixty-four thousand. We'd have to hire an armed guard back to the hotel."

Judy slid the stem of the wineglass between the tips of her fingers. "We're not going back to the casino."

"Oh yes, we are." Monique splayed a hand toward the center of the table. "I have to see how long these last, remember?"

"And I thought you didn't want to do Lenny's bucket list anymore."

"I was perfectly willing to salt my scrambled eggs with the ashes of that list this morning." She jabbed a finger at each of them. "You were the ones who dragged me here."

"You came here on your own four-inch stilettos, Monie."

"I never liked casinos. They give me the creeps." She looked skyward and raised her voice a notch. "There are other ways to cut loose, Lenny. You could have tried just *communicating* with me. We used to be pretty good at that."

"It's done." Judy fortified herself with another gulp of white wine. "Just check the item off the list."

"That'd be lying."

"He told you to see how long a thousand bucks could last in a casino. Here's the answer: It can last just about as long as you please."

"Fine." Monique kicked her chair out and slouched against the back. "Consider item number seven checked."

Judy frowned at Monique's flippancy, but she let the comment pass. Seven items on Lenny's list were done. There were five more to go and six more days of vacation. The list was no longer physically impossible.

Monique's forehead puckered as she glared at the chips. "Now I have to figure out what to do with all this."

"Oh, honey," Judy sputtered, "be creative."

"I'm serious. I was supposed to lose this."

"I'm sure Becky and I can help you figure out how to spend eight grand."

Monique stilled. A strange expression passed across her face. She eased up from her slouch and then leaned forward. With quick fingers she started flicking the tokens to one side or another, making two piles.

Judy's breath caught as she figured out what her friend was doing. "I was kidding, Monie." She seized one of the chips that threatened to slide off the table. "That's *your* money—"

"Unearned."

"—and you should consider it a return for what you've spent on me and Becky. Or think of it as a dozen plane tickets to California for when Kiera goes to UCLA."

Monique shoved one pile toward Becky and the second pile toward Judy. "If I can't lose this money in this casino then I'm giving it to each of you."

Four thousand bucks in Swiss tokens now teetered on the table next to her bread plate.

Becky's thin chest rose and fell. "Monie, I can't possibly—"

"It's play money." Monique waved a dismissive hand toward the ceiling. "And it's all from Lenny, not me. I don't want a damn penny of it. Pay for Brian's hockey gear. Buy Brianna a piano. If I'm going to 'lose' money, I want to 'lose' it to my friends." Monique closed her hand over Becky's wrist. "Take it, Beck. You'll be doing me an enormous favor."

Monique gave Becky an encouraging smile while Becky softly shook her head. Judy looked at the chips pooled by her plate, thinking about a different vacation, a different set of wailing girls, a different sort of chaos.

"What about you, Judy?" Monique settled back in her chair. She looked like she'd just shrugged off a hundred pounds of solid rock. "Plenty of money there to shack up with Bob on the Adriatic coast, if that's what you've got in mind."

Judy's thoughts leapfrogged from one possibility to another. She thought about Lenny's list, and how important it was for Monique to finish it with less stubbornness and more joy. She thought about Becky's impending blindness, the aching load of troubles awaiting the young mother at home. And she thought about her own volcanic yearning for adventure—adventure that could only be seized while she was still far, far away from her empty nest.

The tokens glittered on the table before her. Play money, Monique had called it.

Judy closed her fingers over the pile. Then she thought about the craziest thing a woman in midlife crisis could do with four thousand bucks.

∞ chapter sixteen

As a young girl, sketching thistledown fairies under a maple tree, Becky used to dream that the speck crossing the sky wasn't an airplane ferrying luckier girls to cities like Minneapolis, where she had lived before her father's fatal accident. No, no, it was something far different. Any moment it would careen out of the blue, swoop down, and materialize into something that would take her away from the teeth-aching loneliness of her rural life—a magic carpet, curved and oriental and rimmed with golden tassels.

Now, pressing her head against a soft leather headrest, Becky revised her image. Her mature magic carpet looked a hell of a lot like a Porsche 911 Carrera 4S Cabriolet.

"Can you hear that?" Becky felt soft vibrations through the leather of the passenger seat. "This car actually purrs."

"I hardly need to touch the gas pedal," Monique said, "and it just zooms."

The magic carpet was Judy's idea. She'd pulled up to the hotel this morning with the rental agent in tow to fetch Monique and her international driver's license out of bed.

The car was jewel blue, a little ragtop bonbon of engineering that could rev up to 185 miles per hour in less than five seconds. The seats were custom upholstered in creamy white leather, the steering wheel radiated its own warmth, and the rental cost as much in tokens as Monique had pushed over to Judy at last night's dinner.

Later, Becky thought, when she could get Judy aside for a private conversation, she would offer up her own half of Monique's winnings to split the cost. That money felt like a stash of druid gold found buried in the corner of a garden, magical in a way that was not meant to be spent on orthodontics or hockey equipment, but rather laid upon fairy mounds as tribute, pierced and worn around the neck as a talisman, or paid to a crone to redact a curse. And right now this magic carpet was sweeping her away from care and worry in a way that left her breathless and a little stunned.

"Wave to Lichtenstein, ladies." Judy sprawled sideways on the narrow backseat of the car, eating from a bag of Zweifel Pomy paprika chips perched on her abdomen. "The map says it's about twenty miles that way."

Monique waved distractedly. "Do you see how this car is handling these curves? When I get home my minivan's going to feel like a Big Wheel."

They'd just passed through the border checkpoint between Switzerland and Austria at St. Margrethen/Höchst, on their way to Munich. It was a four-and-a-half-hour drive from Interlaken. With every mile they drove it was getting easier for Becky to allow her troubles at home to grow smaller and smaller in the rearview mirror.

"So much better than the trains." Judy lifted a peppered

chip for emphasis. "No nauseous swaying back and forth, no annoying tourists, no sticky gum on the seats, no rattle of train wheels—"

"Hey," Becky said, "train travel is romantic."

"You like the smelly toilets, too?"

"Of course not."

"The crackle of unintelligible vital instructions over 1950s-era sound systems?"

"That happened once, on the milk run to Brussels."

"The molded plastic seats not wide enough to accommodate a certain middle-aged woman's well-rounded ass?"

Becky turned against the seat so she could eye Judy in a space meant for packages from Gucci and Henri Bendel rather than a healthy woman from Jersey. "Hey, how's that backseat working out for you?"

"I'm lolling on the finest leather. My shoes are kicked off. And if we want, we can change destinations on a whim." Judy took a crisp bite of a chip for emphasis and then talked around the crumbs. "Hey Monique, let's go off road and get completely lost."

Monique's grin could have lit up a room. "You're the devil."

"We could head off to St. Petersburg. Spend some time in Moscow. Let the rental company come looking for us on the steppes."

Becky's mind flooded with images of the striped soft-serve domes of St. Basil's Cathedral in Moscow's Red Square.

Monique said, "Two words restrain me: Grand larceny. Oh, and the fact that Kiera may object if I spend the next ten years in a Swiss prison."

"Are you sure of that?" Becky asked. "Last time I eavesdropped she was barely on texting terms with you."

The sidelong glance Monique sent her was secretively gleeful. "Three texts yesterday, all in a row."

Judy's bark of laughter filled the inside of the car. "I told you that all she needed was time."

"Mind, they were petulant texts, scolding in her Kiera way, but I still take that as a step forward." Monique checked the road in the rearview mirror. "How long have we been driving now, ladies?"

Becky flicked her wrist to look at her watch face. "An hour and a half?"

"So you're saying that, for an hour and a half, I've been sitting in the driver's seat of a Porsche, tooling through Switzerland, and now Austria, around the southern point of Lake Constance." Monique ran her fingers over the stack of controls. "That's an awful long time for this to be a hallucination, or some residual effect of the absinthe."

"Oh, honey," Judy murmured, "it's four thousand dollars of real."

"I feel so odd. I feel like I'm *watching* myself drive."

"This half-blind woman is looking directly at you," Becky said, "and you do appear to be actually driving."

But Becky knew what Monique felt like, all the same. She'd spent half her youth with her head in the clouds. After her father died, her mother moved them back to the farm in western Minnesota, a place where the nearest neighbor was a mile and a half down the road. That neighbor was Milly Hanson, and she'd been collecting Social Security for two decades. With no close neighbor kids and a school filled with oversize corn-fed farm boys and ruddy-cheeked mean girls who'd laughed at her sketches, it had been easier to just live in her drawings amid the bee-hum glade of a woodland cottage.

"You know," Judy said, "the Germans have an expression for that sensation of detachment, that sense of seeing yourself doing something even while you're doing it."

Monique snorted, "So it's not just the ventilated seats?"

Judy said something in German, a swift, effortless, and guttural sound. "Literally, it means you feel like you're walking beside yourself."

"I'd have to be walking darn fast to keep up with this baby." Monique reached for the radio dial. "But I get it. Right now I am more tuned in than this bad German pop station. In fact, I'm going to give that feeling my own special name. It's called *Porsche*. As in I'm feeling really Porsche right now."

"I'll have a shot of Porsche," Becky added.

"Honey," Judy added, "let's go upstairs and Porsche."

Becky exchanged an amused glance with Monique.

"What?" Judy exclaimed. "Am I wrong? It's just incredible, the way this engine rolls and growls. It's just like sex."

"Clearly my ovaries are dead." Monique made an abrupt, humorless laugh. "Or maybe I just don't remember sex."

"Sure you do. All this vibrating and purring and yielding skin." Judy released a long, satisfied sigh. "I need to get me one of these when we get stateside."

"No way," Becky said. "Sports cars are the answer to a man's midlife crisis. You were jonesing for an Italian lover, if memory serves."

"What the hell would I do with an Italian lover when I've got Bob the Mormon Stallion at home?"

Becky chuckled along with Monique and Judy because it was expected, but then her breath hitched and a shudder went through her as if the Porsche had rattled over a pothole. Sex was something she used to have with Marco, before mortgages and motherhood settled a whole world of worries in bed alongside them. What they'd been having furtively between bath and bedtime these past years, well...it wasn't the revving excitement or the purring vibrations she felt riding along in this Porsche.

Becky pressed her head against the window as an excuse to hide her face. Judy hummed in the backseat to bad electro-pop music as Monique wove the car through the lines at the German checkpoint at Lindau. Becky tried not to feel guilty as she willed her troubles to recede again, to diminish in the side mirror like the checkpoint booth as they passed through. The past couple of days had been a crazy-sweet interlude, a gentle loosening of the knot that had tightened in her gut over too many years.

She tried to rustle up a good memory to distract her again, and ironically the first one that popped in her head had everything to do with Marco. She'd been young and working as a pastry chef in the little kitchen of a ritzy restaurant, daring to gaze across the stainless steel worktables where Marco labored as a sous-chef. It was an electric shock to glance up and meet his brown eyes through a haze of steam. She remembered her nervous expectation in the late hours, after the kitchen had been cleaned up, when the staff gathered to have a beer or a glass of wine to unwind before heading back home. She'd finish her wine, sling her bag across her back, and pause a moment hoping that fine Italian prince with the long-shoreman's shoulders would finally offer to walk her to the subway. So many nights he'd look at her, just look, as she bantered with the Mexican dishwashers. So many nights he'd duck his head and focus on peeling the label off his beer.

One particular day she'd been exhausted, her lower back aching, her feet sore. But when Marco muscled up the courage to offer to walk her out, the jolt of adrenaline had erased all weariness. The January cold bit her cheeks as they stepped out onto the New York streets. The heat of his knuckles brushed against hers as he moved close to let some partiers pass them by. His skin felt rough, as if crystals of sea salt still clung to the backs of his fingers. She tensed as they touched, just imagining what those fingers would feel like scraping against the underside of her breast.

The heat that surged to her skin countered the chill on her jean-clad thighs. She knew she was blushing. She hoped he would blame her flush on the cold. They'd barely exchanged words as they walked, just pleasantries about his classes in architecture, the taste of the raspberry sauce she drizzled over cheesecake, murmuring little nothings that covered up what they both were thinking.

What they both were hoping for.

He broke first. He just stepped in front of her. Those broad shoulders blocked out the world. He thrust his fingers in her hair, and she stumbled two steps backward. The bricks of a storefront dug into her back. His eyes, inches from hers, were bright with wanting. The juniper-berry taste of his breath.

The whole city could have gone up in flames and she wouldn't have moved an inch.

Yeah, she remembered great sex. That was the magic carpet that had finally swept her away to a castle in the suburbs and to the birth of her strong little elf and her bright little fairy. Judy was absolutely wrong. Sex like that was a hundred thousand times better than rolling down a European highway in a Porsche.

Zooooooom

Becky jerked away from the window. A car reeled out from her peripheral vision and shot past so fast that she barely registered the color. It sped ahead a few car lengths and then zipped in front of them.

Monique said, "Looks like we're not the only ones with hot cars on this road."

Becky pressed her hand against her sternum to keep her heart in her chest. "Tell me that you saw him long before I did."

"He's been looming larger and larger in the rearview mirror for a while now. Nice wheels." Monique grinned. "Not as nice as ours, though."

"It's a sign." Judy straightened up and put the bag of chips on the floor before leaning between the seats to squint at the road signs. "We must be on an autobahn."

Monique nodded. "Practically every major highway in Germany is an autobahn, Judy."

"I always thought the autobahn was one road." Becky

stretched out her toes against the dark flooring. "You know, like one wide straight road through the heart of Germany, where all the rich guys with their fancy cars burned up fuel by speeding from Frankfurt to Berlin. Like a go-cart track for yahoos."

"The guy who passed us wasn't tooling around at"—Judy peaked over the steering wheel and squinted at the smaller print on the odometer—"a mere sixty miles per hour."

Monique said, "He was a crazy driver."

"Then it's time to join him. What do you say, Monie? Ready to check another item off the list?"

"Down, girl. We only just entered Germany."

"Are we on an autobahn?"

"Yeah."

"Are we in a hot sports car?"

"Uh-huh."

"Then give me one good reason why you're not blowing our hair back going one hundred miles an hour?"

"Speed limit." Monique gestured behind her. "Back there at the checkpoint. There was a speed limit sign for sixty kilometers per hour."

"Which feels like ten miles an hour," Judy said.

"It's about forty miles an hour, which I'm now surpassing. And not all German autobahns allow you to go as fast as you want, you know."

"Monique, see that sign?" Judy pointed toward the side of the road. "The blank white circle with the diagonal black line?"

Becky, temporarily blinded by the glare, saw nothing more than a white blur as they passed quickly on by.

"I'll tell you what it means," Judy said as Monique didn't answer. "It's the universal sign for 'no speed limit.'"

"And you know that because...?"

"I read German. Punch it, Monique."

Monique's knuckles tightened on the wheel. "Too many cars. Can't do it now."

"It's wide open up ahead."

"You really are the devil."

"Rumor has it that this baby can do a hundred and eighty miles an hour."

"I'm *not* doing a hundred and eighty!"

"How 'bout a hundred and fifty then?"

"No way!"

"One twenty?"

"Lenny said—"

"Oh, so we're back to a literal interpretation, are we?"

Monique's answer was a sharp glance in the rearview mirror then a hard press on the gas. The car engine revved and the Porsche thrust forward, throwing Becky back against the passenger seat. The vehicle ate up the asphalt. Becky tugged her seat belt until she felt the comfort of resistance. She looked straight ahead, where her vision was most sharp, and saw a gray ribbon of road, the car that had sped past them long out of sight.

"Come on, floor it." Judy leaned back and clicked her seat belt on. "We're not a bunch of soccer moms, are we?"

"I am!" Becky gasped as they zoomed past an Audi on their right. "Clearly we're not on some rural back road any-more."

"Somewhere," Judy said, raising her voice a little over

the rising pitch of the engine, "Audrey's braking foot is twitching."

"And Gina's," Becky added, "is pressing harder on the floor."

Monique made a strangled little laugh. "We're going eighty-five."

Becky glanced at the speedometer, the needle straining to the right. "My minivan would be shaking in protest by now."

Monique pressed even harder on the gas. She shifted gears, and the car lunged. Becky had the odd sensation that it moved faster than they did, that the car itself was trying to zoom out from under their seats. They approached an underpass only to zip through it. She'd hardly registered the pass of the shadow before they were zipping under a second, shooting by cars in other lanes at a rate that made the palms of her hands tingle.

Monique's voice was high and tight. "Ninety!"

"That BMW we passed," Judy said, "isn't that it up ahead?"

Monique's voice was a warning. "Judy, this isn't a race—"

"You're not going to let some weenie in a BMW," Judy said, "beat our sweet little Porsche, are you?"

Monique made a little grunt and pressed even harder on the gas. They were flying over these gentle hills, riding the rim of the curves that sent her body leaning to the left and to the right. The car's purring matured into growling, the power beneath them a palpable thing.

Then suddenly she was laughing. The effort stretched her face muscles in a way that felt achy, unfamiliar. Judy whooped and Monique squealed and Becky surrendered to the hilarity, even as some small voice in the back of her mind whispered, *this is a fairy tale, and all fairy tales end.*

She waved the little voice away.

Right now she was laughing.

Right now she was happy.

Becky leaned against the window of the Porsche as Monique navigated through the streets of Munich in search of their hotel. The neighborhood they passed through smelled sour-sweet, of hops and fermentation. In the back Judy took a long, dramatic breath and exclaimed it smelled like Okto-berfest.

Becky nestled further into the soft leather. She couldn't help but compare this large, industrial city to the little me-dieval town of Landsberg am Lech that they'd all visited an hour ago. They'd opted for a pit stop to stretch their legs and indulge in a late-afternoon snack to hold them over until the feast they'd be digging into tonight, under one of Munich's Oktoberfest tents. It had been like stum-bling through a forest and coming upon a German fairy-tale town. The place was full of charming towers—the Bayentor with its crenellated roof and artful brickwork corners, and the fanciful Mutterturm with its conical green caps—both of which she'd sketched. Ludwig Street boasted colorful four-story stone buildings cheek by jowl, topped with steep-pitched red roofs. She and the girls had lingered longer than they'd intended. They bought a gelato from a riverside ven-dor and watched the swans swim in the turquoise water like three little Gretels drugged by magic candy.

Judy stopped humming long enough to glance out the window. "I think those are the Oktoberfest tents back there," she said, gesturing down a street. "Are we close to the hotel, Monique? It'd be nice to just walk to them."

"Once we made the decision to come here," Monique said, "I made a point of choosing a hotel as close as possible to the Weisn."

Judy said, "And you got one at this late date?"

"Lucky I guess."

"Lord, you must have paid a fortune for it."

"Not really. It's nicer than the one I'd reserved before. In the original itinerary we were supposed to be in Munich days ago, and *that* room was hard to find and expensive. But someone must have cancelled because I found this one on the first try. Becky, keep your eyes open for Parkstrasse."

Becky blinked rapidly as the twilight washed the world to gray. "Judy and I should switch places. I can't help you anymore."

"Wait—there's the street." Monique hit the signal and glanced over her shoulder to change lanes. "We're just a few blocks away now. That road we just passed was my marker, to tell me that I'm close."

"Monique," Judy murmured, "are you sure this place isn't a dump?"

"We're arriving in Munich in a Porsche. You think I'm parking this thing on the street in front of some rent-by-the-hour hotel?"

"But there shouldn't be a decent bed available in a sixty-mile radius."

Monique shrugged. "It got good reviews."

"It's Oktoberfest. Everyone leaves here soused or hung-over but happy."

"There it is." Monique headed farther down Gollier-strasse. "The big red building with the sign."

Judy's head popped between the seats, and her eyes widened. "Hotel Ludwig?"

"Yup."

"Well I'll be damned."

Monique pulled the purring vehicle to a stop in front of the building. "We've got the four-bedroom apartment too. One bedroom more than we need."

Becky snorted, "Not if we can get Judy an Italian."

A valet approached the car, and reflected in his eyes Becky saw a feverish appreciation for the jewel-blue confection that they'd just parked. She stepped out of the vehicle feeling like a high roller, when in reality she had a desk full of bills, no income, and a six-year-old minivan approaching one hundred thousand miles waiting at home.

Monique came around and tossed the keys to the valet with breezy, grinning aplomb. Falling into step behind her— it was starting to go from twilight to dark—Becky followed Monique through the glass doors of the hotel while Judy came up from behind. Judy put her German to good use instructing the valet to unload the trunk. No doubt he'd be baffled when he saw their battered, worn, decidedly non-designer luggage.

The hotel lobby was a well-lit modern place. A sparse collection of blond wood chairs clustered around a low table by the front window. Monique approached the desk but Judy physically stopped her and walked on ahead, speaking in confident German to the woman at registration.

Monique turned to Becky with a conspiratorial roll of her eyes. "You know she's going to be like this when she gets home too."

"Bossing everyone around? Swearing at will? Renting little sports cars?"

"Poor Bob."

"I wouldn't pity him too much." Becky eyed her friend, now leaning across the registration desk. "She seems so happy these last few days. So much happier than when she was back home, obsessively mowing her lawn."

"Oh, lord. My lawn. I forgot to arrange for someone to mow it." Monique let her eyes flutter shut for a moment. "You know what? I don't want to think about going home right now."

"I hear you."

"I don't know if it's the Porsche or something else. But I haven't done anything this crazy in years. I haven't had this much *fun* in years."

Becky was about to tell her that it felt like they'd stepped through some portal into another world. A world where the sun always shone and troubles fluttered away and, with a wave of a magic wand, bills disappeared, princes never left you, and disease would never touch your children. Judy's cry of surprise interrupted her.

Judy gaped at the woman at the registration desk, who rumbled an explanation, her open palms suggesting a state of affairs outside her official ability to remedy. Judy slapped her hands on her head. Then she swiveled on one heel and joined them by the chairs.

"Well," Judy said, "you're not going to believe this."

Monique said, "They bobbled our reservation?"

"Oh, no, we've still got the four-person apartment. But now I know *how* we got it."

"My epic skills in navigating online registration forms, of course."

Judy shook her head. "It's October third."

Becky said, "Is that some kind of German national holiday or something?"

"This year, it's the official closing day for Oktoberfest."

Monique leaned into Judy. "You mean *opening* day."

"At noon today," Judy said, "the riflemen fired their gun salute on the stairs of the Bavarian monument, and that was it."

"But it's not 'Septemberfest,'" Becky said. "It's Oktoberfest."

"Which apparently begins in September." Judy waved her arm in the general direction of the city. "All afternoon they've been closing down the tents. The whole city is in extended-hangover mode. I think the woman at the registration desk is still drunk."

An odd light gleamed in Monique's eyes. "Well, there it is. I guess I can't check Oktoberfest off Lenny's list."

Judy's head shot up. "You absolutely *can* check this off Lenny's list. It's still Oktoberfest until midnight."

"Technically." Her eyes narrowed. "I suppose."

"Technically and in spirit," Becky countered. "Tonight we'll take a walk to where the tents were and, in Lenny's honor, we'll spill some microbrewery Bavarian beer."

"No roasted duck," Judy lamented. "No dumplings. No pastry at the Café Kaiserschmarrn tent. We came here in a Porsche. We came for Oktoberfest. I want to dance with drunken Germans in lederhosen!"

The words echoed through the room. An elderly woman passing through the lobby stopped in her tracks. The worker at the registration desk shot them a glare. A crowd of college-age men, shuffling through the front door, winced at the noise then tugged their coats closer as they headed toward the elevator.

Judy slapped a hand over her mouth. "I can't believe that I just yelled that."

"You said it in English," Becky said.

"Most Germans speak English!"

Monique snickered. "Then everyone knows you're macking for men in lederhosen. And I thought you had a thing for Italians."

"I don't know, Monie," Becky said, "do you think we can distract her with a few drunken Austrians?"

"It has worked before."

"Stop!"

Becky struggled to control herself. For Judy's sake she really did try to choke down the laughter. She tried so hard that tears squeezed out the corners of her eyes. She glimpsed Monique's face contorted with the effort. Only when Judy's laughter spilled out between her fingers did Becky allow the hilarity to overcome her for the second time that day.

She thought of Brianna's Tickle Me Elmo that giggled with one press of his hand. With a second press, the doll's laughter rumbled, just as Becky's had in the Porsche that afternoon. But a third press set Elmo vibrating in the kind of convulsive glee Becky witnessed in Brianna sometimes, when the girl was exhausted at dinner and Brian started monkeying around and shoving peas in his nostrils. It was a whole-body seizure, a roiling hilarity that set shoulders shaking and made her fling her head back to gasp in air.

That's what seized the three of them now, as they bent over in the lobby. Becky gripped Monique's shoulder as a stitch clutched her ribs. Each time Becky tried to straighten up, she would catch Monique's laughing brown eyes, or Judy's arcing gray ones, and the laughter would seize her all over again.

She knew she would remember this moment. It'd be branded in her mind more than the castles she'd seen in Germany or the food she'd eaten in Paris or the jewel-blue Porsche she'd traveled in. This memory sizzled with the same intensity of the midnight kiss from Marco, of Brianna red-faced with laughter nearly tumbling off her chair.

Joy had felt for so long like something snatched away, a magic ring stolen, now forbidden and undeserved.

If she could only find a way to bring it home.

chapter seventeen

"Judy," Monique said, gesturing to the ugly, rock-like lump rolling in her friend's hand. "I hate mushrooms."

"It's a white truffle." Judy lifted her palm into the Italian sunlight. "Does this look like one of those dirty lumps you buy at the local grocery store?"

"A truffle is a fungus, and funguses are grown in piles of manure."

"These aren't grown in manure. They're routed out by specially trained pigs or dogs or something."

"Ooh, yum. Fungus *and* dog spit."

"And when they're fresh, they retail for two thousand bucks a pound." Judy shaved off a little piece of the thing with the edge of her Swiss Army knife. "They're harvested between September and December so right now they're prime and in season. How can you say no?"

"If I'm going to have a truffle, it'll be the chocolate kind."

"Philistine."

Monique folded her arms. "Do you guys know what a virulent fungus does when it attacks the human body?"

"Stop projecting your fears on this succulent *trifola d'Alba*."

"In any language, it's still a moldy tumorous growth."

"That's like saying a Porsche is just a car." Judy nudged one slice aside with the tip of her knife and then cut off another. In the shade of the stone wall Judy offered a piece to Becky. "How 'bout you, Beck. You feeling adventuresome?"

Becky seized it. "I'm so in."

Monique watched as Judy slipped the sliver onto her tongue. To Monique the truffle—and all the mushrooms piled on the little cart nearby—smelled vaguely pungent, like old cheese and musky moss. The scent threatened to turn her stomach, but not Judy's apparently. Judy's eyes fluttered closed. As she chewed she lifted the shriveled, ill-formed thing to her nose. Her nostrils flared as she breathed in the scent.

"Tonight I'm having pasta with truffle butter," Judy said. "Two servings at least."

Becky held out her hand for another bite. "We're staying here for dinner, yes?"

Monique shrugged. "We'll stay the night if you want." She was sure they served more than just truffle pasta in the little restaurants around the square. "I saw a sign for a pensione down that side street."

"Thank goodness we didn't start this trip in Italy." Becky popped the thing in her mouth. "You'd need a forklift to pry me away from here."

Monique let her gaze pass across the town, a pastry sweet of a medieval village perched on the height of a hill. They'd spent yesterday morning visiting the castle at Neuschwanstein, the afternoon at a late lunch in Innsbruck in Austria, and they'd crashed at night in a pensione outside

Verona. Lenny's list had them attending the wine and truffle festival in Alba, but as they traveled through northern Italy, Monique knew she and the girls wouldn't make it that far west. Especially when the little town of Neive loomed into sight.

They'd all glanced at one another. Sure, the truffle festival at Alba had donkey races and locals in medieval costume, truffle-seeking forays and live music...but this little village amid the barbaresco vineyards was nearly free of tourists and full of cheese and wine shops, quiet and seemingly unexplored.

They hadn't exchanged a word. They drove into town and found a parking spot near the top of the hill where, between streets and buildings, there lay a breathtaking view of the surrounding vineyards.

Becky said suddenly, "Is that your phone ringing, Judy?"

Judy probed her belly pack as the sound repeated. "Nope, not mine."

Monique realized that the ringing was coming from her pack. She fumbled it off her shoulder and pulled out her cell phone. "It's Kiera." Monique panicked when she saw notifications for six texts, but as she scanned the contents she relaxed. She did a quick calculation of the difference in time zones. "I guess she's awake now. She must have finally seen the photos from Neuschwanstein I texted her yesterday."

"You've got time to answer them," Judy said, flicking her wrist to look at the face of her watch. "The wine tour at La Contea doesn't start for about an hour."

"Can we wander back to that little cheese shop?" Stepping out of the shadow into the sunlight, Becky squinted in the vague direction of one of the narrow streets. "Wasn't it down there somewhere? I want to buy some of that jam made out of grape must. It smelled so good."

"*Cugnà,*" Judy murmured, wrapping her two remaining truffles back up into the paper.

Becky raised a brow at Judy. "You speak Italian now?"

"No, no, I just liked the word. It stuck in my head." She gave a little shrug. "You know, if you start serving that up with toast for breakfast, Brian and Brianna may never eat Welch's again."

"The Swiss chocolate is for them," Becky said. "The jam is for me."

"Well, this lactose-intolerant woman is going to skip the visit to the cheese shop." Monique waved the cell phone. "I'm going to find a place to sit and catch up on these. Text me when the wine tour is about to start, and I'll meet you at the entrance to the cave."

Monique waved as they headed down the hill to a building with a bell tower. She swiveled on a heel and headed in the opposite direction, up to the top of the hill to a plaza she'd noticed when she'd parked the Porsche. Around the side of a building, a stone terrace jutted over the edge of the hillside. She took a seat on the bench against the wall. The seat warmed her thighs and the gritty stone tugged the fibers of her yoga pants. Through a gap in two lower buildings there lay a crazed staircase of red roofs, and beyond, a stretch of combed fields.

She flipped through Kiera's text messages.

Mrs. Lorenzini must have loved this castle. It'll make a great cake.

LOL, Mom, nice hair in this shot should I make an appointment for you at Bangz when you get home?

Grand-mère told me to text you hello and that she hopes you're enjoying yourself. Like it's not obvious.

I bought some clothes at the mall so don't freak if you see the charges on your credit card.

BTW, we finally won a race against Livingston.

Mom . . . when are you coming home?

Reading the last text, Monique felt a quiver of motherly instinct. Kiera could find out the flight information in a flash. The itinerary was pinned on the bulletin board in the kitchen. Clearly her daughter craved something more than her estimated time of arrival, and Monique didn't have to think long about what that might be. Kiera needed reassurance that her mother missed her, that she'd come back soon, and that when she did everything would be exactly the same.

Monique curled both her hands over the cell phone, wishing she could text a full-bodied hug to her daughter. Kiera was such a creature of feeling and sensitivity, still struggling to muddle everything all out like every teenager who'd ever lived. Her daughter probably didn't even see the irony in her yearning for her mother to return, when it was Kiera herself who was truly planning to leave. For the past four years Monique had made Herculean efforts to reassure her that she would always be around. This vacation was the longest the two of them had ever been apart. And now she held in her hand Kiera's plea, uncertain and subtly alarmed, a tremor of growing realization.

Mom might not always be there.

She set her thumbs to the keypad. *Not long now, sweetie.*

I'm taking the red-eye on Friday. Miss you terribly. Can't wait to see you.

She hit send and slid the phone on the bench beside her. She gazed over the stretch of the vineyards, admiring the blush of russet on the fields and a touch of gold here and there. She heard the noise that the text had slipped into the ether. Slipping her sunglasses on top of her head, she raised her face to the sunlight.

Did I do wrong, Lenny? Loving Kiera as fiercely as I do? Loving you as strongly as I still do, holding on to you even now?

In the breeze Monique felt a disturbance in the air, a subtle shimmering of light and sound. The feathery ripple interrupted the chatter of the Italian shopkeeper around the corner of the building. The subtle disruption put a tremor in the high steady whine of a small Italian car laboring to climb up the hillside from below.

She stilled, softly reaching for the wisp of his presence. Lenny had always wanted to come to Italy. He would have loved the slow, bone-seeping warmth of this place. He'd have loved the mossy smell of the streets, the shops with cured meats hanging in the windows, the pungent cheeses in boxes of straw, the bottles of ruby-red wine. He'd have eaten egg tagliatelle, scarfing down the noodles tossed in butter and covered with truffle shavings. He'd have tried the wild boar stew she saw advertised as a specialty of one restaurant, a robust meat in a peppery marinade. This trip to an Italian wine and truffle festival wasn't one of the mysterious little breadcrumb-clues Becky claimed Lenny had sprinkled in that bucket list, mysterious messages from beyond. Of all the things Lenny had talked her into adding to his list, this trip to northern Italy was one she could say without question that Lenny would have enjoyed wholeheartedly.

She willed him closer, aching for the moment he'd settle his big body on this stone bench, when he would finally speak to her in that voice she loved, about the dinner they would have eaten, the wine they would have drunk, the vineyard they would have toured, the drive they would have taken. He'd speak to her of Kiera's growing confidence, of Kiera's college plans, of the wonderful life they would all have lived together.

He was near. She was sure of it.

She missed him so much on this trip.

Finally he would come.

Monique did not know how much time had passed, sitting on the bench with her head leaning against the sun-warmed stones, waiting for that electric charge in the space where Lenny should be. It could have been minutes. It could have been hours. She knew her face had gone wet, because a breeze slipped up the hillside and made the tracks on her cheeks cold.

Then a shadow crossed beyond her eyelids.

She blinked her eyes open. Judy came around beside her. Becky followed more slowly in her wake.

"I see why you ignored your phone." Judy settled on the bench. "This view is breathtaking."

Monique lunged for her cell phone lying on the bench just before Becky, with her peripheral vision issues, threatened to sit right down on it.

Monique fumbled with her phone. "Did you call?"

"Judy texted twice," Becky said. "But who knows about the cell service here? You probably didn't receive them."

Monique looked at the screen and saw that she had two missed texts. Texts she hadn't even heard, though the phone ring was set on high.

"I must have dozed." She tried to force her voice back to normal. "I suppose I missed the winery tour."

"There's going to be another one in English in an hour," Becky said. "We changed our tickets. We didn't want to do it without you."

Monique canted forward to slip the phone into her daypack by her feet and hide the stupid trail of tears that still clung to her cheeks. She tried to wipe them off with the back of one hand while she rifled needlessly in her daypack with the other. She took a deep gulp of air—air somehow cooler and thinner than before—and then squared her shoulders and straightened back up.

"You know, Monie, I've been meaning to ask you a question," Judy said. "It's about something weird that happened last May."

"Last May?"

"I was making sausage and peppers for dinner," Judy continued. "I'd forgotten to pick up some onions at the grocery store. So I came over to see if you had one to spare."

Monique frowned. "Judy, you do this every time Maddy comes home. I buy extras just for you."

"Your front door was open so I let myself in. I was about to call out, but then I heard you talking to someone."

Monique felt a painful little prickling at the back of her neck.

"I knew it wasn't Kiera," Judy said. "Kiera was upstairs. I heard her singing, really loudly. You were in the kitchen with your back to me, running a soapy sponge over a saucepan. You were talking in a low voice, like someone was in the room with you. I put my head around the door but there was no one there. No one I could see anyway."

The prickling intensified and invaded her throat. She couldn't move. She couldn't look at either of them. She felt the shame of it radiating. She stared at the path of moss in the mortar between the paving stones, feeling like a thirteen-year-old whose diary had just been read over the school loudspeaker.

And she became aware, in slow degrees, of a ribbon of collusion between the women flanking her. Maybe it was the way they were both canted back on the bench, still as stone. They weren't picking threads from the seams of their well-worn jeans or idly examining their ragged cuticles or closing their eyes and lifting their chins to the sun. Even their feet were equally still, balanced tensely on the heels of their sneakers.

Monique cocked her head a fraction toward Becky. "You knew this, too, didn't you?"

Becky laced her fingers around one raised knee. "Two summers ago I fetched Brianna and Brian off your swing set, long after dark. The kitchen window was open and you were laughing out loud. I hadn't heard you laugh in so long, Monie. I was so happy for you. I wondered what Kiera had said that made you laugh like that. That's when I realized you weren't talking to Kiera."

"Neither one of us blames you," Judy said. "God knows if something happened to Bob, I'd still be complaining to him that he never makes the bed."

Monique swallowed the lump growing in her throat and pressed back against the stone wall. The rough edge of the mortar snagged in her loosening braids. She was a nurse; she was supposed to understand grief. A nurse saw grief up close on a regular basis. She'd seen it the very week before she'd come here, in the eyes of a young mother and father as she handed over the carefully swaddled body of their twenty-five-week infant—heart-size and far too young to live despite how hard everyone at the NICU had tried. There was no getting used to the distorted faces of the anguished parents. They pressed their hands against their mouths and bit their knuckles as if they could physically hold in the pain.

But four years ago, in that little room with Lenny dying in that bed, she hadn't been the nurse who always sees grief up close. She'd just been Monique, the wife of a burly Louisianan who'd charmed her into his wonderful life. And she'd learned that this is what grieving people did long after they'd buried their loved ones: They pretended they were okay. They went through the motions of living as if their hearts didn't lie dead in their chests. In secret they spoke to the ones they loved as if they were still living and breathing.

But no one wanted to hear the truth. So she'd hid it from everyone—her daughter, her neighbors, her mother, her co-workers, her best friends. What the world wanted to hear was that she'd started "moving forward," or that she was at least working hard to "come out of it," that she was definitely "moving on." So she'd hidden from the world her urge to bite the back of her hand to keep in the words she couldn't bear to speak.

Now the truth pierced her like a needle. "You were right, Beck, about all that stuff you said on the cliff. I talk to Lenny now because I couldn't really talk to him while he was dying."

Monique remembered each time she'd pushed the chair away from the hospital bed in their den in order to fetch Lenny some pureed lentil soup or set the water to boil for chamomile tea or to check on Kiera. She remembered making a grim joke when he brought up the subject of funeral arrangements, chuckling as she waved the whole subject away. How many times had she done that? How many times had she walked briskly out on a weakening Lenny, who asked her to hold on a minute while raising his hand from the sheets?

"You know he's still talking to you, Monie," Becky said.

"No." Her breath came in short fearful sips. She knew the truth now, sitting on this Italian hillside. "He's stopped talking to me altogether."

"Well that's a relief," Judy said. "Otherwise we'd have to call in a priest."

Monique shook her head. Judy just didn't understand. Lenny would never again come and sit on the mattress behind her, or materialize out of the corner of her eye to lounge in his chair in the kitchen, reading a newspaper with her rhinestone reading glasses perched on the end of his nose. She knew this deep down. The wisp of presence she'd sensed in this beautiful place was like the scent of incense lingering in a church long after the parishioners had gone.

"What I meant," Becky explained, leaning into her, "is that Lenny is still talking to you through the bucket list."

Damn the day she'd ever pulled that bucket list out of the drawer. "You guys are calling me out on talking to my dead husband, and yet here you are treating that list like it's a mystic code to be broken."

"It's not much of a code," Becky said. "We've talked about this. The first half is what you gave up, and the second half is what he wants you to do. If you just thought about it for a moment, you'd see it too. You already figured out for yourself what he was trying to tell you with the gambling."

"He wants me to throw my money to the wind," Monique said. "Is that a lesson I'm supposed to embrace in my late forties with a kid about to go to college?"

"He specified the exact amount," Judy said. "The man gave you a *budget*."

Monique frowned.

"There's also a truffle festival on that list." Judy crossed her legs at the ankles and massaged her swollen knee. "And we all know how much you love truffles."

Monique shook her head sharply. "You're forgetting the details. The Alba festival is a wine and truffle festival. Mama likes the red."

"There are plenty of wine festivals this time of year," Judy argued, "but he's urging you to go to a festival for a fungus that you just don't eat."

"It's warm in Italy." Monique held up her palms as if

to pool the sunlight in her hands. "Lenny loved the warm weather. He smothered himself in sweaters come October in New Jersey."

Sweaters that still filled his closet. A closet that she opened on rare occasions, slipping inside and closing it behind her, to breathe deeply of what little scent was left in the woolen fibers.

"If he just wanted someplace warm," Judy countered, "I could have recommended a couple of fine Greek isles."

"It's sort of the same with the motorcycles," Becky said in a tense little voice. "Lenny wanted you to try something new, something you once wanted to do."

"Beck, he called motorcycle owners 'organ donors.'"

Judy snorted. "He knew you wouldn't do anything so crazy as to risk your life—even driving a hundred miles an hour on a German autobahn."

"He didn't supply the Porsche."

"The car wasn't the point. The point was to make you, Miss-I-never-drive-without-a-seat-belt-on, take a risk and do something crazy."

Monique raised a brow. "Like hooking up with Austrian bikers and drinking absinthe?"

Judy pointed a finger toward the sky. "You don't think he's up there, laughing his ass off about that?"

Monique paused. She squeezed her eyes shut. "I can't do this."

"Do what?"

"Speculate."

"It isn't speculating."

"It is. You and Becky are just making this up, reading

Tarot cards, consulting oracles, putting words in Lenny's mouth."

"Like *'laissez les bon temps rouler,'* for example?" Judy asked. "Think about it. This trip to Italy and the visit to Oktoberfest—they're both festivals. What better way to urge you to take some time off to eat well, drink heartily, and enjoy what the world has to offer?"

Monique's jaw began to hurt. "Let's change the subject."

"Not yet," Judy said. "Our last stop is tomorrow in Milan. Remind me again what the final two items on the list are."

Monique played with the sleeves of her hoodie, her mind leapfrogging in its attempts to shut this whole conversation down. "We're visiting the marble monuments at the Cimitero Monumentale di Milano."

Judy murmured, "Ah."

Monique resisted the urge to glare. "So, wise oracle, what do you think Lenny meant by sending me to some Milanese cemetery? It wouldn't be something as simple as admiring the tombs carved by Leonardo da Vinci, would it?"

Becky leaned over, sharing a glance with Judy. "It is rather Dickensian."

Judy shrugged. "Nobody said Lenny was subtle. And sometimes a person needs three ghosts to face the truth."

Monique looked from one to the other. "Are you two really saying I'm supposed to act like Scrooge and finally face my own mortality?"

"No," Becky said. "You're supposed to face *his*."

Becky held Monique's gaze. In the silence Monique noticed that Becky's focus was off just a bit. Maybe it had always been like this. Maybe Monique was just noticing because her mind had gone still and her perception razor-sharp. Becky was looking at her like newborns did, intense on the fuzzy brink between light and dark.

Monique supposed she'd been straddling that fuzzy edge too, for way too long. She'd grown comfortable in a hazy in-between place where Lenny still lived in her mind, a place where she could visit whenever she needed him. She wondered how Lenny knew that she would behave like this. She wondered why Lenny thought—just by sending her to some cemetery far away from the one she'd buried him in—that she would then just let him go.

In the silence Judy dug around in her belly pack and then rustled open a stained and tattered piece of paper. "Yeah, that's it for the list," Judy said. "First it's the cemetery in Milan, and then we're off to see *The Last Supper.*"

Monique fixed her gaze on the staircases of red roofs. She didn't have to think too hard about the meaning of that final item. It glared at her now, a one-hundred-watt incandescent bulb, but she sure as hell didn't catch the significance of it while she'd been taking care of him. She'd been so absorbed making sure he had enough morphine to stave off the pain but not so much to cause his skin to itch or his worst imaginings to rise. So worried about Kiera and how the twelve-year-old was handling the slow wasting away of her father in the den. So worried about tracking the comings and goings of the hospice nurse and the home health aide, so worried about keeping the house together and monitoring what was going on in the hospital where she worked reduced hours.

Maybe all that time he was just trying to urge her to treat

every meal with him like a last supper. Maybe he was just trying to say a proper, and final, good-bye.

Monique gazed over the far vineyards, the rows abutting at oblique angles. She heard the scrape of a shopkeeper's broom on the stones around the other side of the building. She heard wind rustle the leaves of the tree canted at an angle off the mountain. She heard Judy rifling around again in her belly pack and the sound of a knife slicing through something soft.

Judy raised between two fingers a sliver of a white truffle so thinly shaved that it was almost translucent.

Monique narrowed her eyes. "You're kidding me, right?"

"Dead serious."

"Unless that's a magic mushroom it isn't going to make me just accept everything you guys are saying."

"It'll be a step in the right direction."

"I hate you, you know."

Judy smiled softly. "I hate you too."

Then Monique opened her mouth wide. Judy laid the truffle on her tongue like a communion wafer. Monique forced down the rise of bile as the taste burst in her mouth—oddly fragrant and musky but not entirely disgusting. She closed her lips over it and attempted to chew. Becky's arms came around behind her, and Judy leaned forward and hugged her so she was surrounded, encircled, engulfed.

Then, while the oddly fragrant taste lingered in her mouth, Monique remembered that there was one more item on Lenny's list. One more task, beyond the trip to Milan, far more daring than taking a small bite of a warty little truffle. It had been scrawled on the bottom of the original list in a script so spidery it was nearly illegible. Lenny had added it in the last week he was alive, when the cancer had sapped all but the faintest spark of vitality. She'd read it later, tugging the list out from under his limp hands. She'd assumed he hadn't really meant it. In that last week his attention span had shortened along with his ability to maintain the logic of a conversation.

This last task was too crazy to believe.

She was sure of this: It was the morphine that had prompted him to add number thirteen.

chapter eighteen

Judy walked into the refectory of the church of Santa Maria delle Grazie with twenty-four other tourists who'd just been ushered in through a pair of climate-controlled doors to view the famous Leonardo da Vinci mural, *The Last Supper*. They approached the fresco, painted on the end wall, with a communal air of awe. The mural itself was thirty feet long and about fifteen feet tall, far bigger than Judy had ever expected, and the size had an impact that no photograph in any art history book could match.

Becky whispered, "My art teacher would talk about this fresco and his eyes would roll to the back of his head."

Judy murmured, "Clearly he needed to get out more often."

Becky ignored Judy's comment, all hungry eyes. "It's just been through so much. Da Vinci painted it on dry plaster and then sealed it in an odd way. It's been deteriorating since the fifteenth century. They cut a door out of the wall and chopped off Jesus's feet. And in World War II the refectory was bombed."

"Wow. How long has it been since you took Art History?"

"My professor would ramble on about all the references to the number three. The Apostles are grouped in threes. There are three windows in the background."

"Good things come in threes."

"I wish there were more light in here." Becky expelled a frustrated sigh. "I've never seen a real da Vinci up close."

"They bricked up the windows to try to stave off the deterioration."

"Good for you, Judy," Becky said with a smile. "You read the placards."

Judy let the comment lie. She knew about these boarded-up windows not from the placards in the little antechamber, but from listening to the guide nearby lecturing in a low voice to a group of fifteen or so tourists. She'd noticed the professorial-looking man as he'd stepped off a bus outside the church. He was dressed tweedy and he hustled his elderly Italian troops to hurry along to make their scheduled tour time. She understood his haste. She, Becky, and Monique had parked the Porsche in the street to make the tour time that Monique had scheduled back in the States. Only twenty-five people were allowed in the refectory at any given time. Monique had read that casual last-minute arrivals were frequently disappointed, even in the deadest winter of tourist season. This was one part of the itinerary they hadn't dared to amend.

That lecturer, once he'd hustled his people into the antechamber, had barely taken a breath between sentences as he discussed all aspects of the church and the mural in a rich, rolling Italian. Judy had first discovered in Neive that the Italian language was very much like French. She understood a good portion of what he was saying just by parsing out rhythms and recognizing word roots.

She leaned toward Monique to make a remark about the latest restoration but the words died on her tongue. Monique faced the painting, but though her body was present her brooding mind was elsewhere.

Judy wished she could come up with some wise-woman strategy to make her friend feel better. Her stock of emotion-management tricks were useless in the face of Monique's newly unfiltered grief. Judy just couldn't put herself in Monique's shoes. Imagining Bob gone was impossible, like trying to imagine a world without light.

En route to this church they'd done a swift drive-by through the Milanese cemetery, waving at the lovely marble monuments while Judy tried to figure out from the map where Eva Peron and Giuseppe Verdi had once been buried. Monique hadn't seemed interested in that. She was captured by the mourning angels and aboveground monuments and the weeping trees. She told them that the cemetery reminded her of one particular Louisiana bayou plot that held the bulk of Lenny's ancestors, full of elaborate crypts grown over with swamp plants and dripping Spanish moss.

Wise Lenny, if not so very subtle, Judy thought. What Lenny couldn't know was that Monique had buried him beneath a tombstone with a stone angel, close to a willow tree, exactly because the spot reminded Monie of the Reed crypt. Recognizing the parallels, Judy had watched her friend closely, saw the way she looked around the cemetery, saw strong Monie, her dear friend, finally accept her terrible loss.

A bell rang, startling them all. Fifteen minutes was all

they were allowed in the refectory. The guards strode in and herded them toward the door. The rate at which the tour guide spoke accelerated as he and his group, as well as she, Monique, and a stumbling, reluctant Becky were urged toward the exit. Judy lingered as long as she could, looking at the figures at that table and the feast spread out before them, and the man in the middle who knew he was going to die the very next day.

"Speaking of last suppers," Judy said, as they tumbled blinking into the little stone-paved plaza outside the brick church. "I've been looking into where we should eat tonight."

Becky clutched her stomach. "I'm still digesting last night's white truffle risotto."

"Shut up, skinny. There's a famous place called Ibiza, but it's loud and full of fashion celebrities."

Becky shook her head. "Sounds like a headache."

"I agree. That's why I'm thinking we should go to La Latteria. It's tiny, and it used to be a creamery. It's a little off the path, and we can't make reservations, but it's run by real locals who cook real Milanese food."

Judy and Becky glanced at Monique, waiting for her to make a decision. "I'm sorry," Monique said. "What did you ask?"

"Dinner. At a little local place called La Latteria."

"Okay." She gave herself a little shake. "We'll go after we've returned the Porsche to the rental place and checked into our hotel."

Judy was relieved to find the Porsche exactly where they'd parked it, squeezed between a battered Citroën and a tiny

Fiat. She tumbled into the backseat and Monique settled into the driver's seat again. But once settled with her seat belt snapped Monique didn't turn the car on. She paused with her hands on the wheel, staring through the bug-splattered windshield toward the Milanese traffic.

Monique said, "Do you know what got me most about that mural?"

"Oh, where to begin?" Becky melted in artistic ecstasy against the seat. "We were in the presence of an ancient masterpiece. The flawless composition, the use of symbolism, even the distribution of bread and wine on the table was—"

"The expressions on their faces," Monique interrupted. "Each one of them showed a different emotion in a different way. I knew this mural would be amazing, but I wonder if Lenny knew that it would be so . . ."

Monique struggled to find the right word and Judy sensed that there was more to her hesitation than a lapse in vocabulary. Standing in front of *The Last Supper* today Monique's mission—however bittersweet—was finally at an end.

Judy leaned forward between the seats and placed a hand on Monique's shoulder. "Lenny knew what he was taking you to see, Monie. He wanted you to see a well-loved man among his friends, saying one last good-bye."

"Oh, baby, I am going to miss you the most."

Judy ran her fingers over the sweet curves of the Porsche, leaving trails in the fine dust that coated the hood. She and Becky stood sentinel by the sports car, parked in an illegal zone outside the Eurocar rental terminal at the train station. Monique had gone inside to hand in the keys and finish all the paperwork. Their luggage—much added-to since they'd given up the strict itinerary in Interlaken—now stood bulging on the sidewalk, shopping bags slung on the retractable handles and threatening to tip them over.

"You're a sad case." Becky, with her face raised to the Milanese sunlight, gave Judy a squinted eye. "Even a blind woman can see how much you're lusting after that car."

"It's *bellissimo*."

"So shallow. I must warn Bob."

"This is a fine-tuned instrument of absolute freedom."

"Oh, lord."

"This is my Italian lover, and I can't bear to let him go."

Judy traced the length of the car with one finger, from the signature bulge of the headlights, over the rising slope of the windshield, past the strong mesh of the ragtop, down the opposite slope to the rear brake lights. She traced it not caring about the soot that dug under her fingernail or the mark it left in the patina of dust. She wished she could carve her initials in the metal casing. *Judy* ♥ *Porsche*. Then she'd feel like she left something of herself behind with it, maybe the part of herself that Becky was scorning—the crazy, light-hearted, utterly uninhibited woman who'd been born the moment she'd slung her leg over the seat of an Austrian biker's motorcycle.

She wanted to bring this woman back home, but the thought made the tendons at the back of her knees go liquid. She could rationalize the feeling away as due to the long hours spent scrunched in a backseat designed for tiny pure-bred dogs, but that would be an abject lie. She was terrified of what this creature would do once she returned home. She didn't want to morph into one of those postmenopausal women who sought adventure in young lovers or six-cylinder engines. She didn't want to be one of those desperate middle-agers dieting to emaciation and having their faces remodeled in a mockery of youth. Youth was gone. She didn't really want it back.

But the woman she was bringing home to Bob was a fierce newborn thing, emerging from the space between what she'd left behind and what she'd desperately hoped to find: A fresh stage of life, a new and fulfilling purpose. That purpose—whatever the hell it would be—still eluded her. Until she found it this woman returning from Europe with a sense of adventure and lack of impulse control might so easily become a fool.

Monique came up beside her, a sudden shadow. "We're all set. We can catch a train here at the station to bring us back to the hotel."

No one made any move toward the station. They all stood admiring the dusty little car as the working people of Milan milled around them. They stood there, staring, and Judy could feel the perfect alignment of their thoughts.

Monique mumbled, "Tell me it's just a car."

"It's just a car," Becky said, giving it a little pat on the hood, like a mother burping a child. "Just a silly car."

Judy blurted, "We have to do this every year."

Becky laughed. "Rent a Porsche?"

"No, I mean this trip. Maybe not for two weeks. Maybe not with the Porsche. But some time away from our regular lives—we must do it again."

"Judy." Becky sighed. "I have two young kids, a husband on work furlough, and a stepdaughter in college."

Judy wanted to urge her to take the money Monique had given her—the money Judy had refused to take to share the cost of the Porsche—and put it away for next year's adventure. But then she remembered the cost of braces, tutoring, soccer fees, and hockey equipment, and she kept her mouth shut.

But Monique would be an empty-nester next year with Kiera off to college. Monique would be gainfully employed with accumulated vacation time closing in on three full months. Monique would wander foreign roads with her, where folks spoke German and French and Italian and all the food was cooked by others.

"I'm sorry, Judy," Monique said, answering the unasked question. "My heart could not bear another trip like this, not for a while anyway."

An attendant in a shirt sporting the rental company logo jogged his way past them to the Porsche. The familiar keys rattled in his hand. The young man—purebred Italian in the scruffy-jawed, finely shouldered, sexy-eyed mode—gave all of them an amused look as he pulled the door open and slipped into the driver's seat.

Judy thought of the memories as the attendant turned over the ignition. She thought of the hours and hours on the road listening to bad European pop, the bags of paprika chips and overpriced bottles of mineral water they'd shared. She remembered the discussions they'd had about their stubborn, fascinating, brilliant teenagers, about life and men and sex, in the way of women of a certain maturity who respected frankness and wisdom above all. All cocooned in a womb of soft leather while the vehicle hummed around them.

"All right, ladies," Monique said. "Say good-bye."

Becky mewed a soft good-bye, but the word stuck in Judy's throat. She could not raise it to her tongue. She'd been too long in foreign countries. Good-bye was not the right word. It was too casual, like *ciao*. It was too general of feeling, like *auf Wiedersehen*. Good-byes like that could mean you'd be reunited tomorrow, or at the next class, or the next year. Good-bye could mean I'll see you later, or I'll never see you again. The French at least had some distinction. They could say *à bientôt*, I'll see you later; *tout a l'heure*, I'll see you soon; *à la prochaine*, until next time. In English good-bye was used so broadly that it turned all farewells into a casual, meaningless flick of the hand.

The speakers of Romance tongues—French, Spanish, Italian—they understood final partings. They knew there were beginnings, and then there were ends.

Adieu, adios, addio.

Judy raised her hand as the Porsche pulled out of the parking area, revving as the attendant screeched into the street.

She could not say good-bye.

So she blew the car a kiss.

chapter nineteen

The sweeping marble staircase in the Milano Centrale train station seemed a little over the top for grandiosity, even for the Italians. But Becky couldn't help but admire the national dedication to art as she perused the mosaics of winged trains, the bas-relief of a horse-fish, and a standing sculpture of a cherubic boy. She craned her neck to gape at the high ceiling, the magnitude as impressive as any church she'd visited throughout Europe.

But as she reached the center of the main hall, Becky stopped short. Monique muttered something unintelligible and continued to walk ahead of her, but Becky stayed fixed, staring down the corridor that opened on one side of the building. There a soaring iron-and-glass canopy covered a train platform, allowing sunshine to pour in through black crosshatch supports.

Judy clattered up beside her, as one wheel of her luggage had gone wonky. "Looks a little like Gare Saint-Lazare in Paris. Or at least how Monet painted it."

"It's the ironwork."

Becky's fingers itched for a pencil. This dawn-of-the-twentieth-century type of architecture was not something that usually inspired her, but now she found herself wondering how many pages were left in her sketchbook. Her eye followed the pattern of the wrought iron, her gaze enveloped the scale of the room—vast and full of murmur and whisper and whistle and the screech of metal. The opening of the platform at the far end was a glare of Italian sunshine where the train tracks disappeared into a blast of white light.

"Judy," Becky murmured, "where'd Monique go?"

"She's trying to figure out where the Metro is. Apparently these upper floors don't service all the local stations."

With a *thunk*, Becky dropped her backpack to the marble floor. "While we're waiting, I'm going to get a quick sketch."

"Go for it. Our time is our own now that Monique has crossed the last thing off her list." Judy wearily perched herself on the edge of her standing luggage, sinking her elbows onto her knees and her chin onto her hands. "I'd like to spend the next hour or so soaking in a really hot bubble bath—but that's a pipe dream. Even if they have tubs, European hotels still haven't grasped the definition of *hot*."

Becky closed her fingers around the spiral top and yanked the sketchbook out of her pack. Poking around she found a pencil with a bit of a point, and then settling down cross-legged she flipped the sketchbook to an empty page. With quick strokes she sketched the perspective, then set to work on the crosshatching, trying to take in the full scale, squinting a bit to try to focus more carefully on the metal detail, realizing as she did that somehow—during the weeks since she'd received the RP diagnosis and became more aware of her weak peripheral vision—she'd unconsciously adapted to that weakness by bobbing and weaving her head in order to take in the most detail with the center ring of good vision she still had.

As she settled in on the ironwork detail of the canopy, the memory of a certain evening with Marco drifted through her mind. It was the early days then, long before marriage, long before money troubles and Gina troubles dampened the fires. They'd spent the weekend in a sexual haze, giddily besotted, lolling in the loft of her sixth-floor walk-up, an apartment she shared with another art student. In one moment of postcoital bliss he joked that her low-ceilinged, two-room apartment was very *La Bohème,* with its slanted rooftop glass. It had once been a skylight, he'd surmised, before some enterprising owner had lowered the high ceiling of the fifth floor in order to produce the sixth-floor apartment for either maidservants or starving artists like herself.

She'd placed her bed under that skylight. The dawn served as her alarm clock, convenient for the job she'd taken after she'd left the restaurant, baking chocolate croissants and boysenberry scones at a little bakery nearby. With his hands tracing lines in the air Marco had gestured through her window to an office building under construction a few streets away. Lazing in her bed with her head on his broad shoulders, she'd run her fingers across the muscles of his chest as his magical hands made graceful swirls in the air, describing the balance of forces on the lattice-like steelwork.

Now she glanced at the graphite crosshatching she'd sketched and knew why she'd felt the uncontrollable urge to reproduce it on paper.

Marco would love this place.

Her pencil point trembled above the paper. Fear was a seeping cold that came up through the marble floor and bled through her skin to the marrow of her bones. She'd tried very hard not to think about the fact that in twenty-four hours she'd be on her way home. Back to the not-so-imaginary moat that surrounded her crooked little castle, so broad and deep and dangerously unsurpassable that it may as well be full of alligators.

"Okay," Monique said, her footsteps sharp and sure as she approached in full I'll-take-charge mode. "Remember when we said it was weird that the trains were on the second floor?"

Judy jerked out of what must have been a doze. "Yeah?"

"Well, it *is* weird." Monique brandished a map of some sort, frowning as she shook it smooth. "Any train we caught up here would take us to Zurich or Vienna or Budapest."

"Zurich would be good." Becky leaned over the paper and concentrated on finishing the pattern. "I'd take Vienna."

"Look, Monie, we've made a vagabond of her."

"Well, vagabonds walk," Monique muttered, "and the city Metro is underground, and from what I can tell from this map, we've got a hell of a maze to navigate."

"Pack it up, Beck." Judy pressed her hands on her lower back and stretched. "There's a shower and a featherbed calling."

"They've got featherbeds in Budapest." Becky ducked further over her sketchbook. "Young, strong porters too."

"Tempting." Judy's face crumpled in concentration. "Very tempting."

"Stop, both of you. If I don't show up at Newark Airport

the day after tomorrow, Kiera will jump on a plane and drag me back by a fistful of braids."

Becky reluctantly flipped the pad shut and shoved it and the pencil back into her backpack. She straightened up and glanced dreamily at the bullet-nose train just pulling out of the station as Judy readjusted the weight of the shopping bags hanging off the handle of her rolling baggage. With a sigh Becky fell into line behind Monique.

They wound their way through the sea of other travelers, dipping and lacing through the crowds so thick at the stairs. Monique walked ahead of her and Judy behind, a tandem configuration that had sometime during the vacation be-come their default. Down they went, bumping their suit-cases over the stairs, bags crinkling as they jostled. Becky glanced up occasionally to catch sight of the swinging Smurf keychain hanging off the back of Monique's pack and then down again so she could make sure there was no crack in the marble floors that could catch the edge of her sneaker, no placard outside a boutique whose slender brace would trip her up, no errant bag or piece of luggage or dropped umbrella across the path. As they descended into the Metro, where the lack of light in the tunnels washed her sight to gray, she lifted her arm to trail her fingers against the cold wall tiles, feeling the bump of the edges, the rough grout, and the occasional lump whose provenance she preferred not to consider.

"Hold up." Monique buried her head in the folds of the map. Becky stopped abruptly so as not to careen into her. "I think we go left here."

Monique cut across the tunnel. Becky pressed away from

the wall to follow Monique but she was so focused on the bouncing Smurf that she didn't notice that Monique's luggage didn't lurch with the same speed. Becky's toe caught on the underside. She plunged forward—but Judy stepped up, absorbing her weight, cutting off what would have been a complete header.

Judy held firm as Becky suffered a hot surge of embarrassment.

"Are you sure this is the right direction, Monie?" Judy peered over Monique's shoulder. "Here it says to take the right tunnel to the M2—"

"But we don't want the green line." Monique squinted closer at the map. "We want the yellow line, the M3."

"I feel like a hamster in one of Audrey's middle-school science fairs. I thought the green line was the M3."

"Nope, that's the M2." Monique traced something on the paper. "We're taking the yellow line, south, toward San Donato station."

"Left it is, then." Judy settled back on her heels once Becky regained her composure. With a flick of her fingers, Judy tilted Becky's luggage upright when it threatened to tumble. "My doggies are barking. There better be seats on the platform."

Monique surged forward and Becky stepped into her wake, more carefully now. Judy slipped behind her. The heat of embarrassment ebbed into a different kind of warmth, a wave of gratitude that made the back of her eyes prickle. She blinked it away. Her sight was bad enough in this dim light. She didn't need tears blurring what little vision she could muster.

They arrived at the entrance to the platform just in time to hear the ding of doors closing. A train sporting a yellow stripe pulled out of the station. "That was our train," Monique said, as they moved into the light. "But it shouldn't be long before the next one comes."

Judy blurted, "Bench."

Judy made a beeline past a busker who sang something vaguely Eastern European to the distinctly Milanese breed of well-heeled commuters gathered on the platform. Becky followed. Judy settled on the bench with an exhalation not unlike the breath of a train coming to a complete stop. Becky collapsed next to her as Monique sprawled on her other side, drawing her luggage in close.

Judy nudged Becky with her shoulder. "Gosh, that girl looks a lot like Brianna, doesn't she, Beck?"

Becky followed Judy's gaze and saw a young woman standing amid a cluster of people near the platform. The dark-haired girl looked to be about college age, and she was surrounded by younger kids twirling and dancing about. With a flip of her hair the young woman chatted with a woman who must, by the resemblance, be her mother. Nearby stood a short, barrel-chested man who Becky surmised was her father.

"I thought I was the blind one in this group," Becky said. "That girl has about ten years on Brianna."

"Are you talking about that young woman with the yellow scarf?" Monique glanced at the family. "I was thinking the same thing when we walked in. It's the hair, I think. It's thick and wild and the same shade as Brianna's."

"Well you guys certainly have an idealized image of my

daughter at eighteen." Becky let her gaze travel over the girl's chic hip-length tailored coat and the casual curl of a buttery yellow scarf under her chin. "I suspect Brianna's look will veer more toward ripped jeans, work boots, and heavy-metal T-shirts."

Judy barked a laugh. "Don't make Gina your measure for all teenagers."

Becky grunted. "Twenty bucks says that, when Brianna's fourteen, she'll chop off all that heroine hair and gel it into a Mohawk."

"None of my kids have tattoos," Judy said, "and despite a few instances of drunken rebellion and one perpetual student, they're all studying or gainfully employed."

"Your kids aren't real," Becky said. "You had them manufactured in a factory in your basement."

"Gee, Judy, you should have told me," Monique said. "I'd have ordered a few of those custom-made types myself."

"Don't you go complaining, oh mother of a genius." Judy reached over to give Monique a playful slap on the thigh. "And as for Brianna, I've got a prediction. Yeah, Brianna might be the ripped-jeans type, but she'll wear lace stockings underneath. She may overdo it with the eyeliner, but she'll prefer buying her clothes at the thrift store. In her messenger bag she'll be toting an oversize spiral notebook full of acid-free paper, full of drawings of dragons and gnomes, of elfish castles and hard-faced warrior-kings. Off to play Dungeons and Dragons—"

"Skyrim," Becky corrected. "Join the twenty-first century, Judy."

"—then, sooner than you'll hope, she'll find some floppy-haired artistic boyfriend with his jeans slung low on his hips."

"Oh, lord," Becky exclaimed, "are you trying to make me crazy?"

Monique said, "You lost me at the floppy-haired boy-friend too."

Becky glanced over at the young woman, now rocking her mother in a hug. "Maybe it's good that I'll be blind. Maybe it's good that I'll never see the nose rings or the neck tattoo or the raccoon eyes. In my head Brian and Brianna will always have the faces of my sweet, if occasionally irascible, young children."

"Wow," Judy said. "You had to really dig for that silver lining."

Becky shrugged. "Hey, I won't have to contend with the wise-ass expressions or the rolling of the eyes."

Monique made a scoffing noise. "Maybe you should go deaf too, Beck, so you can dodge the snark and the sass."

Judy tilted her head. "Hey, does going blind mean that you'll always see me as a sprightly fifty-something and not the fat old lady I'm bound to become?"

"For twenty years," Becky said, "you've eaten Oreos every afternoon at three. You'll never be fat. But yeah, I suppose I'll always see you just the way you are right now."

"Oh, honey, I'm spending the rest of my life with you."

They laughed as light streaked on the curve of the wall and a rumbling began down the tunnel. Monique leaned forward as the front of the train came into view and showed itself to be the M2, not the M3 that they were waiting for.

A collection of shouts drew their attention back to the

young brunette. The mother dabbed at her eyes with a tissue as her father gave the girl a hug. The kids jumped and wriggled and wrapped themselves around the young woman's legs. A torrent of Italian fell from the mother's mouth, and though Becky couldn't make out a word of it, she recognized the universal, desperate, last-minute instructions of a mother to a child. The young woman nodded and nodded and backed up into the train, bumping her luggage over the space between door and platform, and then lifted her hand as the tone rang and the doors slipped closed.

Judy made a noise, a hitching, wheezed breath. "That's the worst. That wave."

"If Kiera cries when I send her off to Los Angeles," Monique said darkly, "I will lose it. I'll drag her right off the plane."

"No, you won't," Judy said. "You'll let her go, because that's what we do. We birth them and feed them and raise them and give them hell, and when it's time we just let them go."

Becky watched as the train whistled and lurched forward, moving with increasing speed into the tunnel while the family waved until the back lights of their daughter's car disappeared into the darkness. The weight in her chest swelled and rose up and threatened to block her throat.

That's what we do. We just let them go.

Becky sank her elbows onto her thighs. So much of life had already gone. Not just her own eyesight, dimming every moment, no way to grasp it and stop it from fading, no way to hold it tight. Not just her marriage, cracked and withering, bits of it falling apart. Her friends had lost so much too.

Judy struggled to say good-bye to her active motherhood. Monique, to her much-loved husband.

She heard her own tense voice. "We're always losing something, aren't we? We're always saying good-bye."

Monique made an odd, strangled sound. Judy mumbled *no, no, no* but Becky hardly heard the words. The rattling of the train faded down the tunnel. The busker playing the accordion paused in his singing as a hush fell over the platform, bereft now but for a small cluster of commuters, quiet and still and sad in the way of absence.

In that silence Becky sat wedged between her two friends as her mind turned, inevitably, to the troubles at home— to all those things she had not yet lost. Once again fear threatened to smother the flicker of joy she'd nurtured since Munich. She wanted to hold that joy inside her and carry it back home. She knew the only way to do that was to find a way to renew her relationship with Gina and take the first halting steps to repair what was left of her marriage. Such an impossible quest.

Maybe she wasn't meant to do it alone.

Becky reached over and took Judy's hand. "I'm sorry for being such a pain during this trip."

Judy raised her brows. "What's brought this on?"

"A stumble in the tunnels maybe. And a glimpse into the future."

"Well, honey, don't worry about it. I've seen a hell of a lot worse."

"I've been as self-absorbed and moody as any teenager."

Monique snorted. "Welcome to the club. At least you've got a damn good reason."

"Right." Becky reached over and took Monique's hand too. "Like I'm the first person in the world to get bad news from a doctor."

Monique looked down at their joined hands, her lips curving in a small smile. "It's the first time for you, Becky. And for what it's worth Lenny was pretty self-absorbed and moody when he got the news too. Because of this bucket list you might all think that Lenny was nothing but wisdom and soft laughter, but that really wasn't the case. That man could be one stubborn goat, especially when it was time to take his medicine. That was his way of trying to keep control, I think." Monique gave her a look. "You know, acting fierce and independent, like he didn't need anyone."

Becky shrugged. "He should have just realized he'd never make it through the dark times without a little help from the people he loves."

Becky squeezed those hands tight. Tonight, at dinner, she would tell her friends the ugly truth about Marco and herself. She'd confess to the cracks in the mortar of what she'd always hoped to be the most perfect of castles. She'd clung to pride and her own farm-bred Midwestern independence, when she should have been sharing that all was not sunshine in the house of Lorenzini; when she should have been probing the wisdom of her friends for advice on how to keep this prince close.

They pressed against her so tight that she felt like a tottering column now buttressed on two sides. They nudged her, knocking her gently back and forth, sputtering teasing words. She basked in the singular brightness of the moment, like she'd done while laughing in Munich, abseiling in

Switzerland, and listening to Judy in the Porsche, loudly butchering German pop songs.

Monique was the first to lean away. She grew terribly quiet and still. Becky hesitated, wondering if she should say anything, but Judy gave her a quick shake of the head. Maybe words weren't always necessary. Maybe what was important was presence—to hover always like a ghost in the room, summoned when most needed.

When Monique finally exhaled it was as if the widow were trying to expel every last bit of air out of her lungs. "Oh, lord," she said. "Now I think I'm going to have to do this."

Monique looked uneasily at the two of them. The sound of another train began to rumble down the tunnel.

"I have a confession to make," Monique said. "There is one more item on Lenny's list."

∞ chapter twenty

Fifty miles outside of Milan the Ponte Colossus bridge traversed a steep gorge, its slender, arrow-straight supports shooting five hundred feet up from the crook between the wooded hills. Monique stood by the guardrail in the center of the bridge as the wind howled up from the chasm. An Italian hottie in a blazing orange T-shirt stood in front of her, strapping her into the second harness she'd worn on this European trip.

Abseiling had clearly been a dry run. Monique wondered at what point Lenny's playful list-making changed from being a simple distraction from their troubles into a map of deep purpose. Was it midway through when he'd nudged her into choosing abseiling to prepare her for what he ultimately had in mind? Or had he known from the very beginning the lengths he would have to push her in order to convince her to let him go?

A speeding car zipped by, rattling the portable metal fences that separated the staging area from the active road. Judy stood by the bridge rail, peering into the gulf. The breeze blasted her hair into a fluttering halo as she cast a crazed gaze Monique's way. "Sure you wouldn't rather be shopping at the Via Monte Napoleone?"

Monique shrugged. The harness strap dug into her shoulder. "You've seen one Gucci handbag, you've seen them all."

"Shoes? Ferragamo, Tanino?"

"I've got feet like flippers. They won't carry my wide size."

"They've got great prices on Valentino ready-to-wear—"

"Did you forget that I change diapers for a living?"

Judy sighed and carefully stepped back from the railing. She minced her way across cables and gear to stand by Monique's side. "You know that Lenny was tripping on morphine, right?"

"I used to think that." Monique lifted her arms as her instructor checked the buckles and bolts for tightness. "Now I've changed my mind."

"I know he didn't consult you about this one."

"God, no. I'd have nixed the idea in a heartbeat."

"For the record, I'd totally support you if you decided to shuck that harness and call it a day. Thirteen is a terribly unlucky number."

"You're true-blue, Judy."

"I mean, you're standing here with a cherry-red cable attached to your ankles. You've made your point."

"This from the woman who backpacked across Europe?"

"Young Judy had better knees. And different dreams."

"Middle-aged Judy did shots with a bunch of Austrian bikers."

"A task that didn't require a harness."

"Join me anyway." With her arms still stretched out, Monique glanced toward an awning where Becky was receiving instructions from another coach. "Come and join *us*. We'll be the three crazy Americans, leaping off a bridge."

"Have I mentioned how wonderfully liberating it is to say a firm and unmovable 'no'?"

"You'll never be the same after something like this."

"Dislocated joints and broken vertebrae do tend to change lives."

"Judy—"

"It's not all that safe. You shouldn't listen too closely to the words of adrenaline junkies, even if they have meltingly gorgeous accents and visible six-packs."

"Stop." Monique glanced down at the straps and buckles of her harness. "I'm committed. I'm going to trust Lenny on this."

"Maybe that's the difference between you and me, then. I've already made my leap of faith." Judy's face was ashen and twitchy. She looked like she wanted to ask one of the Italian instructors if she could bum a cigarette. "I made my leap twenty-seven years ago when I gave up my wandering ways, married the stud-muffin that is Bob, and gave birth to the better half of a baseball team. So I'll leave the bungee jumping to you."

The word sent a shiver down Monique's spine that had nothing to do with the nippy breeze. She remembered the description in the Milan guidebook. The Ponte Colossus was a favorite place for adventure travelers. It offered four and a half seconds of free fall into one hundred and fifty-two meters of gorge.

That gorge, zigzagging toward the horizon, was a steep V that ended in a sliver of a rocky stream, the roar of the water audible even over the zip of the cars speeding on the road behind her. The instructor finished his tugging and stepped away, then started explaining in his fluent English about how she should approach the leap. He told her to set her palms together, above her head, in a posture of prayer. He told her to leap out, as if diving into the sky.

Despite her determination, her bladder clenched.

Judy pulled the camera out of her belly pack and checked the settings as the instructor turned to take one more look at the main cable. "At least I can take video. I've always been good at that." She glanced up as Becky skipped their way. "I'll video you too, you loon."

"Awesome." Becky stepped into a harness splayed on the ground and grinned maniacally as the instructor slipped it up her legs. "None of the soccer moms will believe me otherwise."

"Certifiably wacko." Judy clicked the camera on. "And not even liquored up to justify it."

"Are you kidding?" Becky shimmied to better settle the straps over her backside. "This is going to be awesome. For once I'll jump over something knowing I can't stumble into a wall or get hit by anything. Unless there's a sudden flock of birds."

"Great. Death by starlings."

"Judy, you know there will come a time when every step I take could be an ass-over-tit tumble onto concrete, right?"

"That's preventable with a seeing-eye dog," Judy said. "Or a cane. Those beeping things at crosswalks."

"Or your arm." Becky's smile grew slow and warm. "But in the meantime while I still can . . . let me fly."

Monique felt that rush of electricity again, that shimmer of visceral realization she'd experienced yesterday in the train station. Somehow, over these past four years, she'd fallen into the trap of viewing life as a series of achingly painful farewells. Since Lenny's death grieving had become an old habit, like a favorite tattered robe, eagerly sought-out and comfortable and the perfect fit. Rather than accept a life without him, she'd wallowed in memories of breakfast on a lazy Sunday morning amid the smell of hazelnut coffee and banana bread and reminiscences of Lenny's quiet laughter as Kiera beat him in yet another game of checkers.

But there could still be joy without Lenny. This trip had taught her that. She'd discovered it while thrilling to the rush of air over the hood of a Porsche, white-noise background to the hysterical laughter of her friends. She felt it even now, amid the fear gripping her because of what she was about to do.

The instructor stood before her, inviting her toward the three metal steps that led up to the top of the bridge railing. She felt a rush of adrenaline, a hundred thousand pinpricks all at once. She breathed in deep puffs, as she'd been taught in Lamaze.

Lenny had gone to Lamaze with her. He'd sat behind her to support her sore back as they'd all sprawled on mats, bellies forward. The instructor had told all the women in the room to practice Kegel exercises, counting repetitions as the men gazed at the ceiling sheepishly, and no one moved in any visible way.

Promise me, he'd laughed in her ear, *that you'll practice those again tonight.*

A bubble of delight stuttered her breathing. She took the instructor's hand and managed the three stairs. The wind slapped her face. It lifted her unraveling braids and suspended them around her head. Four and a half seconds of free fall, the instructor had told her. Expect a pull on the ankles, and then a yank up, and then a fall again, but much easier, followed by random swinging until she became still enough for the team to inch her down to the folks waiting at the bottom of the gorge.

She seized the top of the padded blue pole that served as a brace, burrowing her fingernails into the plastic. With gentle tugs the instructor adjusted the trailing cord behind her. She dared to look down into the yawning chasm but then she jerked her gaze up before she succumbed to vertigo. She focused instead on the blue sky ahead of her, scudded with puffy clouds.

Becky's voice, above Judy's breathy gasp, "You're all right, Monique. You're where you're supposed to be."

There came a hush around her, like the sound of the ocean heard in a shell pressed against her ear. A great calm settled over her. She didn't feel him really. There was no wisp of his presence on the breeze, no faded echo of his laugh coming from far away, no scent of autumn leaves clinging to the warmth of his fleece.

But there was something here. Something warm and embracing and undefinable and so much bigger than the world itself, something whispering the truth she already knew.

Stop being afraid.

Stop being afraid of risk. Stop being afraid of returning to the things she once loved. Don't be afraid of loving something new. For the world is big and sweeping and wonderful, and it lay sprawled at her feet. She deserved to be happy.

She supposed this is what Lenny had really tried to tell her, those precious last weeks of his life.

"*Pronta, Signora?*"

Her heart started that strange pitter-patter again, the swift, trembling skitter in her chest. She loosened her grip on the padding.

Then she lifted her arms like wings.

∞ chapter twenty-one

A swirling fog obscured the skyline of New York City as the plane approached Newark Airport. With a book open on her lap Monique rolled her shoulders to shift the kinks out of them. The trip back to the States was a twelve-hour odyssey including a two-hour layover in London, and now she felt as if sandpaper lined the inner membrane of her eyelids. After rereading the same paragraph a half dozen times, she finally flipped the book closed.

Over the sound system the pilot mumbled instructions to the stewardesses to prepare for final descent. She buried her chin in the silk scarf wound about her neck, feeling the urgency of the looming home schedule with every queasy drop. Kiera's college applications waited, as did the Monday shift at the NICU. No doubt there'd be groceries to be bought, mail to sort through, laundry to be done, bills to be paid. All of this drummed in her head while her limbic brain continued to experience the euphoric moment she'd hurled herself off the Ponte Colossus to free-fall into that Italian gorge.

Becky elbowed her. "Stop pulling at your hair. There's not going to be a braid left unraveled."

Monique suddenly realized she was staring at the frizzy end of one of her braids. She dropped her hand and mentally added a salon appointment to her unwritten list. "I'll make you a deal. I'll stop tugging my hair if you stop jiggling your leg. You're making the whole seat vibrate."

Becky forcibly stopped. "Did Marco text you yet?"

"The phone is off, Beck."

"I'm an idiot." Little white teeth chewed on a lip, swollen and red. "I shouldn't have told him to bring the kids."

Monique slipped the book into the daypack at her feet and then pushed the battered thing under the seat, remembering that Becky had a boatload of issues waiting for her at home, much more serious than hers. "Beck, right now they're leaping around outside customs, bursting with excitement to see you."

"They shouldn't take a day off from school."

"Why? They might miss show-and-tell or adventures with the letter E?"

"I wasn't thinking straight when I spoke to Marco during the layover." Becky pulled the edges of her cardigan across her chest. "I could tell—he hesitated to agree. He took my suggestion the wrong way."

"Beck," she said tentatively, "don't you think you might be reading too much into a bit of satellite interference?"

"He'll think I want them there as a buffer. You know, like they usually are. Two demanding urchins to focus on so we don't have to deal directly with each another."

Becky no longer jiggled her leg, but a new set of vibrations now shimmered between them. During their last supper in Milan Becky had confessed the trouble that had been growing between her and Marco, trouble that until that moment she and Judy had only guessed at. It was a story of deep disagreements and long silences, of ugly compromises and terribly faulty communication. Despite the painful details Monique was relieved that Becky had finally felt comfortable enough to open up and ask for advice.

Monique could only hope it wasn't too late for the couple. Inwardly she felt helpless in the face of such marital strife. She and Lenny had had fifteen years and they'd never really had anything approaching a fight. If something did come up between them—a disagreement over which couch to buy, or a conflict about whose family they should visit over the holidays, or different points of view over how they should invest their retirement money—Lenny had the knack of defusing it with humor. Nothing had ever seemed so grave to unravel the thickly woven rope of their relationship.

Then she let her mind drift down a road she'd never before considered—an act she'd been doing with increasing frequency in the twenty-odd hours since she'd hurled herself into the Italian abyss. It used to be, when she dreamed of what her life would have been like had Lenny lived, that she'd imagined a more mature version of their younger bliss. But in the face of Becky's troubles Monique conceded that maybe she and Lenny had just been lucky.

Certainly they'd never faced the teen years and the distinctive troubles they bring. Had Lenny seen Kiera in a grass-smeared dress after the junior prom, the black strap of her bra dangling, smelling of cheap beer as she stumbled out of her date's car...well, in the face of Kiera's confessional apologies, Monique had chosen to be lenient...but Monique knew Lenny would not have been. His mother was an alcoholic, an ugly truth everyone in his family let simmer in a Southern hush. Monique knew Kiera's behavior would have pushed him well past the limits of his good nature, and triggered a swift and likely ill-conceived response.

She reached over to take Becky's hand, wondering how far she should venture into the thicket of Lorenzini marital woes. "Honestly, Beck, I think you should just stick to the plan."

"That plan is too simple."

Bombs, bombs, buried on every side. "Sometimes the most complicated situations have the simplest solutions."

"I should have left breadcrumbs."

"Huh?"

"Before Gina came, Marco and I were good together. I should have left breadcrumbs," she explained, "to find the road back."

Words failed her. So Monique did the only thing she could think of: She cradled her friend's hand all through the descent. She was still holding it when the plane landed on the tarmac in a gray fog and taxied toward the gate.

Becky released her only to reach across the aisle and nudge Judy, who'd slept through the flight and the jumpy landing.

Judy sputtered awake. *"Où sommes-nous?"*

"We're home," Becky said, "where we speak English."

Judy shifted higher in the seat and then squinted out into the gloom, past the young British businessman sitting beside her in the window seat (Judy, as they boarded, breathed *thank God he's skinny*). "You know, I dreamed we got rerouted. To Sicily. Or was it Madrid? I can't remember. Gawd I'm still exhausted. What time is it?"

Monique flipped her phone up to check the face. "It's almost one thirty p.m. That's about seven thirty in the morning, Italian time."

"I'm going to sleep for six straight days." Judy stretched her arms above her head. "At least it's raining here. Rain means that I don't have to mow the lawn."

The plane finally reached the gate. Travelers began unbuckling their seat belts, standing up, reaching for the overhead bins. Monique gathered her luggage and wiggled out of her seat behind Becky, then headed down the aisle, over the ramp, and into the airport. They followed signs to the baggage carousel where they looked for the fine designer suitcase Judy had bought in Milan to carry all their purchases. The lines for customs were blessedly thin in the middle of the afternoon, and, in spite of the rather random and thorough inspection of her luggage with its bag full of dirty underwear, they were soon walking out into a reception area of the international airport.

Bob saw them first. He raised his hand and waved it wide. Judy darted from her side and made a beeline to her husband. The place was swarming with people so Monique curled her hand around Becky's elbow to guide her—but then she heard the familiar shrieks of two young children. Knee-high out of the chaos, Brianna and Brian bulleted toward them, throwing themselves against their mother. With a grunt Becky dropped to their level, seized them close, and then tried to take in everything they were saying all at once.

Monique stepped away to give them a little privacy, hoping that she'd get as enthusiastic a greeting from Kiera when she got home. She doubted it. After the single plaintive text Monique had received in Italy and Monique's own text reassurance, Kiera's communications had reverted to the curt, breezy, yeah-I'll-see-you-when-you're-finally-home mode.

Marco wandered over to join them, running his fingers through his thick black hair. Monique watched as Becky raised her head a moment and caught his eye. Then, just as swiftly, Becky bent over Brian, shielding her expression with the sweep of her hair, ostensibly to hear something her son was trying to say over his more socially gregarious sister's monologue. Monique watched Marco's smile dim. He flexed his broad shoulders and shoved his hands in his pockets, his chest rising and falling on a sigh.

Monique frowned. Already Becky wasn't following the plan. Monique swiftly changed her expression into a welcoming smile as Marco caught her eye and approached.

He gave her a dry buss on the cheek. "Welcome home, weary traveler."

"It's good to be back."

"Do you believe them?" He tilted his head at Judy and Bob, who were giving the stream of international arrivals a passionate, live-action lesson in French kissing.

"I guess that's what happens after five kids leave home."

His smile hardened like concrete. "So was it a good trip?"

"Fabulous, but for the last twelve hours. We had a rough patch of turbulence over the Atlantic."

Judy and Bob were still at it, not kissing anymore, but now hugging and chatting, their mouths inches apart, rocking back and forth, gazes locked, a couple of fifty-year-old lovebirds. And Becky was still ignoring her husband, using her children as a buffer.

"Hey, Marco," Monique said, trying to break the uncomfortable silence, "do you think I could hitch a ride home in your minivan? I don't think Judy and Bob are going to make it out of the parking garage with their clothes on."

He shrugged. "Sure."

Becky finally rose from her crouch. Her hands were lost in her children's hair and her blue gaze was uncertain. Marco caught that gaze. Without pulling his hands from his pockets, he stretched forward to offer what Monique expected would be a publically acceptable, perfectly perfunctory kiss. But Becky at the last minute lowered her head to whisper something to Brianna which made the little girl laugh and spin away on the slippery sole of one shoe. Becky then petted Brian's head and the boy took a pouting step away. Just as Marco took one step closer, Becky took a step toward him. The result was the dull thunk of Becky's head against Marco's stiff and stubbly jaw.

Marco stepped back, off-balance, clutching his jaw as Becky winced. After a moment Becky's lips twitched, and then Marco's did too. Monique squinted, thinking maybe something had just passed between the couple, a little stuttered spark, a moment of awareness. With more hesitation Marco and Becky attempted to cross the distance that separated them, and then they sealed it with a kiss.

Monique felt a little shimmer watching that kiss—short, but certainly not perfunctory—and her own heart went fluttery. *That* was most definitely in the plan. Fairy tales always ended with a kiss.

She stood patiently while Becky and Marco talked to one another while ignoring the kids tugging at their pants. Their voices were polite, and their words most carefully chosen, but at least they were communicating. Judy and Bob still clasped hands and chatted. Monique waited, taking in the airy space of the international airport, searching for someplace for her gaze to land.

No one waited for Monique Franke-Reed.

The thought didn't hurt as much as it could have. Her leap of faith off an Italian bridge had changed her. This hollow in her chest didn't really feel empty. Already the imprint was filling with a new sense of warmth and fullness, like the welcome burden of a swaddled newborn, clasped close against her breast.

Monique pushed the door open and walked into the house. She dropped her daypack to the floor and jerked her rolling luggage to a stop. She called out her mother's name, but there was no response. Kiera had already texted her that she wouldn't be home from school for another hour, but Monique had expected her mother to be waiting. She glanced at the dining room table and saw a note pinned by a coffee mug next to a teetering pile of mail and a separate pile of flyers from colleges.

Monique picked up the note. Her mother wrote that she hoped to be home before Monique arrived, but first she had to make a quick trip to the Caribbean market in Irvington to pick up dasheen leaves.

Monique smiled, put the note back on the table, and

glanced around her empty house. She'd only been away for two weeks, but her body still suffered that sense of stretching dislocation she always felt when she traveled. She took a deep breath and tried to pull her spirit back into this place. The scent of curry tickled her sinuses. A pile of Kiera's discarded shoes lay heaped just behind the door. Her gaze caught on her mother's knitting splayed over the arm of a chair in the living room, a chair that had been moved so that it sat in a pool of afternoon sunlight.

The breathing emptiness in her home was a palpable thing, like a drop in pressure, like the thinness of alpine air. Lenny didn't live here anymore. She knew this already. But she supposed Becky was right. There was a world of difference between knowing and acknowledging.

Monique slogged up the stairs to her bedroom, hefting her luggage up one step at a time, every knock of the wheels against the stairs reverberating through her bones. She slipped her purse through a patina of dust on her bureau. Mentally she added another item to her list: Give the house a good attic-to-basement cleaning before she went back to work on Monday. She paused to caress the frame of a photo of Lenny and Kiera.

How young he was.

She turned away and hauled her luggage onto her bed. As she unzipped the top bulged open, dislodging a few pairs of underwear onto the comforter. She pulled the laundry basket out of the closet—already half full with Kiera's clothes—and by handfuls she added the contents of her daypack atop a dirty crew uniform and muddy sweatpants.

She was halfway done when she heard the front door swing open.

Kiera's excited, high-pitched voice called, "Mom?!"

"I'm up here, hon."

Kiera took the stairs so fast that Monique hadn't yet rounded the end of the bed before the teenager tore through the hall and into her room.

Kiera, all shiny eyes and widening grin, stopped abruptly at the threshold as if she suddenly realized she wasn't acting nearly cool enough for a seventeen-year-old senior welcoming her mother home from a long trip. Lightning-quick her stance shifted into the usual cock-hipped pose, and she gave her mother a look from head to toe.

"Ma, you're a mess!"

"Shut up and give your mother a hug."

A bit of the little girl was still in her, Monique thought, as Kiera launched herself into her arms and squeezed her tight. Monique could almost believe the young woman rocking in her arms was still that girl, if her cheek wasn't level with Monique's and her hair didn't smell like the fancy coconut relaxant she favored, and the laugh that bubbled out of her wasn't throaty and confident and fully, undeniably mature.

"I'm *so* glad you're home." Kiera pulled away and then bounced on the end of the bed. "Nothing against *Grand-mère's* fabulous cooking, but after two weeks I am just dying for a burger and fries."

"Callaloo for dinner." Monique returned to her suitcase, searching the zippered compartments, wondering where she'd tucked the little ceramic gargoyle from Notre Dame. "*Grand-mère* left me a note."

Kiera puffed out her cheeks and clutched the micro-pouch of her stomach. "Can't you talk her into McDonald's?"

"I doubt it. I'm looking forward to a few cheap American meals myself," she said, gently slapping her own hip, "but it's good to know you see me as a dependable purveyor of fast food."

"If I eat another curried chicken thigh, I'm going to sprout feathers."

Monique tossed a bunch of flyers on the bed. "I've got a boatload of stories for you."

"I've got a few for you too."

"The best part is that I've still got a little money in the bank."

"This is a surprise?"

"Enough so that—if you were so inclined—you could look through those flyers and see if any of them catch your interest. Between what I've got left and my new frequent-flier miles, you and I can afford to do a trip to Europe next summer before you go off to school."

"Oh... we don't have to do that."

"Only if you want to."

Kiera spread the flyers with one finger, cocking her head to read the headings, going still in a way that suggested she wasn't really reading at all.

Monique unzipped pockets, dislodging ticket stubs, train schedules, and her cache of costume jewelry while her motherly senses tingled. "So," she said, "did anything inter-esting happen while I was gone?"

"Well, we won two crew meets but lost the one against Irvington. *Again.*" Kiera braced herself on the heels of her hands, stretching her feet out before her. "And I got my mid-term report—all As except a B in AP World History."

"What do you know, you *are* human."

"It's a high B." Kiera's jaw tightened in determination. "I'll make it up before the end of the quarter."

"Don't break a sweat."

"If it sticks, it'll be like an oil blot on my transcript. I don't want to send a transcript with a B on it to NYU."

Monique paused, noting the mention of New York University less than twenty miles away and not the mention of UCLA, on the other side of the continent. Maybe her fatigued mind was not quite catching the subtext of the conversation.

"It's weird but I found out that UCLA doesn't ask to see a transcript until they let you in," Kiera said into the moment of silence. "They just trust what you tell them. But NYU wants an official one, plus mid-year grades."

"I see."

"Although I have been rethinking UCLA."

Monique opted to stay very, very still, even though she'd found the stuffed fat rat she'd bought for Kiera at the catacombs hiding under her sneakers. "Rethinking?"

"Well, yeah." Kiera feigned intense interest in the sight of her bobbing legs. "It was real quiet here while you were gone, Mom." She slouched back, her head sinking between her shoulders. "In fact, it was sort of lonely."

Monique was a little surprised that Kiera hadn't noticed this before. The house had grown so still since Lenny had died. Lenny had the kind of presence that filled up a place. Monique didn't like to think how desperately this house was going to need warmth and life and noise after Kiera left.

Then her thoughts began to drift, once again, down a road she'd never before considered. She shook the thought free. That idea would have to wait until she returned to work on Monday at the NICU.

Monique tossed the stuffed rat into Kiera's lap. "I understand lonely, Kiera. But quiet? Didn't *grand-mère* drive you crazy playing her calypso music while she cooked?"

"She shut it off whenever I came home. And since it's crew season, I usually didn't make it home before seven. She was asleep in front of the TV by eight thirty." Kiera ran her fingers across the wiry rat whiskers. "You know that I can't go wrong with either school, right?"

"Well." Monique knew she wasn't ready for this discussion, but she couldn't avoid it either. "You did make a point of telling me that UCLA would be the better film school for you."

"It's too far away. And I don't like the idea of you banging around this house all by yourself, drinking wine at the kitchen table on a Saturday night, wandering into Daddy's old closet to smell his clothes."

Monique muffled her own sharp response. Another vice revealed. She'd been doing a pretty dismal job of shoring it up for the world, it seemed. Then again Monique knew she wasn't the only female in the house who occasionally stepped into that closet.

"So I've been thinking," Kiera said, squeezing the stuffed rat. "Maybe it's best that I stick around local for a few more years rather than haul myself across the country."

Monique swung a pair of shoes from her fingers and thought of how wonderful it would be to have her little girl coming home every weekend, sweeping into this house with all the energy she'd inherited from her father. She loved the image of Kiera laying her books and schedules and plans and ambitions all on the kitchen table as she filled the house up with chatter.

But Judy's words rang in her ears. *We birth them and feed them and raise them and give them hell, and, when it's time, we just let them go.*

"No, Kiera."

Monique swallowed hard and lifted the now-empty suitcase to settle it on the floor. She took a seat on the edge of the bed, close enough to touch her daughter if she'd let her, but far enough away to give the girl the space she might need. "You're sweet to consider it. But I'm going to have to say no."

Kiera's brow knit. "What do you mean, 'no'?"

"You can't make this decision because of me. It's too important. You should go exactly where you want to go. You should go where you believe you'll get the best education. If that school happens to be three thousand miles away or even half a world away, well, so be it."

Kiera's lips parted but no words came out.

"You and me, we're really lucky." Monique glanced toward the photo of Lenny on her bedside table. "Your daddy made sure that you and I had the freedom to make these kinds of choices. There was no better man, Kiera. No better man in the whole wide world."

Kiera kept blinking at her, like Becky did sometimes

when she emerged out of a great darkness. "So you're say-ing," Kiera stuttered, "that you don't mind if I apply to UCLA?"

"Nope. Just be warned. I've got a heck of a lot of frequent-flier miles now. If you do decide to go to UCLA, you might find me at your dorm room door more often than you'd like, kiddo."

Kiera's eyes grew round and steady and serious. Con-fusion rippled across her face, confusion and some other emotion Monique couldn't name. "You finished Daddy's list, didn't you?"

Monique nodded, as her limbic brain sent her soaring once more off the edge of a bridge into a cavernous gorge.

"Okay." Kiera nodded sharply. "That's good."

"It was good, Kiera," she said. "It was something that I had to do, more than I even knew when I started."

"Well maybe now you won't be mad at me for what I've done while you were gone."

Monique felt a pinch of unease. "You couldn't have done anything drastic. The UCLA application isn't due until the end of November, right?"

"I really didn't mean for it to go quite so far."

Monique's motherly instincts started to tingle all over again.

Kiera said, "I just thought it'd be better if I checked them out before I go away."

"Check what out?"

"You've been alone for so long, I figured you probably for-got everything. About how to dress, how to present yourself, how to choose sensibly."

"Choose?" The tingling turned to needles. "Choose what?"

Kiera avoided her eye as she launched herself off the bed and into the position that Monique recognized as her spine-straight, debate-team pose. "I'm just a little more *in tune* with that world, you know what I'm saying, Mom? I'm in high school. I deal with this every single day. So I've got more street smarts than you."

"Kiera. Franke. Reed—"

"I used that photo of you from last New Year's Eve. The one taken at the hospital party, when you let me do your makeup and you looked so good? And after working on college essays all summer, I figured I've got the chops now to really write a kick-ass profile. And who knows you better than me, huh? Who can tell the world who you *really are* better than your own daughter?"

The horrible realization sank in. "You signed me up on an Internet dating site."

"I just posted your profile."

"Oh, God."

"I didn't wink at anyone or send an email or do anything else. I left that for you." Kiera suddenly sidled next to her on the bed, seized her hand, and then squeezed the fingers tight. "Don't be mad at me, Mom. I just don't want to leave here, and leave you all alone."

Monique stared in choking disbelief at Kiera's hopeful face, the encouraging smile and the cheeks that were the same shape as Lenny's, but brighter, higher, stronger. She told herself not to be furious—Kiera's heart was in the right place. She meant well. Kiera just didn't know that her mother was developing her own ideas right now, ideas that had a lot to do with a certain determined, sweetly stubborn, abandoned preemie, hopefully still thriving in the NICU.

"Kiera Franke-Reed," she said, "I ought to ground you for six straight months."

Kiera did a little jump, sensing as she always did that she wasn't going to be scolded. "I *knew* you wouldn't be mad."

"Give me a minute to work up some fury."

"But there's no reason to be angry." Kiera bounced on the bed. "You've got three winks already!"

chapter twenty-two

Judy kneeled in the middle of the attic, just in the spot where the sun streamed through the window and heated a square of dusty floorboards. The unheated attic was chilly, but something about the slanting, autumn sunlight and the warmth of the floor under her knees reminded her of the little hilltop patio in Neive, Italy.

She rested there, soaking it in, looking up at the tower of boxes that held the outdoor decorations for Halloween. The blow-up pirate ship. The fog machine. The bags of spiderwebbing and the strings of jack-o'-lantern lights. The plastic skeletal bones to be half buried and the collection of humorous tombstones ("See, I told you I was sick!"). Usually long before now, she would have spread the spiderwebbing over the bushes in front of the house, festooned the porch with the lights, and dragged out the extension cords in anticipation of placing the strobe lights and the equipment for the sound effects.

Instead she just sat here, passing her gaze across the whole sweep of the attic: Over the blow-up pool that hadn't been dragged out to the backyard in at least a decade; the six-foot wooden turkey she put on the lawn every year on November first; the collection of Legos and Polly Pockets and Playmobil castles in labeled boxes in the corner. She eyed the three sets of crutches between the old fish tank and the sagging zip-up rack of graduation gowns and prom wear. She cast her gaze over the tumble of computers and monitors and printers that, considering how swiftly technology changed, were now sliding out of vintage and into pure antiques.

It'd be a nice two-month job putting this room in order, separating the stuff into piles to be junked, donated to charity, given to friends. It was a job that had to be done. Her wonky knee had finally shrunk back to its normal size, once she'd given it a good week's rest. She'd slept well since she'd returned home and was starting to feel human again. Most importantly she'd come to a conclusion she hadn't been ready to face before she'd jetted off to Europe. It would be a good thing, to just let all this stuff go.

But right now, at eleven a.m. on a Saturday, dressed in her ripped and paint-splattered jeans, she found herself thinking—to hell with it. She had more important things to do.

She pushed herself up off the boards. She slapped her hands over her knees and watched the dust puff away, scattering in the air lit by a ray of sunlight. She turned her back on the piles of boxes and ducked her head under the low attic doorway, pulling it shut with a satisfying click before rounding the landing to the stairs.

She passed that plaster crack in the wall she'd been meaning to fill with mesh and spackle. She passed the boys' bedroom she'd been working in before she left for Europe, scraping thirty-five years of paint off the baseboards to restore the original walnut wood. As she reached the first floor and rounded the dining room, she saw the old laptop she'd left open on the table, where she'd spent the last few days Googling crazy ideas.

Bob poked his head up above the Sunday paper as she entered the kitchen and made a beeline to the coffeemaker. She grabbed a cup, filled it, stirred in some half-and-half, and plunked herself in the chair opposite her husband.

She said, "I'm giving all the Halloween decorations to the Lorenzinis."

With slow and deliberate care Bob lowered the newspaper. He gave her that long, steady look that reminded Judy of her uncle George, a Maine lobsterman who liked to keep his thoughts to himself while squinting off at the horizon, as if he were gauging the weather by the swirl of the distant clouds or the direction of the wind.

"It's not like our kids are around here to enjoy them anymore." She planted the cup on the table. "Or even help us put them up."

He bobbed his head in a brief, noncommittal nod as he sought his own coffee cup around the edge of the paper. "Sounds good, Jude."

"Next summer," she added, "I'll give Brianna and Brian the blow-up pool."

"I'll check it for leaks first." He took a long, deep drink. "I can't remember the last time we put that out."

"I'm also thinking of helping Becky out."

Bob paused, his coffee cup in midair.

"You know, in the bakery thing," she explained. "You remember her talking about that on the deck last night. She's going to sell blueberry scones and banana muffins through the coffee kiosk at the train station."

"Oh."

Judy narrowed her eyes on her husband, the man she loved desperately, almost as trim and fit as when she'd first met him, though with a lot less of his golden-boy hair. "You have no idea what I'm talking about, do you?"

"Beck makes great blueberry scones." He feigned scanning the columns of the newspaper. "She eats lots of muffins."

"Becky hunted down the owner of the kiosk. She tempted him with a tray. He's going to put them out for sale on a trial basis." It was amazing that any man could remember every score to every Giants game for the last twenty years, but he couldn't seem to remember what they'd all discussed at a barbecue last night. "You didn't catch that, but I bet you remember the photo slide show Kiera put together about our trip to Europe."

He twisted his lips in that sexy half smile that made Judy's thighs tighten. "I'm still trying to wrap my brain around the sight of you on a Harley."

"Kiera might have overdone it with the Beethoven soundtrack. In any case, Becky may need help baking for a little while until she figures how much she needs to produce in the morning."

"Should I ask what has this to do with the Halloween decorations?"

Sometimes Judy felt as if her mind worked at one hundred miles per hour while Bob's lagged at fifty. "The boxes got me thinking about holidays. The holidays got me thinking about the seasonal jobs available at the mall. Mrs. McCarthy down the street used to work at department stores during Christmas to make a few bucks."

His coffee cup was still frozen in midair.

"We're going to need a few more bucks coming into the house, Bob."

The poor guy's brain was going to explode. "Jude," he stuttered, "you know we'll manage Audrey's tuition. We always have."

"I've got a few other plans."

"Like giving the Lorenzini kids the old pool? Helping Becky out at the bakery?" His eyes brightened. "Finishing the paint job in the boys' room so I'll have a home office?"

"Hell no. That's busywork. A couple of buckets of paint and a few hours of labor ought to take care of that. Maybe I could pay Kiera to do that over her Christmas break. In any case, my plans have nothing to do with home improvement projects and everything to do with bringing in a little more disposable income."

Poor Bob. He was bracing himself for anything. She knew she'd been a puzzle to him these past months, and even more so since she got home, sleeping till noon, tossing frozen meals on the table, regaling him with random non-chronological Europe stories, and completely ignoring the overgrown lawn.

"Did you know," she said, "that there's an adult school at the high school? They run two sessions a year. They pay a nice, tidy sum for skilled professionals to give twelve-week courses."

He mimicked, "Twelve-week courses."

"*Ich spreche gut Deutsch.*" She gave him a little smile. "*Et aussi, français.* I still speak two foreign languages, pretty damn well too."

"I'm still trying to interpret your English."

"Listen carefully, hon. I thought I'd pitch an adult conversation class to the school, in either or maybe even both languages. There's still time for me to write up a full proposal for the spring session."

"Oh." He exhaled, long and slow. "I thought you were going to tell me you're taking up ceramics or something."

"Please. Can you really see me throwing clay, painting watercolors, going to bingo?"

"I'd like to see you doing all three naked."

She flushed and sputtered and then, after a moment, she gave him a slow smile. That part of their life, well...that was really, *really* nice to return to.

"Ha ha," she said. "But I'm serious. A class like that wouldn't take much prep, it'd only be a few nights a week, and it'd make me a few bucks toward tuition."

"But Audrey's tuition—"

"*My* tuition," she interrupted. "For the community college. Did you know how cheap their per-credit cost is?"

"Wait—you're going back to school?"

"They have a two-year master's program."

"Masters?"

"In education, Bob." Judy tapped her fingers on the table. "Try to keep up. I'm planning to blow the dust off my bachelor's degree in German and French. With the master's degree in education, and a certain number of hours of classroom time, I could be certified to teach language classes in about three years."

"Teach."

"High school, Bob. Teenagers." She watched his dear, dear face as she took a long, deep breath that was a little unsteady. "That is, if I can find a school system willing to hire a teacher over fifty."

"They'd be damned fools if they didn't."

Judy sank into herself, touched by his trust.

"But," he said, "if I've got this straight, then this is a more serious commitment than wrapping presents at the mall."

"Thank God."

"A full-time commitment, Judy."

"You might have noticed I'm driving myself crazy bouncing around this house with no kids to take care of anymore."

"I don't know what you're talking about."

"You're a terrible liar. But you've shown admirable restraint."

"It's easy when you're six paces behind."

"Old man."

"Not so old yet." He gave her a wink. "If this is what you really want to do, well, you'd be a damn good teacher, Jude. The kids in your classroom? They'll be the luckiest kids in the world."

Her heart tripped at his words, and she felt a new flush spread through her. She was such a bundle of emotions. She was excited about the idea of teaching, but also anxious at the huge step she was about to take. She felt a swelling gratitude for Bob, who didn't question when she came to him with full-blown plans, and also for Becky and Monie with whom she'd first hashed out her thoughts.

"The job will be great," she said, "and so will the money and the summers off. But I do have an ulterior motive, you know."

He shook his head as he took a sip of coffee. "Albert Einstein couldn't figure out how your mind works."

"With the money I make and no more tuition bills to pay, you and I will finally get a chance to do something guiltless and wonderful and completely for ourselves."

"We did that last night."

"Oh, honey." She came around the table and wrapped her arms around him. "I'm talking about two long, lazy weeks alone with you—in Italy."

chapter twenty-three

Every day Becky built a map in her head. A map of her world, ever-expanding. And so much richer than what she could simply see.

Like now, standing in her hallway, holding a knit cap in her hands. She knew which way it went on—her eyesight had not deteriorated that much. But instead of depending upon her vision, she oriented the hat by running the pad of a finger along the soft inside band until she felt the nub that indicated the seam. Only then did she pull the hat over her head, lining that nub against the nape of her neck.

She also knew, because of the faint creak of the floorboards in the adjacent dining room, that Marco stood right in front of the windows. The old floorboards had gone slightly warped there from decades of exposure to the afternoon sun. He was standing there studying the architectural plans he'd fetched from work—the ones he'd be using next week when he was finally back on the job. She heard the subtle crackling of the curled blue paper as he traced the lines with his fingers.

Then her two kids raced down the stairs, squealing. They plowed into the back of her knees, one after another.

Brian's excited voice, "I won!"

Becky dropped her hand onto his mop of hair, sweaty-warm. Beneath her fingers, she felt the vibrating energy of the boy, all power and movement.

"It was a *tie*," Brianna responded, swinging around to peer up at her. "Right, Mom?"

Becky caressed Brianna's chin and smelled the scent of her daughter's favorite strawberry shampoo. She caught a tress that curled between her fingers and felt, against her knuckles, the tremble of Brianna's excitement.

"One of you definitely reached me before the other," Becky conceded. "But don't ask me which one."

There were certain advantages to having no peripheral vision.

"Rematch," Marco ordered as he stepped into the hallway. "The winner will be the first one who comes back wearing sneakers."

Brian shot up the stairs. Brianna ran after him, wailing, "But I have to *tie* my shoes, and he wears *Velcro*!"

Becky watched until they disappeared around the landing. Behind her Marco's presence was a perfume of sun-heated cotton and ink. His slow laugh rumbled through her, through some parts more thoroughly than others. She didn't turn to face him completely. It was still easier to talk to him when he lingered just out of the range of her vision. Like this she could bear being honest.

"I know you have a lot of work to do," she said, reaching for the scarf she'd hung on a peg behind the door, "so I'll keep them outside for as long as I can. Judy's already at the park with Monique. Judy's walking the dogs so that should keep the kids entertained."

She heard the slip of flesh against cloth as he shoved his hands into his pockets. He leaned into her and spoke low near her ear. "They're still so thrilled that you're home, Beck."

"That'll wear off when I make them clean their rooms tonight. In the meantime I'll take the extra hugs and kisses. Two weeks away must have seemed like an eternity for them."

"Two weeks is a long time for husbands too."

His fingers slipped into her hair. He played with it for a moment, and then he gripped her head, silently nudging her to turn around. With a flutter of nerves she faced him and absorbed the full impact of those melted-chocolate eyes with the impossibly long lashes. The memory of last night shimmered between them.

"I should just go with you to the park." His voice had dipped to that low, lovely timbre that now made her think of a Porsche purring on an open road. "It's a nice day. I could bring the mitts and play catch with the kids."

"Marco, you did that for two straight weeks."

"It rained half the time you were gone."

"And you spent it playing board games." She met his eyes, silently letting him know how much she appreciated how he'd kept the kids, the house, and her world together while she was overseas falling apart. "I know you're itching to work on those plans."

He rolled a shoulder. "I still have a few days to eyeball them."

She traced his jaw, prickly and unshaven. He always tried so hard to be the best at everything. She remembered now that she'd fallen in love with him for just that quality. That had gotten lost amid all her anxieties these past years, worries that had led to nothing. Gina, for all her risky behavior, had never lost herself to drugs, never become pregnant, never crashed the car, or injured herself or others. Brian, her wild man of a son, had never darted into traffic as she'd worried when he was a fury of a two-year-old. Brianna had never developed heart problems from the strep throat that had escalated into rheumatic fever. Marco though on furlough had never completely lost his job.

She was going blind, yes. Someday in the not so far future her eyesight would dim and wink out.

But not today.

"Work on your plans." She patted the muscled swell of his chest. "Then pick us up in an hour and a half. You can drive us all to Brian's soccer game and buy me an orange Creamsicle from the ice cream truck."

His lips twitched. "You've got your cell?"

She reached into her pocket, pulled it out, and waved it. "Don't forget Brian's cleats. He can change in the car."

"That phone isn't on vibrate, right?" Marco's eyes crinkled. "Because you're terrible at picking it up, Beck."

"It's at full volume now. When you call, I'll hear it."

"Promise?"

"I promise."

He fixed his mouth upon hers, sealing the deal. He tasted of strong coffee, taken straight black in the morning. He tasted of forgiveness, and hope, and promise.

Thundering feet soon interrupted along with Brianna's high-pitched, "Ewwww*wwww*!"

"Mommy, Daddy!" Brian's little fists pounded on her thighs. "Stop, stop, *stop*."

Marco reluctantly pulled away. Then he swept Brian up and swung him around. Brianna tugged on the end of Becky's scarf, urging her to hurry. Becky hiked her pack on her shoulder, and in a rustle of coats and scarves and one more quick kiss, she and her kids bounded out the door.

Becky slipped on her sunglasses and followed her guides. Brianna announced that she was the warrior princess that led the queen, warning her of any wrinkle in the red carpet that stretched from their house to the park a quarter mile away. Brian was the knight who challenged all the squirrels and chipmunks who dared to cross their path, who destroyed any broken branches that blocked their progress. When nothing else challenged him, he used one of those sticks to battle invisible dragons.

Becky followed the sight of their little figures, feeling the path beneath the soles of her feet, stretching out her hand as she passed each city tree, noting the thickness, the texture of the bark, the sound of the wind in the drying leaves and the warmth of the sun against her skin despite the chill in the air. Even the most familiar of places could be newly discovered when all of one's senses were put fully to use.

She glimpsed Judy and Monique just as they turned into the park. Judy was leaning forward, telling a story. Monique threw her head back to laugh at whatever Judy said. They were waiting for her at the usual place by the big stone, surrounded by pots of mums, where the new mulch smelled loamy and rich.

The dogs, panting, leaped off their feet as they glimpsed Brian and Brianna, who bounded toward them. Monique and Judy waved at her. She waved right back.

Every day she built a map in her head. A map of her world, ever-expanding. She'd memorized the center of that map by heart.

All the people she loved lived here.

reading group guide

friendship makes the heart grow fonder

Lisa Verge Higgins loves to meet new readers. If your book club has chosen a book by Lisa and you're interested in arranging a phone or Skype chat, feel free to contact her at http://www.lisavergehiggins.com/contact.htm.

1. Here's Lenny's bucket list. How many of these would you like to do?
   a. Take a ride on the London Eye.
   b. Enjoy a scenic cruise down the Rhine River.
   c. Dine at Le Jules Verne at the Eiffel Tower.
   d. Visit the catacombs of Paris.
   e. Go abseiling in Interlaken, Switzerland.
   f. Ride a motorcycle through the Black Forest.
   g. Blow $1,000 in a Monaco casino to see how long the money lasts.
   h. Travel 100 mph on a German autobahn.
   i. Celebrate Oktoberfest in Munich.
   j. Enjoy the wine and truffle festival in Alba, Italy.

     k. Tour the crypts at the Cimitero Monumentale di Milano, Milan.

     l. See Leonardo da Vinci's *The Last Supper*.

     m. Go bungee jumping.

2. Write a thirteen-item bucket list of your own. How does it compare to that of your friends?

3. At the end of the book Monique considers making a drastic change in her life, perhaps by adopting another child. Do you think this will be a good choice for her? How do you think Kiera will react to this life change?

4. Each of the women in this book is facing a loss: Monique has never recovered from the death of Lenny, Judy is grappling with a sudden crisis of identity, and Becky is facing the eventual failure of her eyesight. These losses are in the past, present, and future. Are they equally strong? Which of the characters, in your opinion, is facing the most difficult transformation?

5. It has been four years since Monique lost Lenny, yet she still mourns deeply. Do you have a direct experience of this kind of personal loss (spouse, child, parent, or other close loved one)? How long do you think it should take to regain some sense of normality? Do you ever, really, move on after such a life-changing loss—or do those who grieve deeply simply build a new life around the absence?

6. The marriages of these women are markedly different: Monique imagines Lenny as still present, still commu-

nicating, and idealized; Becky's marriage is tense, full of silences, and clearly in trouble; and Judy's marriage to Bob is earthy, communicative, and grounded. How do their relationships to their husbands hinder or help them in their personal journeys?

7. Judy's journey is a search for self. She starts by looking to her past, to the young fleet-footed girl she once was. Are there parts of your own self that you left behind, perhaps put aside for marriage, motherhood, maturity? What were the dreams you held as a young woman? Are they still viable? Do they still inspire you?

8. Becky and her bête-noir Gina are worlds apart in attitude and outlook. But Becky and Gina share a sensitive, artistic sensibility—not just in their ability to draw, but also in the way they use this talent to express their brightest dreams...or darkest nightmares. If they dared to reinvent their relationship, what could these women learn from one another?

9. At the beginning of the book Monique feels the presence of Lenny so strongly in her life that in private moments she "summons" him, speaks with him, wallows for a few moments in the feeling that he is still alive. Have you ever posed a question to a loved one who has died and knew what his/her response would be? What kind of things bring the memory of a lost loved one most strongly back to you—the smell of her perfume or his aftershave? The feel of an old sweater? The discovery of a letter or an old note?

10. After their last child goes off to college, Bob says to Judy that she's acting like a bird who doesn't realize that the door to the cage is open. Judy remembers an incident with a pet parakeet: One of their children had left the door open, and the parakeet flew out...only to fly right back in. What does this say about Judy's state of mind? Could this analogy also fit Monique's situation? What about Becky's?

11. Becky has not yet lost her eyesight, but the inevitability of it looms. Monique lost Lenny four years ago, but reminders keep the sense of loss immediate and pinpoint-painful. Judy, surrounded in her attic by the memories of a once-vibrant family life, remembers anew all she has lost. Are sharp, sudden, and unexpected reminders of a loss a natural part of the grieving process?

12. Why do you think Lenny added the thirteenth item—bungee jumping—to the bucket list? What final message did he wish to convey to the woman he loved?

13. Judy and Becky know about Monique's "talks" with her dead husband long before they confront her in Italy. Why did they choose this particular time to let Monique know they are aware of her behavior? What did they hope to accomplish by exposing the fact that they know her weakness?

14. Why is Monique so angry at Lenny when she's trying to lose "his" money at the casino? Do you think Lenny knew how much this particular task was going to bother her?

15. Kiera's reaction to the announcement about the bucket list trip takes Monique by surprise. Should Monique have put the trip off for another year, when Kiera would be in college?

16. Despite the anxiety attack and the strong urge to go home, Becky decides to fly to Zurich with Monique to do one more item on the bucket list. During the rappelling Becky discovers that she has no fear of the height or danger of the activity. In fact, she enjoys it with heightened sensitivity. How does this, and the crazy evening to follow, change her mind about leaving?

17. Judy is in many ways a woman torn in two—between "wanderlust," a very fundamental urge to explore new places and "nesting," a just as fundamental urge to revel in her home, neighbors, and friends. Do you think the choices she makes at the end of the novel will satisfy both aspects of her character?

18. Becky is, at heart, an artist and a romantic. How do you think she will channel her artistic gifts as her sight slowly dims?

19. Becky is a woman who still nurses wounds left by the death of her father and still feels the uncertainty of the subsequent upheaval. She has become fiercely independent in order to protect herself from further pain. Unfortunately this also prevents her from asking for help when she needs it. How do you think this quality may have exacerbated the situation between Marco and Becky?

a note from the author

Judy Merrill and I have a lot in common. Like the character in *Friendship Makes the Heart Grow Fonder*, I once spent three months backpacking through Europe. At the time I was in an "in between" phase—between coasts, between jobs, and between being single and being married. With few responsibilities, a lot of time, and a vague return date on my plane ticket, I set out with a happy heart and the sketchiest of itineraries.

This is the kind of journey best done while young. I slept on beaches and in trains or stayed in hostels in the roughest parts of town. I existed on street vendor food at a few dollars a day. Like most women travelers, I was occasionally followed through the squares of foreign cities and had to dodge being groped on subways. I learned in a crowd in front of Buckingham Palace the meaning of the "dead hand."

But, oh, what places I saw! I spent an evening in a castle in the Scottish highlands. I walked the ramparts of Mont Saint-Michel as the roaring tide cut it off from the rest of France. I got mobbed by gypsy children in Rome, saw a bull fight in Madrid, basked in the sun on the rocky beaches of

Nice, gambled in Monaco, and danced to wistful Portuguese *fados* in Oporto, with snakes draped around my neck.

Each day brought a new challenge, a new city, a new friend. I may not remember what I cooked for dinner last Tuesday, but I sure can remember that truffle pasta I savored years ago in Italy. For Monique, Becky, and Judy I had to condense the transformative nature of that experience into two action-packed weeks. But I knew that the discomfort of being pushed out of one's normal routines would provide distraction from their troubles and give them a chance to take a good hard look at their lives.

Back then, like Judy, I was tempted to extend my trip indefinitely. The pack of Germans and Aussies I'd been traveling with invited me to go to the south of France to work the vineyards. But I understood that to stay footloose was to choose a new and vastly different life. I already had a new life—and a hunky guy—waiting for me back in the States. Three months abroad made me understand how much I wanted to begin it.

Sometimes getting lost is the only way to find exactly what you're looking for.